I0691810

Trust Me With Forever

Starry Hills
Book 4

Kayla Chase

Mythical Lake Press, LLC

Trust Me With Forever

Copyright © 2024 Laura Hoak-Kagey

Mythical Lake Press, LLC

Print Edition

Cover Art by Laura Hoak-Kagey of Mythical Lake Design

ISBN: 979-8891560451

Also by Kayla Chase

Reader Note

This book contains thoughts, memories, and discussions about the death of family members and verbal abuse from an ex-partner. I hope I have treated these items with the care and consideration they deserve.

Chapter One

Abby

I nearly groaned as I started to wake up. My head throbbed as if a million tiny needles kept stabbing my brain over and over again. Add in my dry mouth and feeling about a hundred years old, and I knew I had a hangover from hell.

Too bad I couldn't remember how I'd gotten it.

After a deep breath, I finally forced my eyes open, hoping for some clue as to where the hell I was.

The room was mostly dark, with barely any light coming in through the curtains. But wait, whose curtains were those? They looked like some kind of hotel standard fare, an ugly pattern no one would dare buy themselves.

Add in the small table with two chairs, the blasting

air conditioner, and the unfamiliar nightstand right next to my face, and it was clear that I wasn't back at my family's home in Starry Hills.

Or anywhere in Starry Hills, for that matter.

Something shifted behind me, and I froze. Wait, was that a soft snore? Yes, yes it was.

Damn. Had I really hooked up with a guy last night? One I didn't remember?

I slowly rolled over to see who it was. But he had his back and rather wide shoulders to me. His hair was dark, maybe black, and tattoos covered his visible arm.

Tattoos that seemed strangely familiar.

The more I stared at them, the more dread pooled in my stomach.

Because I knew who they belonged to, and it most definitely shouldn't be him.

With a screech, I jumped out of bed.

Rafael "Rafe" Mendoza jolted upright, looked around, and scowled at me. "What the fuck, Abigail?"

Then his eyes took in my shirt—well, it was technically his shirt—and he froze. My heart pounded as his gaze met mine. "Why are you wearing my shirt?"

I crossed my arms over my chest. "I don't know, *Rafael.* We didn't...me and you didn't...did we?"

He ran his hand back and forth over his short hair. I did my best not to stare at his chiseled biceps, let alone his muscled chest, now in full view.

Okay, maybe I did peek and see he didn't have much chest hair. Which I rather liked, because it would make licking his skin easier.

Woah, Abby. Not going to happen.

He finally replied, "I don't know. Although why the hell are you in my bed anyway?"

"Your bed?" Something hit me, and I hugged myself harder. "Did you do this to get back at West?"

My eldest brother, Weston, had recently married Rafe's much younger sister, Emmy. While the two guys had been best friends as children, they barely tolerated each other now.

And what better way to get back at West than to sleep with me?

Tears heated my eyes to think that Rafe, the guy I'd known since I was born, had used me that way.

Rafe jumped up, wearing only a pair of boxer shorts, and shook his head. "No, Abby. No, I would never do that. I can be an asshole sometimes, but I would never hurt you like that. I promise."

Searching his gaze, I wanted to believe him. But believing in men had cost me my dream job, my future, and possibly my reputation, if the details ever came out.

Apart from my family, I viewed all men as potential betrayers.

Why would Rafe be any different?

A small voice in my head said, *Because you've known him your whole life. He was a good man once, and probably still is, under his grumpy exterior.*

Not wanting to cave into believing him, I turned around and flipped on the lights. As I searched for my clothes, Rafe said, "Abby, look at me. Please."

Ever since Rafe had been injured and forced to retire from being a world-famous soccer player, he'd never once used such a gentle voice. At least, not in my hearing.

I looked over my shoulder to find him standing just behind me. He was close enough I could feel the heat of his body, and smell his spicy masculine scent.

The combination made me want to wrap my arms around him and hold him close. But no, I wouldn't do that. Ever. For so many reasons.

After clearing my throat, I took a step back before turning to face him. "What do you want?"

"I can't remember last night, but I know I'd never use you for revenge. Please tell me you believe me." He gingerly took my hand, frowned, and lifted it. "Why are you wearing a wedding ring?"

I looked down, and sure enough, there was a simple gold wedding band on my ring finger. "I never wear rings. Ever."

Rafe lifted his left hand and sure enough, he had a simple gold band too. He dropped my hand and stumbled backward. "What the fuck?" His gaze met mine. "What the hell happened last night?"

His tone poked at my temper. "You make it sound as if this is my fault. I don't remember a damn thing either, Rafael Mendoza. And before you accuse me of tricking you to get your fortune, I don't care about that. I don't ever want to get married. To you, or anyone."

After whirling around, I searched for my clothes. Because if I didn't get dressed and leave, I might do something I'd regret. Like start throwing things.

Rafe remained silent as I gathered my dress and bra. I ran into the bathroom, shut the door, and leaned against the counter. Staring into the mirror, I noticed my ruffled hair, smudged makeup, and the deathly pallor I always got after drinking too much.

I whispered, "Oh, Abby, what the hell did you get up to last night?"

Because after what had happened during my student teaching internship in San Jose, I'd vowed to never date again, let alone marry.

So how had I ended up in a hotel room with my best friend's older brother, with no memory of the night before? Let alone how we'd both ended up with gold bands on our ring fingers?

And if it were true, if we'd gotten hitched, then how the hell could I undo it and keep it from my family?

Chapter Two

Rafe

As I stared at the bathroom door, my head pounded as I tried to process everything that had just happened.

At first, waking up to Abby wearing my shirt had stirred my cock. I'd dreamed of her often in recent weeks, and I thought it was yet another forbidden fantasy filling my nights.

However, then I'd realized it wasn't a dream, and I'd sobered up. Fast.

Especially once Abby looked at me with such sadness and betrayal, as if I'd used her to get back at Weston Wolfe for marrying my sister. I'd tried to convince her it wasn't true—because it wasn't—but her eyes said she didn't believe me.

I'd heard rumblings of how she'd been hurt by some dickwad ex. But her look of pure pain had shown me a sliver of the truth—she'd had her heart broken, stomped on, and set on fire.

Then I'd found her ring and mine, spoke without thinking, and now she'd locked herself in the bathroom.

Part of me wanted to bang on the door and tell her we needed to figure shit out. Because if we had gotten married while drunk, we could easily get an annulment.

But thinking of the media's field day with that made me hesitate. I could just imagine the headlines if or when it got out:

Playboy's New Tactic: Marriage, Sex, and then a Quickie Divorce
Mendoza's Failure at both Soccer and Love
Drunken Vegas Wedding Debacle for Former Playboy, Rafael Mendoza

Me and the media had a strained relationship. Gaining fame and fortune at such an early age had gone to my head. Before my parents' fatal car crash when I was nineteen, my life had been full of drinking and parties and women. Lots of women.

Then my world had come crashing down.

I'd spent years trying to assuage my guilt over my parents' death. Mostly, I'd wanted to keep people at a distance so no one could ever get close to me again.

Because I seemed to hurt anyone who loved me.

So to never have close relationships, I'd continued to act like the playboy the media made me out to be. That way, women never expected something serious, and I could keep friendships superficial.

And even though I'd tried to improve my public image and partying behavior in recent years, if what had happened with Abby leaked, it would undo everything. All the plans I'd made for me post-injury would go out the window.

No one wanted a scandal-riddled man to run a children's sports training facility.

Because while most of my life in the UK hadn't filtered over to the US—soccer wasn't as popular here as in the rest of the world—everything from my past would come out. Everything.

I'd be doomed before I even opened the doors.

I rubbed my hands over my face. How the fuck had this happened? Abby and I argued most of the time. Yes, it usually resulted in us breathing hard and me wanting to pull her close and kiss her. But marriage? No way. I'd never wanted that.

I tried racking my brain, but I couldn't remember anything about yesterday beyond driving toward Starry Hills from my house on the outskirts, sometime around noon the day before.

Lowering my hands, my eyes landed on my phone on the nightstand. Had our marriage already leaked out? How long until I needed to shift into damage-control mode?

As I wondered about hiring a PR firm to help me, my

gaze moved to the wedding band on my hand and an idea sparked. Maybe I'd seen too many movies with my mom growing up, but there had been more than one which had people staying married for a short time, for whatever reason, as only friends. And while I sure as hell didn't want the end result of those movies—the couple fell in love, blah, blah, blah, happy ending—a fake marriage to Abby could help with my PR problem.

If we were together, for say a year, the press would probably barely mention us splitting up. After all, sports stars married and divorced all the time.

And by the end of the year, my training facility would be up and running and already earning a reputation on its own.

The more I thought about it, the more the illusion of marriage started to seem like the solution to my problems.

But there was a catch—what would Abby get out of it?

Then I remembered her ex and the bits and pieces I'd heard since returning to Starry Hills. Did she want to get revenge on the bastard? Ruin him? Merely stand up to him and give him a piece of her mind?

I could help with that. Plus, I had money, lots of money, and maybe she'd agree to stay married in exchange for me granting her whatever she wanted.

As I tried to form a plan, Abby walked out of the bathroom, all dressed and cleaned up. Rational thought left my brain, and I couldn't tear my gaze away from her. The dress was tight across her chest before flaring out around her hips. And then there were her long, long legs. Abby hated being tall, but to me, she was just the right height for kissing.

What the fuck? No, no kissing. If she agreed to my crazy plan, then it'd be for a platonic year of marriage. Nothing more.

"Abby..."

She put up a hand to stop me. "Rafe, please, not now. I just want to go home." She bit her bottom lip and looked off to the side. "I remembered a little about last night, about how we drove here together, although I still don't know why." She paused and added, "I can't afford to hire a car to take me back. So, can you drive us to Starry Hills and agree to say nothing the whole time?"

"Abby, we can't not talk about this. I'm pretty sure we're married, and we need to think about the next steps."

She finally met my gaze again, and irritation flashed in her eyes. "Next steps? There is only one step, Rafael, and that's getting an annulment. We certainly aren't the first couple to drunkenly get married and regret it in the morning."

Her words shouldn't sting. After all, we weren't even really friends.

And yet, they did. Part of me wanted to cross the room, haul her against me, and say maybe it wasn't a complete mistake.

But that would be confusing lust with more, and I could always find another woman to fuck later.

Think of that. You'll be going back to England soon for a few weeks. Find some discreet pussy there. Your teammates can hook you up with women who know how to keep a secret.

And yet, the thought of meaningless sex with a woman who saw me merely as a trophy left a sour taste in my mouth.

"Rafe?"

I snapped back to the present. Realizing I needed to act fast, I asked, "Is there anything you really want in the world, Abigail? Be it a thing, an action, or what have you?"

She blinked. "What are you talking about?"

I took a step toward her. "I have a proposal, but it'll only work if I can give you something in return for your help."

After a beat, she rolled her eyes. "If you expect me to say I'm dreaming of your dick, you'll be waiting a long time."

"What?"

"Oh, come on. We never did it last night, and now that you remember, you're trying to think of ways to get into my pants. Well, no, Rafael. I don't want your cock anywhere near me."

Ouch. Well, that was the dump of cold water I needed.

After clearing my throat, I said, "I'm not talking about sex with me, Abigail. More like, do you want revenge on your ex? Or maybe to own a house? Something along those lines?"

She took a step backward. "What do you know about Travis?"

"Ah, so he has a name."

She narrowed her eyes. "I don't want to talk about him."

"I could help you get back at him, you know. Say the word, and I'll hire as many people as it takes to ruin the bastard."

Her eyes searched mine. "Okay, now you're not making any sense. Why the hell would you want to help me like that? You've been in and out of Starry Hills for months, and rarely said two words to me, even when I tried being nice at first. And now you're wanting to know about some of the most painful moments of my life? Or, if I have revenge plans?"

"Was I really that much of an asshole to you?"

She blinked. "Yes. If you can't recognize that, then I'm not sure you're the guy I remember growing up."

Now she'd touched a nerve. "I'm not that fucking innocent boy who left at eighteen. Life happened, shit happened, and if you're waiting for me to joke and smile and think the world is full of rainbows and butterflies, you'll be in for a hell of a wait, Abigail."

She gave a harsh laugh. "You're asking me if I think the world is nothing but happy? You lost your parents, but so did I. Then I lost half of my brothers for years and years. And eventually, I lost *him*, too, even if I never really had him to begin with."

Her voice cracked, and it was like a dagger to my heart. And suddenly, I wanted to find every person who'd hurt her and make them apologize. Maybe even grovel.

Except then I'd be in that group, too. I *had* been a dick to her in recent months. However, facing my little sister and learning how she'd felt responsible for our parents' death when it had clearly been my fault—combined with Weston Wolfe being there for Emmy when I couldn't—and well, it'd made me hate the world even more.

But Abby hadn't deserved any of my bullshit. I still remembered when we were younger and she was always so cheerful and happy. She and my sister had always thought they were the sneakiest kids ever as they followed me, West, and our other good friend, Mark, around.

However, something had happened to that little girl, much like something had happened to me.

The urge to protect her and try to make amends for being an ass coursed through me. Maybe time apart from her family, with me at her side to fight whatever battles came her way, could help Abby heal or at least move past the ass who'd broken her heart.

And even if it wasn't with me, I wanted to try giving her the happy future she deserved. Helping my sister's best friend would also be a good step toward making amends for the pain I'd caused Emmy.

Of course, that meant convincing Abby to say yes to my plan. To do that, I needed to step up. I blurted, "I'm sorry, Abby."

She blinked. "Um, excuse me?"

"I'm sorry. I *was* a jerk to you, and I shouldn't have been. You were one of the few who didn't give me the side-eye whenever I first showed up back in Starry Hills last year."

Her face softened a fraction. "Then why were you so

mean to me? I could never figure that out. As far as I know, I've never done anything to hurt you or upset you or anything like that. Unless merely being West's sister is enough to merit your vitriol."

I ran my hand over the top of my head. "Of course not. What's between West and I has nothing to do with you."

"Then why?"

Fuck, was she really going to make me talk about feelings and shit?

I wasn't about to spill my heart out, but I had to give her something. Otherwise, my plan would be a no-starter and I could kiss the success of my training facility good-bye. "Being back in Starry Hills is hard for me."

Would that be enough for her?

But when I saw the flash of curiosity in Abby's gaze, I knew it wouldn't be. She said, "And yet, you continue coming back when you could live anywhere in the world. Why?"

I blew out a breath. "I'm trying to find where home is, now that I can't play soccer any longer. I loved Manchester, but I never quite fit in. Just talking about something from my childhood would get blank stares from most of my teammates and friends. We all take for granted shared TV shows and foods and traditions and all that. Plus, I fucking hate tea and the coffee in England can't compare to what they make at the Starry Eyes Bakery."

Abby smiled. "True, Amber is a whiz with that espresso machine of hers. Anytime I try to make it at home, it's just not the same." She tilted her head. "But really? Coffee and talking about the old Disney Afternoon is what made you want to come back?"

There was more, of course. But I wasn't about to spill everything.

"Part of it. But hell, even now, I'm still unsure if I want to stay in Starry Hills for the rest of my life. I like seeing new places and trying new foods. But it'd be nice to have a place to call home, somewhere permanent. I haven't really had that since I was eighteen."

"You did change teams a lot for a few years there, didn't you?"

It wasn't the first time that Abby had revealed how she'd followed my career over the years. "Yeah. Plus, I like living somewhere with land and a little bit of peace, which is harder to get when you're a famous footballer in the UK. Er, I mean, a soccer player."

"Emmy says you have a house in Starry Hills but have never invited her over. Why?"

"You're nosey, aren't you?"

"If you want nosey, then talk with my Aunt Lori. I'm just a concerned childhood friend." She sniffed. "You've been a jerk to Emmy, too. You need to fix that."

"I know."

She blinked. "You do?"

"Yes. But it's complicated. Probably like it's complicated with your brothers sometimes."

"I guess." She paused and asked, "Why did you ask me if there was something I wanted? Was there a point to it?"

"There was." I took a step toward her and lifted her hand with the ring on it. "What would it take for you to keep this ring on for a year, Abigail?"

Chapter Three

Abby

Of all the things I'd expected Rafe to say, "What would it take for you to keep this ring on for a year, Abigail?" hadn't been one of them.

I blinked and blinked again, trying to process his words. Maybe the Abby I'd been as a little girl would've been ecstatic at his question. But grown-up Rafe was definitely not the fun, mischievous, and secretly sweet boy from my childhood.

Not that I was thinking of being married to any man.

Still, my curiosity got the best of me and I blurted, "Why? I'm guessing that means you want to stay married for a year?"

"Exactly."

"You're still not making any sense, Rafe. What's going on? Why are you even asking me that?"

He shrugged one shoulder. "While I'm not as big of a deal here in the States, news of our marriage will soon hit the tabloids in the UK and other places in Europe. And if we get annulled right away? It'll look even worse, given my past, and eventually it'll make it over here, too. And before you say I deserve all the press and attention because I was a public figure for so long and it'll just blow over, bad press might crash my new business venture before I even get to open it."

I was still trying to process him wanting to stay married for a year when my brain caught onto the last part. "Business? What business?"

He released my hand, retrieved his phone, and turned it toward me. I took it and looked at the picture— it was the old horse breeding place on the outskirts of Starry Hills. I remembered it because my parents had taken me there to finally get my own pony as a little girl.

Once the owners had passed away and it shut down, it'd felt as if another piece of my childhood had vanished along with it.

Rafe's voice garnered my attention. "I bought the Santos place last year, and I'm turning it into a sports training facility for kids and teens. There will be a more specialized program for those who need extra coaching to try and make it to pro. But there will also be several programs for both local teams and summer programs for anyone."

I glanced back up at Rafe, only to find excitement shining in his eyes. After all the months of him scowling and frowning and looking out of place, I barely recognized this version of him. "This is your new passion, isn't it? Now that your injury has ended your soccer career."

He shrugged nonchalantly. "Sitting around, filling my days with endless entertainment, would drive me crazy. This would give me a purpose, a reason to get up every morning."

Growing up, Rafe had never sat still. Soccer had become his entire world, and now that he couldn't play any longer? I'd worried about him. "I can tell it's more than something to pass the time. You're a lot like your sister in some ways, and one of them is that you can't hide your excitement. Emmy is like that with weddings, and now for you, this place is it."

"Maybe." He shuffled his feet. "At any rate, I've been trying to clean up my reputation for years. I always knew at some point my body would give out, and I'd have to find something else. But if there's any whiff of scandal, it'll spread like wildfire and probably ruin my chances with the training facility." He paused and searched my gaze. "I know it's a lot to ask, Abby. But if it's purely a marriage of convenience, one we keep for a year as a ruse and nothing more, my business has a better chance at succeeding. Plus, I'd help fulfill any dream you have in return." I opened my mouth to say it was crazy, but he blurted, "Will you at least think about it?"

The rational thing was to run downstairs and ask how to get an annulment before we left the city. I'd remembered that we were in Las Vegas, but not why we'd decided to come here. Only that we were here and, in fact, married.

But as I glanced down at Rafe's phone again and saw the picture, I couldn't stop thinking about how happy he'd been as he'd talked about his new business. More so than I'd ever seen him be as an adult.

It was crazy to even consider his proposal. And yet, showing up in San Jose with Rafe on my arm and rubbing it in Travis's face was tempting.

But would that really make me feel better? I could be sensible and ask Rafe for money and then travel. Or ask for a house. Or a million other things that might give me a future now that teaching was off the table.

Regardless of what I asked for, it would still mean telling my family and friends about our marriage sooner rather than later. Could I really do that and lie to my family for an entire year?

As if sensing my dilemma, Rafe spoke up again. "I will also promise you a few things now if you say yes: I will protect you as long as you're my wife; I'll give you whatever is within my power to give; and you'll be safe with me. I'll never touch you or kiss you or try to be a dick and demand marital rights."

I raised an eyebrow. "Marital rights? Which century is this?"

"That's what you focus on?"

Considering his words about never kissing me had caused disappointment to rush through me, yes, it was better to focus on bickering with him. "I'll think about it. But before I even do that, I have some questions."

"Okay," he said slowly, as if afraid of what I might ask.

I snorted at the image of tall, muscled, badass Rafael Mendoza being afraid of me.

The man in question peered at me with concern. "Are you still drunk, Abby?"

"No, I'm not drunk. Like you're one to ask, Mr. Wake-Up-Married-And-Hatches-A-Plan. I mean, who asks someone to stay married for a year for PR purposes?"

"Fair point. So, what are your questions?"

I gave him his phone back. "How will it all work? Will we live together? Will you be in Starry Hills the whole time? Or will you jet off and leave me for long periods?"

"Do you want me to leave you alone?"

That would be the easiest route, for sure. Because there was something Rafe probably didn't know, something I rarely admitted to myself—that I'd had a crush on him since I was eight years old. At one time, I'd wanted to kiss him and marry him and have his babies.

But his hurting Emmy had changed all that. Well, mostly. But attraction wasn't something I could turn off, and it took every bit of strength I had not to gawk at his boxer-clad body again.

However, learning what little bit I had about Rafe this morning only made me want to spend more time with him. If I could help him and Emmy fix things and make them closer, that alone might be worth it.

And to do that, I needed him around.

So I replied, "I'd rather you not disappear for weeks at a time, at least without telling me. And..."

"And, what?"

"Well, I've never really been anywhere outside the US. I'd like to see England and Scotland and Italy and, well, anywhere in Europe, really. It's like a starter traveling place for me. Maybe later I can be more adventurous and go to India or Peru or Kenya." Realizing how that might sound clingy, I quickly added, "Only if you're okay with it."

"You're the one who'd be doing me a favor, Abby. I'll do just about anything to repay it if you say yes."

Even kiss me?

Wait, woah. No. I needed to stop that crap right now.

I focused back on our conversation and poking the bear a little. "Anything, hmm? So if I wanted a million dollars in quarters, you'd do it?"

"Why the fuck would you want a million dollars in quarters?"

"Maybe I want to be like Scrooge McDuck and have a money vault I can admire."

"He swam in it, and I somehow think it'd hurt to swim in coins. Bills might work. But even then, they'd be covered in germs."

"Coins would be easier to clean."

He sighed. "Are you really asking for this, or is this another test?"

"It's called teasing, Rafe. Have you never heard of it?"

He grunted. "Yes. But asking for a vault of coins is just bloody ridiculous."

I smiled. "You just said bloody like a Brit."

He growled. "It happens. I spent nearly twenty

years there. I even had to adjust my pronunciation for some words, just to be understood. Twenty being one of them. Twun-tee and not twun-dee like we say here."

"Twun-tee. That was your jersey number, too. That must've been a pain in the ass. Oh, wait, arse."

I couldn't help but giggle. And as Rafe frowned harder, I laughed even more.

Eventually he asked, "Are you finished? I don't know about you, but I'm starving. I need bacon and coffee to tame this hangover."

"Sausage is better."

"Oh, hell no. You didn't just say that."

"Yep, I did. My aunt has a special recipe for home-made sausage that makes bacon look like junk food."

"Well, that just means more bacon for me. Let's have some shitty coffee, find food, and we can drive back. I can be silent, but I can also answer any other questions you might have."

"Any question?"

"Related to my proposal, Abigail. I reserve the right to stay quiet if you bring up silly shit like the coin vault again."

I sniffed. "It's not my fault that you're so serious. You're getting close to forty, after all. So I guess that means you're no fun."

"Yes, because all twenty-six-year-olds talk about swimming in money vaults," he drawled. "And I'm thirty-six, not nearly forty."

"Closer than I am, Grandpa."

"Abigail."

His warning tone only made me laugh. "Is that supposed to work on me?"

He ran his hand over his hair—that seemed to be a habit of his now—and said, "Maybe? You're different from the other women I've been with in the past. Not that we're together or anything. But you know what I mean."

Ah, yes. His legion of former women. I'd read about that over the years. Teenage Abigail had been devastated. But now? It was his past and had nothing to do with me.

Even if he was my husband.

Husband. Weird to think of Rafe as that since I never thought I'd have one after what happened with Travis Doucey.

But, nope, I wasn't going to waste brain cells thinking about that douchebag. So I focused on Rafe. "Well, I am a Wolfe sibling, after all. If you were looking for someone to fawn over you or bat her eyelashes or be demure, then you've got the wrong fake wife."

"I wouldn't want a woman like that as my wife."

For a second, we stared at each other. The way he said, "my wife," all low and growly, almost possessively, made me shiver.

A woman could get used to that.

Not that it was for real. He was probably only practicing in case I agreed to his plan. Because if I did, we'd have to convince the world it wasn't a ruse.

My stomach rumbled, and I actually didn't feel sick. The aspirin I'd taken in the bathroom had helped already.

I gestured at Rafe. "Get dressed so we can eat. I can't wait to steal all the sausage and you can have the tasteless bacon."

"You really don't want to start a bacon versus sausage war, Abigail."

My lips twitched. "If we stay married—which I still haven't decided—I suspect we'll have a lot of mini-wars about stupid stuff all the time. It could be fun."

He groaned, and I laughed. I watched as he grabbed his clothes and headed into the bathroom. I covertly checked out his ass and muscled thighs. Damn, he was toned. Soccer players were lean, and I liked that.

Not that it mattered. So I took out my phone as a distraction and gasped as I opened up my social media account. Because there was a picture of Rafe and I smiling, me dressed up, and both of us in what looked like a chapel.

I deleted it and hoped my family hadn't seen it. Because if so, keeping this a secret—even if I decided not to stay married to Rafe—would be impossible.

Chapter Four

Abby

Aunt Lori: Abby, where are you? You promised to help me get ready for the Valentine's Festival.
Me: Oh, crap. I totally forgot. Sorry! I'll be home soon.
Aunt Lori: What, did you go home with a hot guy last night? I hope you took pictures. <heart-eyed emoji>
Me: Um, no to the man and pictures.
Aunt Lori: Then I have a friend, and her son is quite the looker. And single. I can arrange a date with him.
Me: <sighing emoji> I've told you before, I'm not on the market right now.
Aunt Lori: It doesn't have to be forever. Just for a little fun between the sheets. <fire emoji>
Me: Aunt Lori! Just no!
Aunt Lori: I'm older but not dead, dearie. There's this

new retired guy who moved into town recently and all
the older women are circling. Younger ones, too. But I'm
biding my time. My chance will come.

Me: Then focus on that, Aunt Lori. Find a man of
your own.

Aunt Lori: I can do both! I'll show you the picture of
my friend's son when you get home. You are getting
home soon, right? Otherwise, I'll have to get West to
help me instead. And he just got married.

Me: <sighing emoji> I'll be home soon. Don't you dare
bother West and Emmy!

Aunt Lori: I'll be waiting, hottie picture and all, when
you get here. <heart emoji>

After breakfast with Rafe, he'd driven us home
to Starry Hills, and as soon as he got onto the
freeway, I promptly fell asleep. Part of it had
been exhaustion, but the other part had been that I was
overwhelmed with what to do about my accidental
marriage. I needed to take a walk through the orchard or
around Emmy's fields or anywhere without Rafe nearby
to clear my head.

Eventually, he dropped me off at the entrance to my
family's property so I could walk to the house and avoid
Aunt Lori's keen eyes. Before I shut the door, he said,
"When do you think you'll have an answer?"

I searched his gaze. "I don't know. But at least give
me a day or two. Right now, I just want a shower and
some fresh air." I paused, debated shutting the door

and avoiding the question, but decided to blurt, "Would you seek out other women while we were married?"

I had no right to ask that, of course. The marriage would be a fake one.

And yet, after my last humiliation, his answer was important to me.

Rafe didn't hesitate. "No. I'm loyal, Abby. It's why I stayed with the Dragons so long when better offers came. Even if it's in name only, I'd never betray my wife that way."

The part of me that broke after everything with Travis said Rafe's words were bullshit. I shouldn't trust him. He was a man, after all. And they'd say anything to get you into bed.

Except, Rafe wasn't proposing that. Maybe, just maybe, he'd keep his word.

Except, he won't. Why should he? said the voice inside my head.

Wanting to growl and snarl, I took a deep breath and merely nodded instead. "I'll think about it. That's all I can promise."

"That's all I ask for, Abigail. Text me when you want to talk again."

"I will, thanks."

I shut the door and watched Rafe drive away until he vanished from sight. Turning around, I walked down the road and tapped each fence post I walked past.

The combined familiarity of the tapping and the sight of still-dormant grapevines helped calm my mind a little. I was still in no shape to make a huge decision—

that would require some sleep—but the peace and quiet of my family's land always made me feel better.

It was strange living back here again, after living with Emmy. And yet, I wasn't going to stay with a pair of newlyweds and the twins. I probably could've found a place in town for myself, but I hated living alone. Some people loved it, and that was fine. But all it did was give me time to think of who else might leave me next.

I was happy that my friends were finding love and getting married—even if one of them had married my brother, of all people—but as their families grew, I worried they might not have time for me. Then I'd end up that awkward single person lingering at the edges of the room.

Sure, everyone would try to set me up. And I had wanted to find love at one point. But after being tricked and conned by Travis, I didn't know if I could trust any man outside of my family.

So awkward single person it was. Although at some point, I'd have to get over living by myself. Once Beck and Sabrina started having babies, there'd be less and less room for me in the house.

You could live with Rafe for a year and then buy your own place.

Before I could dwell on that, I reached the front door, and it promptly opened, revealing my brother, Zane. He was one of the twins born before me and had only recently come back from deployment as a Navy SEAL because of his injuries. He'd mostly healed but still couldn't lift anything heavy or stand still for long periods of time.

He asked, "Where the hell did you go yesterday?"

I raised my eyebrows. "I didn't realize I had to report my every movement to you."

As soon as the words left my lips, I regretted it. Zane and I were still trying to find our footing with each other after being apart for nearly ten years. So I quickly added, "Sorry. I had too much to drink last night, and I'm cranky."

"Sugar might help. There are some chocolate chip cookies in the kitchen that I made."

"You're a baker now?"

"I can sit on a stool and let the stand mixer do most of the work. So, yes. I bake now."

Since we'd all learned that Zane would rather be stabbed in the eye than talk about his physical shortcomings since his injuries, I teased, "Don't get too good at it and put Amber out of business."

He rolled his eyes. "I can make exactly three things right now. I think Amber's bakery is safe." He lowered his voice, "I'm mainly learning to bake so Zach stops being such a grumpy asshole. He has a sweet tooth but avoids the bakery at all costs now. And with Avery moving in with Emmy, he's going to need someone to feed him."

Avery was our niece, West's daughter from his first marriage, and a twin herself—her brother was Wyatt. She also loved making cookies.

I also knew why Zach avoided the bakery—because of Amber King. After loving Zach for years, she'd finally started dating someone seriously, and Zach didn't like it. However, the situation was entirely his fault—he'd never shown any romantic interest in Amber—and at this point, he either had to do something to swoop my friend off her feet or let her move on.

A timer beeped in the background, and Zane cursed. "They're going to burn."

He walked—okay, more like shuffled because of his back injury—and I followed him into the kitchen. The yummy scent of cookies filled the air, and I swiped one off the cooling rack. After demolishing one, I picked up another. "These are pretty good. Make sure to hide some for me so Zach doesn't eat them all."

"Look at what the cat finally dragged in," Zach said from behind me.

I didn't even turn around and gave him the finger. "I'm going to eat all the cookies just for that comment."

He stopped next to me, grabbed the cooling rack stacked with cookies, and held it out of reach. "I'll just take these."

"Are you ever not annoying?"

He raised a dark eyebrow. "I was being nice before you threatened to steal all the cookies, but no more." His eyes looked over my face. "Why do you look like you went to hell and back?"

I flipped him off again. "Says the man who will have to find some woman who pities him to wake up to that face every day."

Zach grinned. "Now I know you're tired because that's not your A-game, Abby. I'm sexy, and you know it."

I made retching sounds. "Just no. I already have to

work at not imagining Emmy with West. Don't push me over the edge."

And I suspected I'd soon have to do the same with my brother Nolan and my friend Katie, even with the whole Katie-refusing-to-see-Nolan thing right now.

Zane jumped in. "Zach might have to move away if he ever wants to see a naked woman again. No one in Starry Hills will give him a chance."

After swallowing my cookie, I said, "I'm sitting right here. And I don't want to hear about Zach and naked women."

Zach ignored me and sighed dramatically. "It's true. They keep turning me down, apart from old Mrs. Easton."

Zane smirked. "There's something about an older woman that can be fun."

"Older, yes. But she's seventy-two and I draw the line at septuagenarians."

"Since when do you know words like septuagenarians?" I drawled.

Zach gave me the middle finger. "I read. Not all of us are fancy college graduates."

Memories threatened to break free, ones about my mentor teacher's betrayal and how I'd never teach like I'd always wanted to do.

I grabbed a few cookies and headed toward the door. I heard Zach say, "I'm sorry, Abby. Come back!" But I kept walking.

However, instead of going upstairs to shower and crash into bed, I went outside and walked toward the apple orchard. Memories of my mom were the strongest there, especially since she'd tried to make it a fun place to play after my dad's death when I was seven.

As the bare branches came into view, a sense of peace fell over me. Here, my mom had given so many hugs and kisses. My dad had even chased me and the twins around the trees when we'd been young. Not to mention my friends and I had climbed the trees as kids and pretended they were ship masts and we were pirates on the open sea.

After all the chaos with Rafe this morning, plus Katie's current dilemma with Nolan's ex-bitch, and even Zane struggling with the changes to his body after being discharged from the Navy SEALs, I needed some peace and quiet.

Except when I approached the center of the orchard —where the Wishing Tree, stone arch, and bench were located—Nolan paced back and forth, running his hands through his hair, muttering something.

I'd guessed for a while that Nolan was in love with Katie. And while one of my greatest fears was that another of my best friends would get married and eventually forget I existed, I couldn't be selfish. Two people I loved deserved happiness.

And so I went to talk to my brother and see how I could help him with Katie.

Chapter Five

Rafe

Emmy: By the way, you're coming to dinner next week.

Me: I am?

Emmy: Yes. I won't take no for an answer. You and West need to learn how to get along.

Me: Can't we just go out to lunch, me and you?

Emmy: No. I'm having a big family dinner here. 7 o'clock on Saturday. Don't be late.

Me: So the entire Wolfe family will be there?

Emmy: Yes. And I will send them to hunt you down, if you try to bail.

Me (typed but deleted): If you only knew that I was married into their family, too. For now.

Me (actual reply instead): I'll be there.

Emmy: Okay, see you then. <heart emoji>

As I reread the exchange with my sister, part of me wished it was a little less distant and formal. And yet, it was entirely my fault that it was. I'd been the one to stay away from Starry Hills since our parents' funeral. I'd also given up custody of Emmy when I was nineteen. True, I hadn't been mature enough to raise a little girl at that point—we were nearly ten years apart—but I'd also blamed myself for making her an orphan.

I still struggled with that guilt, to be honest. Although Emmy kept telling me it wasn't my fault that our parents had died in a car crash, even though they'd been driving to the airport to come see me play soccer in England.

A knock on my front door brought me back to the present. Few people knew where I lived on the outskirts of Starry Hills, but one of them would be my wife.

And sure enough, as I opened the door, Abby stood there. She wore jeans and a sweater, her dark hair long around her face and shoulders. With her cheeks flushed from the cold, I could barely tear my eyes from her face. When had the annoying little sister of my best friend turned into this fucking gorgeous woman?

She raised her brows. "Can I come in, or are you going to stand there and stare at me?"

Clearing my throat, I waved her inside and shut the

door behind her. "How do you know I wasn't staring at some bird shit in your hair?"

"There aren't a lot of birds in February, Rafael. Have you been away so long that you forgot about that?"

"There are birds year-round. It's not my fault that you haven't paid attention."

She rolled her eyes. "Remind me again why I married you?"

Neither of us had fully remembered the reason yet, and she knew it. "I was drunk."

She flipped me off. "Maybe I should just leave, asshole."

Sighing, I reached out and grabbed her hand. Ignoring how icy they were and how I wanted to rub them warm again, I replied, "Sorry. I'm going to work harder at being nice to you."

"I don't want you to be too nice, though. I like bickering with you sometimes."

I frowned. "You do?"

"It's like a sport in my family." She shrugged one shoulder. "It keeps life interesting."

"I've never had a woman want to argue with me."

"Well, as we've already established, I'm not like the other women you've been with. I'll never fit into a size two dress, for one thing. Or wear four-inch heels."

I wanted to growl that her curves were perfect, but held back. If we stayed married, it would be platonic. The sooner I accepted that, the better.

However, I didn't want her to keep harping on herself, so I said, "I like that you're tall."

"Only because you're an inch taller than me. Trust me, when the guy is short and his eye line is right at your boobs, it's a little creepy."

"Well, that's something else I can offer—if you stay my wife, I'll glare and chase away any guy who talks to your chest and not your face."

The corner of her mouth ticked up. "The boob-staring police? Is that a new department?"

"I would only serve one woman. Everyone else would have to fend for themselves."

She tapped her chin. "That *is* a tempting reason. But I think I need a little more about the specifics, which means we need to talk."

I'd been dreading "the talk" for days now. Because yes, it'd been a little over a week. Abby had been helping Nolan and Katie with their whole scandal showdown with some actress. What was her name again? Oh, right: Wendy Webster.

But apparently Nolan and Katie were in love and together and would become yet another couple I barely knew but would be jealous of.

Not the time to think about that. I gestured toward the kitchen. "I've been practicing my coffee making skills. I also have brownies. They were your favorite at Emmy's sleepovers as a kid. I don't know if they still are, but I figured I should have something in case you're hungry."

She sat on a stool at the kitchen island and turned toward me. For a few seconds, she frowned and studied me. Then just as quickly, her face returned to her default—as if she were about to smirk at some remark or other. "Chocolate is always a good choice. But only put out a few and hide the rest, though. Brownies are definitely one of my weaknesses, and I can't stop eating them, even if I'm full."

"Can't say I'm the same with sweet stuff." I went to the espresso machine. "What do you want?"

She smiled, propped her arms on the counter, and said, "A latte with a pretty chocolate design on top?"

"Think you're outsmarting me, don't you? But guess what?" I removed one of those stencils they used for exactly her request. "I came prepared."

She laughed. "Point to Mendoza. However, the jury's still out about whether it tastes any good or not. If not, then you owe me a coffee from Starry Eyes Bakery."

Her comment gave me hope she would agree to the year of marriage. However, I wanted a little more playfulness with Abby before broaching that topic. Even though it was something so simple—bantering over coffee—it was more fun than I'd had in a long time.

Not wanting to think about how it was my own fucking fault I hadn't made many friends over the years, I focused on making the best damn latte in the world.

After I finished and placed the mug and some brownies in front of her, she sipped her drink and closed her eyes. "Mmm. That's pretty good."

I should make a remark or gloat or say something. However, I could only stare at the milk foam on her upper lip. I wanted to lean over, lick it off, and kiss her before spreading her wide and fucking her on the counter.

I stumbled backward and rattled the espresso machine on the counter. Abby's eyes flew open, but I busied myself making my own cup.

"It's actually pretty good, Rafe. I hadn't expected a famous soccer player such as yourself to know how to make a latte."

"You can't train for or play soccer twenty-four hours a day."

"No, but as a pro, it probably consumed most of your time. And speaking of your career, it's one of the things you have to promise to talk about if you want me to remain your wife."

Your wife. The words on her lips sent a little thrill through me.

Okay, I must've had too much caffeine this morning because this was Abigail Wolfe we were talking about. Putting aside how love wasn't for me, she was my little sister's best friend. One who deserved so much better than me.

Think of your training facility. Right. Abby was part of a plan, one that would benefit the both of us, if she agreed to it.

I turned around. "So tell me what's on this list of things I have to agree to."

She swallowed her bite of brownie. Too bad there wasn't any chocolate on her lips for me to lick off.

Focus, Mendoza.

Abby replied, "Well, the main ones are that we need to be honest with each other, you need to work on fixing things with your sister, and at the end of it, I want a big favor. I'm still not sure what it'll be yet, but I have a few options—ranging from you buying me a house to destroying an ex to introducing me to some of your soccer friends."

The thought of introducing Abby to other footballers —er, soccer players, yes, I needed to start thinking that way again—made me want to punch something. Or someone.

Which was ridiculous, as she wasn't mine in any way. *Except she is your wife.*

I replied, "You can have just about anything, Abigail, provided I have enough funds left over to run my business and get it going."

She raised her eyebrows. "Just how rich are you, then?"

"Enough."

"That's not very honest."

I shrugged. "Too many former teammates got wrapped up in being rich and turned into complete assholes. I try not to. I buy what I need, donate to a few charities, and save or invest the rest. If you're looking for ten private jets, a yacht, or some other such crap, I don't have it."

"I get seasick, so no thanks to a yacht, anyway."

Part of me was relieved she didn't push the money thing. My fame and fortune had always been a double-edged sword, for many reasons.

I asked, "You get seasick? Really? But you loved swimming in Lake Tahoe when you were little. Or even Lake Sonoma."

"Ah, but swimming is different from being on a boat.

I know it's weird, since riding horses never really bothered me and most cars are okay. But boats are the worst. I learned that in high school during our classes' senior trip to Catalina Island. Thank goodness for the BFF Circle hiding how much I puked my guts out. Luckily, I found a bracelet to help me on the way back."

The BFF Circle were Abby, Katie, Amber, and my sister, Emmy. They'd been inseparable since elementary school.

And they'd been a nuisance to teenage me and West.

Not that I was going to think of West, who was yet another person I'd pushed away after my parents' death.

I focused back on Abby. "I don't get motion sickness of any kind."

"But there has to be something that bothers you. Tell me."

"Is this some kind of test, then?"

"Rafe, I'm just trying to get to know you a little. If you can't even talk to me now, here in your kitchen, then how will you fare when the world is watching us if we stay married?"

"Will you be okay with the attention? Because the world, especially in Europe, *will* be watching us."

"You're changing the subject. But my answer? I think so. As long as you don't have an ex who will send an army of fans after me."

"If you mean someone like Nolan's ex, then no. My longest relationship only lasted a few months."

Fuck. Why had I shared that with her?

"Well, West went from no serious girlfriend ever to

married to widow to married again. So I won't hold it against you. However, you still haven't told me something that bothers you."

She stared at me expectantly. It should be easy to answer her.

However, I wasn't one of those people who blurted things out freely. Hell, my default was to obsess over things—soccer or sex—and forget about my problems.

And while I didn't know Abby well as an adult, as a kid, she'd loved to share everything and be the life of the party. I hadn't seen much of that side of her since returning to Starry Hills, but I suspected that part of her still existed.

So if I wanted her to remain my wife, I'd have to try and meet her partway. So, even though it was like pulling teeth, I replied, "I don't like roller coasters that go upside down. They make me feel sick, and one time as a boy, I had to rush to the bathroom and throw up."

She shuddered. "I also don't like the ones that go upside down or have a lot of turns. The one time we went to Disneyland before my dad died, I always stayed outside with West for the roller coaster-like rides. Don't tell him I said anything, but West doesn't like Space Mountain. At all."

"So if we go to Disneyland, we can avoid the faster rides with the huge lines and save loads of time."

"That would be perfect. To be honest, I always felt guilty going with the BFF Circle or my family and someone offering to wait with me."

I hadn't been to Disneyland since I was a teenager, but now I really wanted to take Abby. Buy her a silly hat, take a picture in front of the castle, and maybe even hold her close while we watched the night show.

Of course, that would only happen—maybe—if she remained my wife. So, even though I wanted to talk and tease Abby some more, it was time to get serious. "Have you made a decision yet about whether you want to stay married to me for a year or not?"

She nibbled on a brownie before answering, "I'm open to it, but I need to know a few more details first. What will the living arrangements be? How much time will you spend in Starry Hills versus England and elsewhere? How much do I have to play up the role? What will we tell our families? That kind of stuff."

I sat across from her and downed the last of my coffee before answering. "Well, you'd live here with me, but you can sleep in the guest room. And I'll be spending more time in Starry Hills than Manchester. I'll need to make a couple of trips to the UK to tie up a few things, and you can come or stay here, your choice."

"I'd like to go, if my family can spare me."

"You want to keep working for them? Because you don't have to. As my wife, I'd take care of you."

"Thanks, but I need to keep busy."

Probably to avoid getting stuck in the past, or thinking about her ex, or whatever shit had gone down in San Jose.

I could just nod and say that was fine. I had no problem with Abby working for her family.

And yet, I sensed she wanted more than to give tours or conduct wine tastings. So I blurted, "I plan to have a tutoring center at my training facility, mainly for the local community. However, I don't have anyone to run it yet. Maybe you could do it."

For a few seconds, she stared at me, her expression unreadable. Just as I thought maybe I'd fucked up—she could be done with teaching, for all I knew—she asked, "Do you have a curriculum? Or would I have to make it? What are your projected student numbers? Is it only for paying customers, or for anyone?"

Her questions gave me hope that she was interested. "There's no curriculum yet, especially since it'll depend on what people need. You could always hire help, for subjects you don't know. And the center would be free and open to all students in Starry Hills. Anyone who comes from out of town will have a sliding fee, depending on their situation."

She shifted in her seat, and then again, as she bit her bottom lip. I stared hard at her teeth and plump mouth, until her voice nearly made me jump as she said, "I'm interested, but there's something you should know about me before you offer me the job. Especially since this whole fake marriage thing is to protect your business's reputation."

I frowned. "What do I need to know?"

She looked off to the side. "During my student teaching internship, my mentor teacher seduced me and tricked me into believing he was in love with me. So imagine my surprise when he announced his engagement to someone else on my last day." She finally met my eyes, her expression sad and shameful. "And if I ever breathe a word of our affair to his now wife, he's going to tell everyone I only got a passing grade because I slept with him. Not only that, he threatened to tell the world lies about me sleeping with students, too." She sighed. "So you see, staying married to me might not be the best idea, after all, Rafe. I could bring a bigger scandal than any annulment."

Chapter Six

Abby

Emmy: You're coming to the big dinner West and I are hosting, aren't you?
Me: I should be there.
Emmy: I miss us living together, you know.
Me: I know. But it wasn't feasible for me to stay.
Emmy: Is everything okay? You've been kind of quiet recently. And there haven't been any emojis.
Me: I'm fine. I'm just trying to figure out what to do with my future since I don't want to live with my family forever.
Emmy: You can always come back to work for me, if you want. Although I know your heart isn't there.
Me: Trust me, I'm working on the future. But enough of

my problems. Enjoy your new hubby and kids! I have to go help Aunt Lori.

Emmy: I'm here if you need me. Love you. <heart emoji>

Me: Love you, too.

I t was only fair that I told Rafe of Travis's threats and blackmail, and I hadn't even shared all of it. My ex had said that if I tried teaching anywhere in California, he'd go to the police about me seducing students. He even had a few teacher buddies who would back him up.

I'd tested him out to see if he was bluffing by interviewing in Santa Rosa not too long ago. But as soon as the interview was over and they'd offered me the job, Travis had sent a naked picture of me. It had originally been of us, but he'd had someone Photoshop it so that it was me with some teenager.

It'd made me sick, but I'd gotten the message and turned down the job. My family thought I hadn't gotten it, but it wasn't as if I could tell them the truth. My own naïveté and lust had caused my shitstorm, one that I'd have to figure out at some point.

Rafe deserved to know the truth, though. And honestly, I'd expected disgust to flare in his eyes and for him to tell me to fuck off.

However, anger flared in his gaze as he curled his fingers into fists. "Who the fuck does he think he is?"

I blinked. "Pardon?"

He stood up fast, and his stool crashed to the floor. "That asshole's the one who took advantage of his position of power. He's the fucker who treats women as toys to use and discard. He should be the one fucking punished, not you. Why hasn't your family helped you with this? Nolan has the money to make that asshole pay."

I blinked, trying to wrap my head around Rafe's reaction. I finally made my mouth work again. "Well, they don't know about it."

"Why not?"

"Why do you think? Oh, let me just tell Aunt Lori about how stupid I was, how embarrassed I still am, or how sick I feel that anyone thinks I'd take advantage of high school students, take advantage of *children*, like that."

"But you don't deserve to be punished for what he did to you."

"And I agree. I tried to call his bluff once, but..."

I shut my mouth. Given how angry he already was, I shouldn't tell Rafe any more.

However, he stalked around the kitchen island and gently took my chin between his fingers. "What happened when you tried to call his bluff, Abigail?"

For a second, I wanted to be a brat and tell him to mind his own fucking business.

But the mixture of tenderness and anger—for me, not at me—made me pause. "Why do you care, Rafael?"

"Because for the moment, you're still my wife, and that makes you mine to protect."

"Protect? What, is this like the eighteenth century and the British are coming?"

"Don't do that, Abby. Don't change the subject with a joke."

For a few beats, I stared at him. Talking about this was hard, harder than anything else in the world. Because I'd been an idiot, and it wasn't easy to admit that. Not even to myself.

Could I confide in him about my screw up? He'd be the first one to hear the details. And given how he was more stranger than a friend at this point, it might be easier.

At some point, his finger started to stroke my jaw oh-so-gently, and I nearly hummed. What would it be like to be Rafe's wife? To kiss him when I wanted, lick every inch of his body, and be there to cheer him up when he had a bad day?

What would it be like to have a man who'd stand by me instead of tossing me aside for a richer, prettier version?

Would he be someone I could trust? Lean on?

A small voice said, *Don't believe in fairy tales, Abby. You learned that lesson already.*

I stepped away, and Rafe released me. Part of me wanted to rush back to him, but I held my ground.

He repeated, "What else did he do to you? Tell me. I can't make a decision without it."

I swallowed and tugged at my top. Could I do this? Could I really reveal more of my past to this man? A man I'd once idolized but now argued with constantly and barely knew at all?

Damn it, Travis really had screwed me up. Because I never used to hesitate in sharing stuff about myself. If anything, I had always shared too much.

For a split second, I wanted to run home and cry. I missed that version of myself so much.

His expression and voice softened. "Just tell me, Abigail. I've known you your whole life, and one mistake from your past isn't going to make me run for the hills."

"It might if it ruins your new dream."

"I doubt it can."

His cocky words sparked anger inside of me. And before I could become trapped inside my own head again, I blurted, "My ex has a deep fake video of me having sex with a former student. The original footage had been of me and him, but he had someone alter it, to the point most people will think it's real. And the worst thing of all is that I hadn't wanted him to take the video at first. But he convinced me it would please him, and I let him record us. But I never thought, I never..."

My voice cracked as my eyes heated with tears. I turned away and placed my hands over my face. One stupid night from my past had the potential to ruin my life and future and might even land me in jail because it looked so real.

How could I have been so fucking stupid?

That was a question I asked myself every day and never had an answer.

Rafe's soft voice was right behind me as he said, "I'll find a way to destroy it, Abigail. You have my word."

After lowering my hands, I dared a glance behind

me. At Rafe's determined look and clenched jaw, I nearly believed him.

Almost.

Don't be that naïve again, Abby.

A harsh laugh escaped me. "As if it's that easy. He has buddies to back up the story, probably some copies stored in the cloud, and who knows what else. He's a coach and might've even gotten students to agree to be witnesses. If it gets out, I'll probably get arrested."

"No."

"What do you mean, 'No'?"

"No. You're my wife, Abby. And no matter what it takes, I'll help you."

"I haven't said yes to your plan yet."

"Do you want to say no?" He stepped aside and gestured toward the door. "If so, feel free to walk out and we'll never speak of this again. I'll get the annulment and it'll be our drunken secret. But if you want to stay married to me for a year, then know I'll protect you against that asshole ex and anyone else who threatens you. That's now part of the deal. So, which will it be?"

I searched his gaze, glanced at the door, and back again. "But my past could ruin your future."

"You have no reason to trust me, I know that. But I take my promises rather seriously. And I will keep that bastard from hurting you, hurting us, hurting anyone else. If my future gets ruined, it's because of my actions and no one else's." He gestured again. "So, are you going to leave? Or will you stay and be my wife?"

The easy route would be to run. After all, with time,

I suspected Travis would tire of threatening me and leave me alone.

But what if he doesn't? What if he gets off toying with people?

And yet, if I stayed, it meant trusting Rafe, trusting a man unrelated to me to not hurt me.

As long as you keep your feelings and heart out of it, you'll be okay. Friendship is different from a relationship. Betrayal can still hurt, but it's not as devastating.

I blurted, "Will you promise to tell me what your plan is before you go after him?"

"Yes."

His words rang with truth. And yet, my cynical ass still didn't want to believe him.

My first option was suffering for who knew how long, hoping Travis would tire of his games. Or, I could agree to remain Rafe's wife and hope he didn't come to regret being married to me when the whole Travis thing eventually blew up. Because, yeah, me marrying a world-famous soccer player would probably set off my ex and make him act out.

Rafe put out his hand, palm up. "Let me help you, Abigail. Please."

I stared at his hand, my heart thudding inside my chest, and made a decision.

Chapter Seven

Rafe

I t took every bit of restraint I had not to rush out the door, find this Travis ex of hers, and beat the shit out of him.

Just thinking about Abby receiving threats from some man who'd manipulated her, used her, and discarded her made me want to kill him.

And with her revelations, any thoughts of letting Abby refuse my offer had gone up in smoke. She needed protection, and I would be the man to give it to her. However, the hard part was convincing her to let me take care of her for a year.

So I gave her choices and did my best to let the truth shine in my eyes and ring in my voice. Although after what that bastard had done to her, I wasn't sure how she could trust any man ever again, except for maybe her family.

I waited as she stared at my hand, wanting to say more but knowing I had to be careful with this woman. She'd been hurt, badly, and she needed to have choices and control. Maybe I could've convinced her with arguments or made her feel guilty about embarrassing her family or any of the similar shit her ex probably would've done.

But while I was far from perfect, I wasn't someone who used and abused women, be it with words or fists. And so I waited.

When Abby finally walked forward, I held my breath. But instead of heading toward the door, she gingerly placed her hand in mine. I curled my fingers around hers and asked, "Are you sure?"

She nodded. "As long as you know the risks and won't blame me for them later."

"I won't fucking blame you, Abigail. I blame the ex. What's his last name?"

"I'll tell you later, maybe once you've cooled down and we've set up a routine. But not now. I'm tired of talking about him."

I squeezed her hand. "Then we'll table it for the moment. Besides, we have more important things, anyway, like moving you into my place as soon as possible and telling our families."

She groaned. "That's the part I dread the most—telling my family."

"Because I'm not the catch they were hoping for?

Were they waiting for a billionaire philanthropist instead? Hmm?"

She rolled her eyes, and I nearly smiled since it meant the fun, more confident version of Abby was returning. She replied, "Being rich and sexy, of course you're a catch, even if you're not a billionaire philanthropist. However, you're also Emmy's brother, and West kind of doesn't like you right now."

"You think I'm sexy?"

"Really? That's what you focus on?"

I tugged her closer, and she came, but stopped about six inches away from me. "We'll talk about how you think I'm dead gorgeous later. For now, we need to decide when to tell our families and also practice being a couple."

"Dead gorgeous? Is that more Brit speak?" I narrowed my eyes, and she laughed. "Fine. I'll stop pointing it out unless it's really funny. As for our families, you're going to Emmy and West's upcoming dinner, aren't you?"

"You want to tell everyone at their first dinner after getting married?"

"Well, it has to be soon. Unless you want to wait to have me move in here."

"No."

She blinked. "Um, that was growly and quick."

Shit, she was right. But for some reason, I craved her being around me. I wanted her close, both to talk with her and to protect her.

Yes, to protect her. That was the reason.

Liar.

I focused on the topic at hand. "It'll look better, from a PR perspective, if the news of our Vegas wedding slips out."

"True. Well, then Emmy and West's dinner is probably the best time since everyone will be there. However, that means we have a lot to do in the next few days, and not just me packing everything up in secret. We need to decide what kind of married couple we're going to be."

She tugged, and I reluctantly released her hand. After sitting on a stool, she peered into her empty mug and sighed. "Oh, caffeine, you would've made this easier."

I went to the espresso machine. "You just have to ask, Abigail. I won't say yes to everything, but at least ask me. For the next year, you're not on your own. We're a team."

"Sorry, I'll try. But I'm not very good at directly asking for things. Well, since *him*."

I turned and leaned on the island, so I could be at her eye level. "That's one of my requirements for this marriage then: you have to ask me for what you want. I might say no, but I will give you a straight answer."

"That's going to be hard. But that means you have to do it too."

I put out a hand to shake. "Let's seal our deal, shall we?"

"Shall we?" I opened my mouth to stop her mocking, but she placed her hand in mine and shook. "We shall."

Her soft, warm hand fit perfectly in mine. She wasn't tiny and delicate and someone who'd break if I fucked her too hard.

Not that I was going to fuck her at all.

I quickly released her hand and turned to make her another latte. "As for the type of marriage we're going to have, I think we should stick to the truth as closely as possible."

"Hmm, but waking up married in Vegas, with no memory of how, isn't really going to endear you to my family, Rafe."

After turning on the machine, I decided to test the truth with her. "You've fancied me for a long time, Abigail. I'm sure your family won't be too surprised at what happened."

For a few seconds, only the hum of the espresso machine filled the room. Then Abby appeared at my side, leaned against the counter, and crossed her arms over her chest. It took everything I had not to stare at her plumped up breasts.

She said, "Explain yourself, Rafael Mendoza."

"You had a crush on me as a kid, right?"

"Er, yes, but—"

"And Emmy let slip that you've followed my career all these years."

"Maybe, but—"

"And we had a moment, right after I was pulled over for driving on the wrong side of the road and the cop let us off with a warning. You remember the one."

Her cheeks heated. "It wasn't a moment. We were arguing, and you kept staring at my mouth. You're the one who leaned in, not me."

I faced her and raised an eyebrow. "The truth, remember? You leaned in, too."

"So, I'm attracted to you. I can't control it. However, it doesn't mean I want to kiss you and make love to you and have your babies."

For a split second, I imagined Abby round with my child, my hand over her belly as our baby kicked.

Then I pushed it away. I wasn't going to have kids. I'd fucked up too many lives already in the past. I didn't need to hurt anyone else.

Because even though I didn't want to, I seemed to hurt everyone I'd ever loved.

Abby's voice softened. "What were you thinking about just then?"

As I tried to think of how to reply, something vibrated in Abby's purse. Then again. And again.

She sighed. "If that's another group chat this early in the morning, I'm going to murder whoever started it."

I watched her walk over to her purse, unable to take my eyes from her hips. What would it be like to hold them as I fucked her from behind?

Stop it, Mendoza. You can't touch.

But Abby's next words cooled my lust. "She knows about our wedding."

Chapter Eight

Abby

Amber: So why were you in a chapel with Rafe
Mendoza?
Amber: Did you actually get married?
Amber: I haven't been on social media and only just
now got your DM.
Amber: Abby, this is important! Why were you in
Vegas with Rafe and then sent me a message and picture
about being married?
Amber: Abigail! If I have to hunt you down to get some
answers, I will.

I nearly dropped my phone as I read Amber's texts. I didn't remember sending anyone pics or messages. And given everything that had happened lately with Katie—Nolan's ex had been bullying her and getting her fans to troll Katie—I'd been avoiding social media in general.

But I quickly opened the right app and, sure enough, I'd sent a message to Amber with the picture I'd deleted and a note about being hitched. Something about it being fun and how it'd keep Aunt Lori from asking me questions about San Jose.

The fact I'd contacted Amber wasn't a surprise. Out of the BFF Circle, she could keep a secret the best. Emmy was pretty good too, but these days I felt guilty about asking her to keep things from West. And even drunk, I'd probably remembered that.

Of course, my messages now complicated things because Amber would want to talk about it. Plus, she would also watch everything Rafe and I did closely.

Resisting a sigh, I blurted, "She knows about our wedding."

Rafe was at my side in the next second. "Who?"

"Amber King." I explained about drunk messaging her and added, "We're going to have to rope her into our master plan, to some degree."

"Why?"

"Thinking about it, this could be a good thing. Amber can say she knew about us. Combined with Emmy knowing about my childhood crush—yes, you were right about that part and only that part—my family might buy it better."

"Buy what better, though? Have you remembered the night we got married?"

I wished. All I remembered were fuzzy moments of laughter. "Not yet. However, I might have a story that'll please my family. We can say that we kissed, had explosive chemistry, and ended up getting married in Vegas as a spur-of-the-moment type of thing."

He raised his eyebrows. "You want to tell your aunt that we got horny after a kiss?"

I rolled my eyes. "You must not know my aunt very well. You haven't been to many dinners at our house, but she full-on teases Beck, West, and Nolan about breaking beds now that they've found love." He looked dubious, so I added, "Do you really want me to show you some of the texts she sent? They'd make anyone blush."

"Er, no. I believe you."

I smiled. "Maybe I should show you a few, just so you get to know my family better."

"I can get to know your family without reading your aunt's lust-filled messages."

I laughed. "You'll get a few soon enough. She'll add you to the group chat before you can blink."

"Maybe I'll keep a second phone, one for emergencies, and then I can ignore the other one."

"She'll just ask you about her comments when you next see her. Aunt Lori loves teasing and annoying us with emojis. And since she helped raise us, putting up with it is the least we Wolfe siblings can do."

Sometimes I forgot about how much my aunt had given up to take care of us. After her husband had been killed in action—he'd been a Navy SEAL—she'd moved to Starry Hills to live with us kids and our mom.

He grunted. "Okay, now I'll feel like a dick if I try to ignore her."

After searching his gaze, I said softly, "You're a much sweeter person than you let on, Rafe. Aren't you?"

"On second thought, maybe I should get that second phone..."

I could tell he was teasing and did my best not to smile. "Well, you can try, but she'll find out your second number. From me."

He narrowed his eyes, and I batted my eyelashes, acting all innocent.

Just as Rafe opened his mouth, my phone beeped again. And again.

A quick peek told me that Amber hadn't given up, and I said to Rafe, "I need to answer her or she'll just keep messaging me." After typing a quick reply, I met his gaze. "I'm going to talk with her tomorrow, so we need to figure out what our marriage will look like to the outside world. Will we be the kind of couple who touches all the time? Holds hands? Or will we be the type who only show affection in private? Maybe somewhere in between?"

I knew what I wanted, even if it'd be dangerous. But I wasn't about to blurt that I longed to hold Rafe's hand again.

Even if it'd probably lead to another "moment" and us nearly kissing.

Not for the first time, I wished I could remember the night we'd gotten married.

He replied, "It's going to take more than an hour or two to figure things out. So we'll sketch out the basics today and after you talk with Amber tomorrow, we can practice being a couple in private."

At his heated gaze, a jolt shot through me and ended between my thighs. Part of me wanted to know if he would kiss me, strip me, and make love to me. You know, just so we didn't have to lie about the wedding being consummated.

Like that even mattered in modern day. And yet, if it would make the marriage even more legal, I'd be willing to strip and fulfill a long-held fantasy of mine.

It would only be sex, and nothing else. My heart was off-limits. But nothing said I couldn't have a little fun.

Anything to erase Travis's criticisms and manipulations and maybe finally banish his words about me not being very good in bed.

Rafe stepped closer, stopping about a foot away from me. He was only an inch or two taller, and yet he made me feel smaller and more delicate for once. Having height, wide hips, and extra weight often made me feel like a giant who'd break any man if I rode him.

You're sexy and a catch. Don't let Travis's words hurt you further.

Which was easier said than done.

Rafe lifted his hand and traced my cheek with his forefinger. I leaned into his touch, and when he cupped my face, I closed my eyes and sighed. His hands were big and warm and a little rough.

But more than that, being near him felt...safe. Which didn't make any sense.

His voice was lower than before as he said, "I won't bring up past women unless I have to, but it's common knowledge that I always touch and hold and show affection to any woman that I'm with. So I'll have to touch my wife in public, Abigail. Often."

The way he said my full name, deep and growly, made my eyes fly open. But his expression was unreadable, even as he stroked my cheek.

His eyes were a deep brown, almost black, and he had some of the longest eyelashes I'd ever seen on a man. It nearly made me smile, as it was a huge contrast to his rugged jaw, chiseled cheekbones, and faint dusting of scruff on his face.

Scruff that would tickle my inner thigh as he licked my pussy.

Holy crap, how was I ever going to fall asleep being in a bed only a few rooms away from his? The whole marriage consummation thing was starting to look more like a necessity, otherwise I'd never get anything done.

I finally croaked, "Okay."

His eyes searched mine. "If I ever make you feel uncomfortable, you tell me. Poke me, step on my foot, or whatever to signal for me to stop, and I will."

For a second, I merely stared at him. My past experiences with men, even beyond Travis, had often involved creative ways to avoid an unwanted touch or kiss.

Maybe you've been with the wrong men.

Even so, I wasn't about to instantly throw down my barriers and think Rafe really wanted to be married to me.

Cynical AF Abby, that's what I needed to be.

"Get too handsy, and I'll punch you in the balls."

He blinked. "Noted."

"My brothers are overprotective, too. All five of them. Think you can handle that?"

"If you're trying to scare me away, it won't work, Abigail. Over the years, I've had to face hundreds of adrenaline-filled men on the pitch. I can handle your brothers."

"Ah, but those men were merely playing a game. I'm their only sister."

"Just a game? Are you trying to start another argument?"

"Well, technically, it *is* just a game. Sure, you got paid millions of dollars to play it. But at the end of the day, the world won't collapse without soccer. Oh, sorry, *football*."

His hand darted to my side, and he tickled me. I squealed and tried to get away, but he merely followed me until he had me pinned against the counter.

As soon as his front touched mine, his fingers stilled, and I quieted. His heat and scent surrounded me, and I wanted nothing more than to wrap my arms around his neck, pull his head down, and kiss him.

Would it be hard and desperate? Or slow and lingering?

Would it be better than when I'd kissed him in my dreams?

Would it make me forget about everything and everyone but him?

Time passed slowly, like hours, and eventually Rafe cleared his throat and backed away from me. "I think we can act the part of a married couple just fine. The dinner is in three days, so we have time to practice some more. Well, a little. I have some meetings with my other head trainer and a walkthrough to do with the contractors."

"Oh, right. Your business." I bit my bottom lip and hesitated.

"Ask me, Abigail. Always at least ask."

"Can I see where the tutoring section will be?"

He nodded. "It's not finished yet, but in a way, that's good. You can tell me what needs to be changed and I'll see it done."

"Just like that?"

"Of course. You know more about teaching than me, so why wouldn't I listen to you? And don't worry about the costs. That section is partly a gift to the students of Starry Hills, and I want to give them the best."

I should say thank you, make an excuse, and then head home.

However, I blurted, "You seem to love this town. So why did you stay away for so long? And don't say because you were busy with your career. Growing up, you doted on Emmy. You laughed hard with West, and even Beck. And then you left and didn't come back for over a decade. Why, Rafe? Why did you abandon everything that once mattered to you?"

Chapter Nine

Rafe

I'd waited for this question to come up. While I'd talked with my sister about our parents and why I'd stayed away, Emmy hadn't shared those conversations with anyone but her husband.

Not that I'd revealed everything to my sister. But she knew enough.

However, as Abby's gaze searched mine, the usual desire to run away to forget about the past didn't appear. I wanted to walk toward her, hold her, and maybe even share a little of myself.

But that would bring us closer, and given my track record, I'd end up hurting her.

It was best to keep my distance. "You know what it's like to lose your parents. If given the chance, wouldn't you run away from the place that reminded you of them and never come back?"

"That's a bullshit answer, if I'd ever heard one."

I blinked. "Excuse me?"

"You heard me. Starry Hills might remind you of your parents, but Emmy was here, too. Unless you're saying that to avoid memories of your parents, you'd be willing to never see your sister again? Because I thought you loved her."

"That's not fair."

"You promised to be honest with me, Rafe. So tell me: did you miss Emmy while you were away?"

"Of course I did."

"Then why did you stay away so long? Yes, coming back would've been painful, but you could've managed it. Remember, I lost my parents too. I know how much it hurts to walk through their favorite spots, eat at their favorite restaurant in town, or even keep up holiday traditions." She paused, searched my gaze as if debating something, and then added softly, "Some of my brothers ran away for a while, abandoning me and the family. But even if they didn't come back for a long time, they still kept in contact. Something you never did with Emmy."

"It was better that way."

She frowned. "Why?"

I could tell her that I hurt anyone who cared about me.

But then she might decide to cut her losses and walk away. And greedy bastard that I was, I didn't want her to run away from me.

Not wanting to think about why, I replied, "I was

young and wanted to see the world. You can't expect a teenager or guy in his early twenties to think about his little sister."

She studied me for a few beats before asking, "How am I supposed to believe that you'll help me, let alone trust you enough to live with you for a year, if you keep lying to me?" She twirled, picked up her purse, and looked over her shoulder. "Text me when you're ready to be honest."

With that, she dashed out of the room and soon the front door slammed shut.

I stared at where she'd been standing and ran a hand over my hair. Abby was no fool, and I'd known that. She —rightly so—wasn't going to put up with my crap.

However, as I stood there trying to think of my next move, one thing she'd mentioned replayed inside my mind: *Some of my brothers ran away for a while, abandoning me and the family.*

So many people had abandoned Abby over the course of her life, even if they hadn't all been intentional.

Her parents. Her brothers. And even the guy who'd supposedly loved her had used and discarded her.

And me, at the end of this.

No. I wouldn't completely abandon her. I'd do whatever I could to help her, ensure she could have the future she wanted, and protect her for as long as she needed.

And what about the truth? Will you share that too, no matter what?

With a sigh, I rubbed my face. That would be a dangerous slope indeed. Because I couldn't get too close to Abby. If I did, I might start wanting something I couldn't have.

To distract myself, I went and made another cup of coffee, downed it, and got ready to visit my training center. Burying myself in work would help me forget about my wife and the future I might have with her if things were different.

As I strode into my other head trainer's office, Mark Shelton looked up from his desk and whistled. "What the fuck happened to you? You look as if someone just kicked your dog."

I growled, "Nothing."

He raised his black eyebrows. "Look, I'm not going to pry as long as it doesn't affect your work. But the second it does, you're going to tell me."

I plopped into the chair in front of Mark's desk and picked at the armrest, trying to decide just how much to tell him.

As teens, we'd been close. But while we were business partners now—he'd lost his chance to play professional football because of a college injury and had become a high school coach, and I'd headhunted him to help with my training facility—we were still trying to figure out the adult versions of each other.

His voice filled the room again. "Why the hell are you wearing a wedding ring?"

Fuck. I'd put it on after Abby had left and must've forgotten to take it off. "No reason."

"Some people might smile and nod and never question your famous-ass self, but I remember when we were seven and you ran screaming from Mr. Winter's possessed goose." He leaned back in his chair and crossed his arms over his chest. "So tell me what happened, Rafe. Because you'd never just wear a wedding ring for no reason."

I noticed the firmness of his jaw and the glint of determination in his dark brown eyes. That look hadn't changed from when he was a teen, which meant Mark wasn't going to let this go.

Well, you need to start practicing your story anyway. Test the waters with Mark before trying it on Abby's family. "I got married, that's why."

He blinked and then shook his head, as if to clear it. "I need to know more than that. Start talking."

"Why? It won't affect my work. Well, mostly. My wife's going to head the tutoring center."

"Wait, what? I'm your partner, Rafe. We're supposed to decide that kind of shit together."

Even though I could've afforded to fund this place myself, Mark had insisted on investing and having a share of the business. I'd offered him a ridiculous salary just to sign on, but he'd refused. "You're right, I'm sorry. But my wife is a qualified teacher, and I know she'll be good at it."

"Okay, now I'm intrigued. Who is she?"

I hesitated before deciding what the hell, and answered, "Abby Wolfe."

Mark's eyebrows shot up. "Abigail Wolfe, as in

West's younger sister? That one? She's what, fifteen years younger than you?"

"Ten. And yes, that Abigail Wolfe."

"I didn't even think you were dating anyone."

Well, here goes. Time to try out our story. "It was kind of unexpected. It started with a near-kiss and we ended up married in Vegas."

"Do you love her?"

I shifted in my seat. "Since when do we fucking talk about love?"

"Because that's the only way her family isn't going to kick your ass. I'm sure they've heard about your actions over the years, while you were playing soccer in the UK. Her brothers aren't going to like it."

"I can handle her fucking brothers."

"You still didn't answer the question."

I blew out a breath. Best to stick as close to the truth as possible. "We care for each other and are giving it a shot. I'm sure once Abby explains it, her brothers will calm down a little."

"I'm not so sure about that."

I growled. "It's not like I'm some criminal. So I have a past and was wild when I was younger. By all accounts, so were you."

"I partied in college, like everyone else. And I couldn't care less about your past, as you've worked hard to get this place up and running, and I admire that." He leaned forward. "But Abby has had a hard time. You've heard the rumors, I'm sure."

"Don't fucking listen to the rumors."

He put his hands up in front of him. "I'm sure most

of them are bullshit. But over the last year or so, her family has been circling around, trying to protect her. And if even a smidgen of the rumors are true, she deserves far more from a husband than giving it a try."

I knew that, of course. But I *could* help Abby with her ex problem, which might give her a better future.

Not that I could tell Mark any of that. As much as I trusted him, I wouldn't share Abby's secrets.

"We decided together to try and see if this marriage could work. And there's so much about her that I *do* like —she's smart and sexy and devoted to her family. Plus, since we grew up together, she knows me better than any other woman in the world."

Mark searched my gaze before eventually nodding. "It's not my job to meddle, although I can't speak for my wife."

His wife, Ashley, had been trying to fix me up ever since I'd returned to Starry Hills. And now that I had a wife? She'd probably suggest romantic things I could do to win Abby over. "I can handle Ashley, don't worry."

"I'm more worried about the Wolfe brothers. And yes, I know you said you can handle them. But you weren't around when Abby was in high school. My wife's cousin was in her class, and that poor girl...the Wolfe brothers scared the shit out of most of the guys in her year and above."

Not wanting to wonder if they'd also protected my sister just as fiercely—Emmy had moved in with the Wolfe family when she was ten—I replied, "If I can deal with entire countries being pissed at me for making a mistake on the field, then I can handle some overprotective brothers."

"If you say so." Mark studied me and then shrugged. "I'll leave it alone for now. As for our meeting with the contractors later today..."

As Mark went over his concerns and proposed some possible changes, I focused on my business and what it needed. This was my new purpose, something to give my life meaning after soccer had been ripped away from me, and I wasn't about to fuck it up.

Chapter Ten

Abby

Aunt Lori: Are you sure you don't want to join me and my friend on our trip to Disneyland next week? <airplane emoji> <castle emoji> <roller coaster emoji>
Me: No, have fun! I have plenty to do here.
Aunt Lori: You need to leave the house more, Abby.
Me: I do leave the house.
Aunt Lori: I'm not talking about the grocery store or a drive-thru. Ever since you moved back home, you've been hiding most of the time. Won't you talk to me? <sad eye emoji>
Me: I'm going to West and Emmy's dinner. That's out.
Aunt Lori: I guess that's a start. Besides, Rafe should be there. He's yummy to ogle. <hearts for eyes emoji>
Me: Please tell me you're not going to ogle Rafe.

Aunt Lori: I'm older, not dead. And since I'm still waiting for my chance with that new guy, looking is all I have. Besides, Rafe is RAWR. <overheated emoji> Imagine him tackling you for the ball.
Me: He played soccer, not football.
Aunt Lori: It's a fantasy. I can do whatever I want.
Me (typed but deleted): He's my husband! Stop it! He's mine and mine alone.
Me (actual reply instead): That's my cue to leave. Tell your fantasies to your friend. <heart emoji>

Every time I walked into Starry Eyes Bakery, I looked around to see if anyone was staring at me or pointing or whispering. It was stupid, but I always worried that someone would learn about what had happened with Travis in San Jose and it'd spread like wildfire. Sure, most of the town would have my back. However, there were always assholes who loved nothing more than to make others feel like shit so they could feel better about themselves.

Then I spotted Amber's blonde head behind the counter. She waved at me, and I forgot about everyone else. After finishing with her customer, the other woman working took over and Amber rushed toward me. "Abby!" As soon as she was next to me, she whispered, "Let's go upstairs so we can talk."

There was a small one-bedroom apartment above the bakery that had been rented out to a former employee for years. But she'd recently moved away, and Amber had finally convinced her parents to let her live there instead.

Although, to be honest, I was surprised that her dad and stepmom had agreed to it. They took advantage of her kindness and need to take care of everyone and instead spent all their time and energy on her younger brothers.

Once inside her apartment, Amber blurted, "What happened with you and Rafe?" She glanced at my hand and added, "Where's your ring?"

Since I'd been here a couple times before, I headed toward the kitchen and grabbed a soda from the fridge. After opening it and sipping a little, I finally replied, "It's complicated. Explaining it will take a while, so we'd better sit down."

Amber plopped onto the couch, hugged a pillow to her chest, and said, "Start talking."

I quickly recapped waking up married, my lack of memories, and my agreement to remain married to Rafe for a year. Once I finished, Amber frowned. "Wait, so it's all for pretend?"

"Yes, and it's a secret from everyone but you, me, and Rafe. If the truth leaks out, the press will have a field day and that'll defeat the purpose of our year-long marriage —to protect the reputation of Rafe's business."

"Of course I won't tell anyone." She leaned forward. "But just promise me, Abby, that you aren't doing this because of your childhood crush on Rafe. He's not the same person he once was, and I don't want to see you get your heart broken again."

Ignoring the latter part, I replied, "I know Rafe's not

the same person. I barely notice he's a guy at all." Amber raised her blonde eyebrows, and I added, "Well, okay, he's hot and I'd be lying if I said I wouldn't sleep with him. Just once, mind you. But men and trust and relationships aren't for me."

She took one of my hands and squeezed. "I wish you'd tell me more about the asshole who hurt you, Abby."

I studied her brown eyes and hesitated. Amber was probably the person I knew the least out of the BFF Circle. Not because she wasn't one of my dearest friends, far from it. After coming back from San Jose, she brought food and stayed every day until I finally ate something.

However, she was the quietest in the group, the peacekeeper, and probably had trouble being heard when there was Katie and, until recently, me, since I'd been loud as well.

I blurted, "I'm sorry, Amber."

She frowned. "For what?"

"For probably steamrolling you more times than either of us could count."

"Don't worry about it." She shrugged. "I enjoy watching you and the others argue with each other. I'm better than I was, but I'll never be the outgoing personality or the center of attention. And you know what? That's okay. It's taken me dating Jay to realize that."

I smiled. "I'm glad you found a guy who appreciates you."

In other words, I was happy she'd finally gotten over my clueless brother Zach.

She cleared her throat. "Well, mostly. I don't know if Jay is my forever, but I'm willing to see where it goes." She gestured toward me. "But right now, we're talking about you. What happened in San Jose, Abby? If I'm to help you and Rafe keep up your ruse, then I need to know as much as possible. I swear I won't tell anyone." She put up her pinky. "Pinky swear I won't tell anyone."

Smiling, I hooked my pinky around hers and shook. As kids, we'd done pinky swears all the time; they were extremely serious for us.

Once we both released each other, I sipped my soda again and sighed. "Well, here's what happened..."

And I proceeded to tell her about falling for Travis, thinking we were in love and would get married, and his ultimate betrayals of announcing his engagement to someone else and later his blackmail.

By the end, Amber stood up, threw her pillow to the ground, and stomped on it. "I'm going to fucking kill that bastard."

I blinked. "Um, what?"

She paced the room, gesticulating wildly. "How dare he! He's probably taken advantage of other intern teachers before. Maybe I should look into it. If there's a way to bring him down without using your name, then he would finally get what he deserves without hurting you."

I also stood. "Now, now, I know you love true crime podcasts and like to do online research for stuff. But please, Amber, promise me you won't do this. Rafe already said he'd take care of Travis, and no offense, but he has a lot more resources and contacts."

"I won't do anything to embarrass you, but I'll quietly tap my own resources."

"Amber..."

She took my hand. "Abby, trust me. I'm probably the most cautious person you know, right?" I nodded, and she added, "Maybe I can find something to help Rafe. But let me at least try."

At the pleading look in her eye, I finally nodded. "Fine. But that, and my pretend marriage, needs to remain a secret from everyone, Amber. Even Katie and Emmy."

"I know. Emmy is going to be the hardest, though."

"I'll eventually tell her, I promise. But until West and Rafe make some kind of truce, I don't want this to ruin any progress Emmy has made with her brother."

"I'll help when I can. But Abby?"

"Yes?"

"Remember, you can talk to me anytime. Pretending for a year will be hard enough without having someone to vent to. No doubt Rafe will irritate you or make you mad at some point."

I blinked. "Irritate me? What are you talking about?"

"Well, for example, Jay always leaves the toilet seat up. Or he seems to save his farts for right after he gets under the covers. That kind of stuff."

"Well, if anything comes up, you're my go-to. But only if you promise to vent to me, too."

She bit her bottom lip and then nodded. "Okay. Although I try not to complain, if I can help it."

"Everyone needs to complain sometimes, Amber.

When it comes to best friends, it's okay not to be perfect."

After giving me a quick hug, she said, "Thanks, Abby. After so many years of trying to be perfect for my stepmother, it's hard to change, but I'll try."

"Wait, I know your stepmother can be critical, but this sounds like more than that. What haven't you told me?"

She shook her head. "Maybe later. If I don't get back downstairs soon, Sofia will kill me. And given how she's the reason I got into the true crime stuff, she'd get away with it too."

Amber winked, and I laughed. But I mentally made a note to ask Amber about her stepmother later. Just imagining my friend suffering over the years and never saying anything made guilt swirl in my stomach.

I'll do better. They'd all been there for me over the last year or so, and now it was my turn to step up.

The alarm on my phone went off, and I disabled it. "Well, that's my cue to go, too. Rafe's going to show me around the tutoring center."

Amber hugged me harder this time, and I hugged her back. She said, "Good luck, Abby."

She whispered something I didn't quite catch, but it sounded like, "I hope it works out for you."

Not wanting to think about fairy tales or Rafe being a man I could actually trust, I said my goodbyes, headed to my car, and drove to the old horse farm.

Chapter Eleven

Abby

Rafe: Make sure to wear your wedding ring. My business partner knows we're together.
Me: Knows what, exactly?
Rafe: That we're married, but not about the agreement.
Me: What about me working for you?
Rafe: I told him, but try to impress him when you get here since I should've talked with him first.
Me: Who's your partner?
Rafe: Mark Shelton.
Me: West's childhood friend?
Rafe: Mine, too. So, do you have the ring?
Me: Yes. I just finished my visit with Amber, and I'm heading over. Talk to you soon.

The weight of the ring on my finger felt ten times heavier than it actually was. This would be my first time acting as Rafe's wife in public, and I only vaguely remembered West and Mark hanging out in high school, when I'd still been a kid.

Which meant this would be our first real test. Because if we couldn't convince Mark we were a real thing, then we had no hope in hell of convincing our families.

I finally reached the end of the long driveway to the old Santos place and nearly did a double take. When I'd gotten my pony as a kid, the sprawling complex had mostly been open and fenced, with horses grazing everywhere. The main building had been a small barn, with a house not far away.

But now? The barn had been expanded and modernized. It still had the feel of the former place, but was freshly painted—brick red with white trim—and had glass entry doors, updated windows, and a new roof. It looked like a modern-take on what a barn should look like.

There was also a paved parking lot, and I could see some nearly completed sports fields. There were probably more I couldn't see since the property sprawled for acres and acres. However, the soccer field was closest, and I could make out a baseball one in the distance, too.

I pulled into a parking spot, exited my car, and took a deep breath. Time to play the part of Rafe's wife.

After entering the glass doors, my jaw dropped at the reception area. It had been painted and filled with furniture, but it was the pictures on the walls that caught my attention. There were old Starry Hills High and Starry Hills Middle School team photos, some newspaper ones from championships, and even one of Rafe mid-kick in his Manchester Dragons FC uniform. Also, there was one of Mark Shelton in his college uniform, from when his football team had gone to the college playoffs.

Rafe's voice echoed in the large space. "What do you think of the reception area?"

Tearing my eyes from the walls, I turned to find Rafe and Mark standing nearby.

Mark was older than I remembered, but he had the same black, curly hair, dark brown skin, and dark brown eyes. He flashed a smile—the one that had dazzled my friends and me when we'd been younger—and I smiled back at him.

Show time. I walked over to the pair. "It's amazing! The school photos will make kids feel more at ease, and including your picture and Mark's, show what you can accomplish. It's perfect."

Maybe I imagined it, but I swore Rafe stood a little taller. "That was my goal. There are better players than me, of course. But since they'll see me and Mark, I put us on the wall."

Mark snorted. "If I hadn't blown my knee, I would've been far better than you, Rafe." He put out his hand. "You probably don't remember me, but I'm Mark Shelton."

I shook his hand. "I do. You and West used to play baseball together."

As soon as I said it, I mentally cursed. Bringing up West probably wasn't the best thing in the world.

Mark nodded. "Yeah, but that was a long time ago." Rafe gave him a look, and Mark cleared his throat. "Nice to see you again, Abby. We'll talk more later, for sure. I want to hear all about your plans for the tutoring center."

"I want to apologize for Rafe offering me the job without talking to you first. But I promise, I have tons of ideas and want to make it work."

Mark nodded. "I can't wait to hear your plans. We can talk a little after the tour."

He waved and headed into the bowels of the building. As soon as we were alone, I said to Rafe, "You've done more than I'd expected, given how you only returned to Starry Hills late last year."

"I did a lot of research while abroad and was ready to hit the ground running." He gestured to the door. "Ready for the tour?"

He put out his hand, and I debated taking it. We were alone, which meant we didn't have to play the part.

But I couldn't resist placing mine in his. He squeezed, and a little thrill shot through me. I liked how his hand made mine look small, how it was so much warmer than mine, and how I could feel his wedding ring against my fingers.

Mine.

Wait, no. Not mine.

Thankfully, Rafe tugged me along and started his tour, telling me about the indoor training rooms, the locker rooms, and the theater-like room to watch replays of other players. I loved watching his eyes light up as he talked, banishing the grumpy, scowling man from my family dinners.

It reminded me a little of how he'd been when his parents had still been alive.

Eventually he stopped in front of a set of doors with the words, "Tutoring Center" painted on them. He released my hand and said, "Close your eyes, Abby."

I raised my eyebrows. "I thought you said it was still under construction, which means I'll probably trip and fall on my face."

"I'll make sure you won't, I promise." He gestured at my face. "Close your eyes. Please."

My first instinct was to say no and charge into the room. Rafe hadn't really done anything to prove he was trustworthy yet.

However, at the pleading look in his gaze, I acknowledged that I *was* married to this man, would be for a year, and I should at least give him a chance.

I closed my eyes. A second passed and another before I felt Rafe's heat behind me. Then his breath danced against my ear as he whispered, "Walk until I say stop."

His hands came to my shoulders, and a jolt of heat spread throughout me. Combined with his breath still on my ear, I wanted to lean back against him, feel his hard body against mine, and ask for his hand to travel down, down, down until he reached my clit and made me scream.

Thankfully, his voice broke my mini-sex fantasy. "Walk, Abigail. I've got you."

He pushed gently against my shoulders, and I

followed his guidance. He steered me left and then right, and eventually he said, "Stop and open your eyes."

I did and stared right at a plaque on the door that said, "Abigail Wolfe, Tutoring Director."

It was a simple brass plaque with my name, and yet my throat tightened at the sight. "I thought I'd never teach again."

"Well, you're going to kick some ass here, Abigail. It won't be long before I'll be fighting off head hunters."

I laughed. "You're rather optimistic."

"No, you worked bloody hard to become a teacher, to fulfill your dream from childhood, and that tells me how much you care about educating others."

He was right—I'd wanted to be a teacher since I was about five years old. "You remember that?"

His hands gently squeezed my shoulders. "You tried to make me and West your pupils that one time, when we were trying to dig a swimming hole in one of the fields."

"I forgot about that! How you ever thought a giant hole in the middle of a field—one with cows in it who could fall into the hole before it ever filled with water—would be a good idea, I never understood. It was stupid."

He chuckled, the sound almost rusty. How often did Rafael Mendoza laugh?

Before I could think too hard on it, he replied, "You told us it was dumb back then, and said we should play school with you. Then we'd know better for the next time. You even got us to sit down for about ten minutes, somehow. Even as a little kid, you were stubborn."

My lips twitched. "That is kind of the Wolfe family motto—stubborn bastards till the end."

Rafe laughed. "Fits."

After turning around, I raised an eyebrow. "Pot meet kettle."

"All right, all right. Yes, I'm a stubborn bastard. You have to be to make it as far as I did. But when it comes to this tutoring center, I bow down to your expertise."

I glanced at the plaque again and then back at my husband. "Not Abigail Mendoza?"

"If you want, I can change it." He lowered his mouth to my ear and whispered, "But you're already doing me a huge favor and I didn't want to take your name from you without asking first."

My throat tightened with emotion. Would any of the guys I'd dated before think to ask me about such a huge change?

No, rang through my head.

How was Rafe still single?

I would find out, whatever it took. There had to be a reason he'd acted the playboy so long. And yes, I did think at some point it had become acting. Because this sweet man would've yearned for more than just endless, meaningless sex.

Wouldn't he have?

Not wanting to think about his parade of women before me, I turned back to the door and stared at my name. Abigail Wolfe had gone through so much, nearly hit rock bottom, and had struggled to think of what to do with her future.

But now, I could do some good here. The passion to

teach stirred to life inside me. More than that, I wanted to be a version of myself I actually liked. Not one who moped and hid and scrambled to deal with her past mistakes.

A new name would make it easier to try and be that version of me.

"I think I'll be Abigail Mendoza, if that's all right with you."

His hands went to my waist and squeezed. My eyes shot to his, and something stirred in Rafe's gaze, something I couldn't name.

His voice was low as he said, "I like it. A lot. Mrs. Mendoza."

As a little girl, I'd created Barbie weddings with me and Rafe. But it'd been a child's fantasy of platonic kisses and setting up house and us moving around the world as Rafe played soccer.

But as an adult? Hearing Rafe call me Mrs. Mendoza sent a shiver down my spine, in a good way. "Well then, Mr. Mendoza, are you going to show me around my office now?"

And maybe we could celebrate my new job with me sitting on a desk while you kneel before me, spreading my legs, and then...

Interrupting my dirty thoughts, Rafe guided me into the room. It was empty of furniture, and I tried not to be disappointed.

Not that Rafe would go down on me at any point in our marriage. However, it still felt like my fantasy would always be for that to happen.

He said, "I didn't want to decorate it for whoever

took the position since I don't know what the hell you'll need. But you can decorate it however you want. Even if you want to hang up 'I heart Rafe' posters, I'll make sure they're made."

I rolled my eyes. "Ego, much?"

"I was voted the best striker in the world one year."

"Were you? Hmm. I must've missed that."

I hadn't, but it was entirely too much fun to tease Rafe.

He said, "It's easy to tell when you're lying, Abigail. You knew. You followed my career."

"Maybe for a while. But eventually, I got too busy."

I waited to see if he'd call me out again because I had followed him up until he'd retired. Even when he'd hurt my best friend, I hadn't been able to completely forget about Rafe. At first, right after his parents died, I kept looking to see if he was sad or hurting or miserable. But trying to gauge emotions through a screen, while he played an intense game, hadn't worked.

His breath danced across my ear again. "I'll make sure you get a packet with all the necessary information about me and my career. Because the students will ask about it, and you should know."

"Wait, I have to take a Rafe Mendoza 101 class now?"

He chuckled, and the sound made me want to lean back against him and feel the vibrations of his chest.

Woah. Get a grip, Abby.

He said, "Something like that. Although you'll have to create an Abby Wolfe Mendoza 101 class for me, too. I need to know as much as possible about my wife."

His hand moved from my shoulders, down my sides, and settled on my waist. For a second, I held my breath, waiting to see if he'd pull me against him.

But after a few beats, he dropped his hands and stepped away. His voice sounded rough as he said, "I have some work to do. But look around and let me know what you need."

With that, he left. As soon as the door clicked closed, I let out a breath and rubbed my hands over my face. Being alone with Rafe had already become dangerous, and I'd only agreed to stay married to him yesterday.

Dropping my hands, I glanced around the room. Once we figured out the basics of how we'd act as a couple, this place would become my focus, my distraction.

Because Rafe would never really be mine, and becoming a workaholic would distract me from wishing he could be.

Chapter Twelve

Abby

Zach: I found some cardboard boxes for you. Are you going to tell me what they're for yet?

Me: Can't a girl have some secrets?

Zach: Well, that depends. Are you building a giant box fort? Because if so, I want in.

Me: <eye roll emoji> I'm not seven years old. So no, I'm not building a box fort.

Zach: Hey, I had to ask. With you moving back home, I thought maybe you were going to start reliving your childhood. You placing a frog in my bed would be next, and I need to be prepared. <winking emoji>

Me: I never did that! It was Zane.

Zach: Naw, it was you. We both watched you do it. That's why we put the worms in your bed.

Me: I still have nightmares about the wriggly things against my feet!

Zach: Hmm, maybe Zane and I should try to pull some pranks again. It'd be a nice welcome home present for you, to feel a part of the family again.

Me: How old are you?

Zach: You're the one wanting to make a box fort.

Me: <middle finger emoji> Has anyone told you that you're a man child lately?

Zach: I resent that. I can dress and wash myself, thank you very much. I even have a decent job.

Me: That's a pretty low bar, Zach. <sighing emoji> Just tell me where you put the boxes.

Zach: I can't because I didn't hide them. Zane did. And not even I know all of his hiding spots. It should be fun finding them.

Me: Fine. I'll ask Zane. I love him more anyway. <tongue out emoji>

Zach: Love you too. We can go box hunting together when you get home. <grinning emoji>

That evening, I paced Rafe's living room and kept looking at the stairs. Part of me wanted to go and snoop a little, but another part of me knew that wasn't the best way to start a marriage.

Marriage.

Twisting the ring on my finger, I paced faster. Rafe should be home soon to begin our married couple lessons, and my heart raced and my palms sweated.

Not because kissing him or touching him would be a chore. I'd dreamed of kissing Rafael Mendoza since I was a little girl. The hard part would be not taking it further, keeping my heart walled off, and not allowing memories of the boy he'd been to cloud my judgment about the man he'd become.

Remember, he hurt Emmy. Plus, he's been away a long time, and he'll probably leave again, too. Don't get attached. Don't do it.

Although remembering the placard with my name on the door and him giving me the choice of my last name softened me a little. Then the man had gone and listened to my ideas of how to tweak the tutoring center and praised me about the suggestions.

Those things reminded me of the boy he'd been so much. Maybe a part of the old Rafe had survived after all.

Stop it. Don't go chasing rainbows.

I was about to distract myself with texting my annoying brother again when the front door opened and Rafe called out, "Abby? Where are you?"

Well, here goes. "In the living room."

I stood near the fireplace for extra warmth. Well, and to put as much distance between me and the entryway as possible.

Rafe walked in, his hair ruffled and his jaw dark with late-day stubble. I wanted to run my fingers over his cheek, his nose, his lips. Would they be soft or hard?

Damn it, why did he have to be so sexy?

He eyed the fire and then met my gaze. "It's not that cold."

It was true. But building the fire had distracted me for a few minutes, and there was something comforting about the crackle and pop as it burned. "I get cold easily. I'm also that person who needs four blankets at night in the winter, and two pairs of socks."

"Wait, doesn't your family keep the heat on at night?"

"Yes, but not high enough for me."

Maybe you could warm me up.

Rafe tossed his jacket on the recliner and walked toward me. It was hard not to stare at his long, lean legs. But his gait was a little off, especially with his right leg. "I thought your injury was healed."

He stopped walking and frowned. "It is."

I met his gaze. "But you're almost limping."

"It acts up sometimes, especially when it's cold. But that's not important. We don't have a lot of time until we have to go to my sister's dinner in two days, so let's focus on how we're going to act and what we're going to tell them."

Part of me wanted to push, to find out just how bad his injury had been.

However, I had five older brothers and I'd learned early on that asking about any sort of weakness usually made them prickly and uncomfortable. Not that I'd given up completely with Rafe. But we hadn't even moved in together yet. I needed to pace myself.

I plopped down onto the sofa and patted the spot next to me. "Come sit by me."

He didn't waste time settling next to me, close enough that his leg brushed mine and a thread of heat shot through my body. The smart thing would be to move away and keep my mind clear. But we wouldn't be able to do that at Emmy's dinner, or any event for the next year, so I needed to learn how to ignore the way Rafe affected me.

His left leg bounced in place as he said, "How far we go in public for PDA is up to you, Abigail." He studied the painting over the fireplace, one that looked a lot like his family's ranch when we'd been kids. "I know what I said before, about always being affectionate. But I don't want to make you uncomfortable." He finally met my eyes again. "I'm not like that bastard who took advantage of you, and I'm determined to prove it."

I softened a little. "I may not like how you abandoned your sister or friends, but I can't ever imagine you blackmailing me with altered sex videos."

He clenched the fingers of one hand into a fist. "I'm sorry that's the bar you have to set, Abby. It's way too low. You deserve better. Better than him, better than me."

My brows drew together. "Better than you?"

He waved a hand in dismissal. "I don't know why I said that. At any rate, we should focus on how we'll act in public and what to tell our families. If...if you want to kiss in public, then we'll have to practice that now."

Rafe shifted in his seat, and I bit back a smile. He was nervous. Somehow, the world-famous playboy was nervous.

Then it hit me—maybe he didn't want to kiss me. I was his sister's best friend, after all. Maybe he thought of me as his sister, too.

His looks from before don't support that, do they?

Maybe. But Rafe had wanted honesty, so I was going to try my best to do that. "If it makes you uncomfortable, we don't have to. But I wouldn't mind if we had to kiss."

Oh, crap. Had I really said that?

Rafe's eyes turned heated and his voice was husky as he said, "I wouldn't mind, either."

For a few seconds, we merely stared at each other and my heart raced as I squeezed my thighs together. After all these years, was I finally going to kiss Rafael Mendoza?

He leaned forward and cupped my cheek. As his thumb ran back and forth across my skin, my lips parted and I couldn't tear my gaze away from his mouth. Would his kiss be gentle and tender? Or, desperate and devouring? Somewhere in between?

Stopping a few inches from my face, he whispered, "Time to finally kiss my wife."

A shiver ran down my spine but I barely had time to notice as we both closed the distance and his lips met mine.

At first, he was soft, gentle, and took his time merely teasing my mouth. But something inside me burst, and I threaded my fingers through his hair and moved closer.

With a growl, his tongue seamed my lips and I opened, groaning as his tongue stroked and explored and tangled with mine.

Somehow I moved to straddle his lap, and Rafe placed a possessive hand on my hip, holding me tight as his mouth continued to devour me. Each nibble and lick and swirl made me moan even harder and my clit throbbed, wanting more, so much more.

His hand on my hip moved to my ass. He kneaded and squeezed as his mouth continued to tease and claim. When he pressed me closer, I didn't resist. The moment his hard cock pressed against my clit, even through both our clothes, I cried out.

Rafe broke the kiss and quickly moved me to the sofa cushion. He stood, walked to the fireplace, and stared into the flames.

My mind tried to catch up with what had happened. I breathed heavily, reveling in his lingering taste in my mouth. The memory of his cock pressed against me made me want to drag him back and demand more.

No kiss had ever made me lose myself like that, to the point I would've fucked him on the couch if he hadn't stopped us.

How was I supposed to live with this man for a year and keep things platonic?

His voice was low, so low I could barely hear it as he said, "You should go now, Abby."

Frowning, I stood and tried to meet his gaze, but Rafe continued to stare into the fire. "Why? If we act like that, then it should convince anyone we're a couple for real."

His gaze shot to mine. "You were acting?"

No. It was the best kiss of my life.

"Yes. Why waste time fumbling around when we're both experienced enough to know how to kiss?"

His eyes searched mine, his expression unreadable. Could he tell I was lying?

Finally, he looked back at the flames and replied, "Well, I'd rather not take it that far in front of our families. Speaking of which, I need some time alone to think about the holes in our story. I'll call you tomorrow and we can finalize things."

"But the dinner is the day after tomorrow. Shouldn't we talk in person to get used to each other more? I can stop by tomorrow."

He shook his head. "I have a lot to do at the training center tomorrow. Sorry."

As he drummed his fingers on the mantel, I wanted to ask if the kiss had affected him as much as me. Or, was he trying to spare my feelings? For all I knew, he'd kissed twenty women the same way and he didn't want to encourage me.

Not wanting to go down the rabbit hole of comparing myself to his former partners, I nodded. "Fine. Call me when you can. But it's probably better if we arrive separately to Emmy and West's place. That way, they won't know right away we're a couple and we can judge the best time to reveal the news."

"I agree."

I waited a few seconds, wondering if he'd say anything else. But Rafe just continued staring into the fire and ignoring me.

So the kiss meant nothing. He just wants me gone. I'm the inconvenient future roommate.

It shouldn't hurt, and yet it did.

At least it reminded me that being married to Rafe was purely transactional.

Before I could do something stupid, like cry, I cleared my throat and said, "I'll talk to you tomorrow."

Not waiting to see if he looked up, I turned and grabbed my purse from the table in the entryway, exited, and rushed into my car.

I took a second to stare at Rafe's house, remembering the kiss and how I'd felt in his arms—safe, desired, an equal.

Then I quickly took a deep breath and locked it away. He'd been my childhood crush, true. But tonight had been the wake-up call I'd needed. From now on, this would be a giant production, one where I played a character to the world but dropped it when alone with Rafe.

The hardest part would be keeping it up around my family. Once this was all over, I only hoped they would forgive my deception. Especially once they learned about the favor I collected from Rafe and his help at hopefully taking care of Travis.

Because at some point, I'd have to share what he'd done to me.

Of course, that meant surviving the year and not screwing up by doing something stupid, like falling for Rafe all over again.

Not wanting to dwell on it, I turned on the car, blasted some music, and headed back to my family's house. The sooner I got home, the sooner I could start a fight with one of my brothers and forget about everything else.

Including the most magical and consuming kiss of my life.

Chapter Thirteen

Rafe

Me: Just an FYI, I have a surprise for everyone tonight, Emmy.

Emmy: A good kind of surprise? Or, more like I need to duck behind furniture kind of surprise?

Me: Somewhere in-between. But I need your help with West.

Emmy: Uh-oh, now I'm worried. Why?

Me: He might not like it.

Emmy: That's unhelpful, Rafe. What's going on?

Me: You'll see soon. But I'd rather not end up dead tonight.

Emmy: Don't you trust me?

Me: I do. But it's not just my secret to share. Please, Em. Will you keep West from murdering me?

Emmy: I'll try, but I can't make any guarantees.
Me: That's good enough for me. Thanks, sis.
Emmy: You'd better bring some macarons with you, then. I'm craving them, and Avery can't make them yet.
Me: Wait, are you pregnant?
Emmy: No! I just want some fancy cookies.
Me: Consider it done. See you soon.

T he drive to my sister's house had felt like an hour instead of fifteen minutes. Not just because of dreading West's reaction to Abby and my news, but also because I was both hesitant and looking forward to finally seeing Abby again.

Since our kiss the day before yesterday, I hadn't talked with her in person for more than a few minutes here and there at the training center. Oh, we'd finalized our story over the phone. But even then, it'd lacked the playfulness from before I'd nearly made her come on my lap.

Fuck, just remembering her hot mouth and tongue twirling with mine as she pressed against me made my dick stir. It'd been one kiss, just one, and we hadn't even been naked. And yet, I'd dreamed of it both nights and spent way too much time wondering what would've happened if I hadn't stopped it.

Which had been the right thing to do. I wasn't about to take advantage of Abby, especially after what that bastard had done to her.

And yet, her sweet moans and her taste and the feel

of her ass in my hands made me want her every second of every day. How the fuck had one kiss changed her from my sister's best friend—attractive, but just another woman—into the person constantly invading my thoughts? I craved Abigail Wolfe like nothing I'd craved before.

Oh, wait—Abigail Mendoza.

My wife.

Maybe I should eventually claim my wife?

No, don't do it. Don't make things complicated.

Thankfully, I pulled up to my sister's place before my thoughts could turn dangerous again. She lived in the same white, two-story house we'd grown up in, which sat a short distance from the red barn where Emmy held most of her wedding receptions. I turned off the ignition and stared at the house, one where I'd been loved and cared for and had never thought I'd be thirty-six years old and without either of my parents.

Parents who were dead because of me.

I'd been here a few times over the last four months or so, but it never got any easier. Even though Emmy had redecorated the inside, making it her own, each room still held a ton of memories. Happy ones that only twisted the knife of guilt in my heart even more.

As I took a deep breath and willed myself to get my ass out of the car, my sister's new stepson, Wyatt Wolfe, bolted out of the front door toward me. He'd been quiet and a little shy at first, but now he was a lot more open and always asked questions about my soccer career. Ever since I'd helped start up a local soccer team for him and his friends, he'd seen me as some kind of hero.

I opened the door, and Wyatt skidded to a halt. "Uncle Rafe, you came! Emmy said you would, but Dad said you probably wouldn't. I'm glad you did! Did you bring the jersey? Did you?"

I couldn't help but smile. Usually, Wyatt's twin sister was the outgoing one. Wyatt only seemed to get like this around me. After reaching over, I picked it up and held it out. "Here you go."

He held up the red and white jersey of the Manchester Dragons, but on the back, it had "Wolfe" for the name.

"Thank you, Uncle Rafe!" He tugged it over his head. It was a little too big, but the boy was in his grow-ing-like-a-weed stage, and I'd wanted to play it safe.

"Glad you like it, Wyatt. Is everyone here already?"

I took out the container of macarons and shut the car door. Wyatt replied, "Yeah, you're the last one. But you're still on time, it's just everyone's early tonight. Something about Aunt Lori bringing fancy wine and Katie bringing fancy cheese and they didn't want to miss out."

Given how the Wolfe siblings always acted like they'd never eaten before in their lives when they got together for meals, it didn't surprise me. "Well, then let's join them."

Wyatt plucked at his jersey. "This is awesome. I can't wait to show my friends. Asher has a San Jose Earthquakes jersey with his name on it, but this is way better."

"A friend of mine plays for the Earthquakes." I lowered my voice. "But the Dragons are better."

Wyatt put his arms out like wings and shouted, "Roar!"

I couldn't help but chuckle. Normally, I hated talking about my time as a pro soccer player—I loved the game and hadn't done it for the fame. But Emmy had confided about how Wyatt had struggled to make friends at first, after moving to Starry Hills. But the jersey I'd given him for his birthday had started talk with some of the students and he now had a best friend.

The front door opened just as we reached it, and Wyatt's twin sister, Avery, stood there. "Another jersey? Why, Wyatt? You have too many already."

"This one is better."

"It's still boring and ugly."

"Just like your face."

"Wyatt!"

He laughed, and she chased him outside, around the front yard. I watched them for a few seconds before my sister's voice made me turn around. "Thank you for getting him that personalized jersey, Rafe. He's talked about nothing else for days."

Before I could reply, she hugged me and I awkwardly patted her back with one hand.

When she stepped back, I handed her the container of macarons. "Just like you asked."

"Wow, these are from a fancy San Francisco bakery."

"Only the best for my sister."

Her gaze met mine, and she narrowed her eyes. "Amber makes amazing ones, too. I think you're buttering me up for something."

I placed a hand over my heart. "Never."

"Okay, now I definitely know you're up to something." Her face sobered, and she whispered, "It's not going to ruin the night, is it?"

"I...hope not."

Before my sister could say anything else, Aunt Lori—she made everyone call her that, even me—appeared next to Emmy. "Rafe! I'm glad you came, lad. Come on. Everyone's waiting inside."

After looping her arm through mine, she tugged. Given how she was over a foot shorter than me, it was almost comical, but I followed her lead.

She added, "You somehow always end up being the last one to arrive. But I made them wait to start dinner. A young, strong man like you needs his food."

I studied the woman in her sixties, her black hair streaked with gray, and tried to determine if Abby had told her about us being married yet. But her expression was merely amused and smiling, and I couldn't tell.

We reached the dining room, and everyone fell silent as West and I stared at each other.

I no longer harbored any bad feelings toward the man since he clearly loved and worshiped my sister. And yet, he refused to accept my apologies for how I'd treated him and Emmy, saying I had a long way to go before I made things up to my sister.

As if I didn't know that. Even now, thinking about how she'd thought I'd stayed away because I blamed her for our parents' deaths made me feel about two inches tall.

I decided to break the tense silence. "Hello, West."

He grunted and replied, "Hi."

The one syllable was filled with anger and loathing. Not for the first time, I missed my friend growing up.

This is your own fault, Mendoza. So just accept it and stop wishing it was different.

Emmy rushed to her husband's side. "Why don't you sit down while I check on Beck, Sabrina, and Abby in the kitchen? Dinner should be ready."

Aunt Lori shook her head. "I'll go."

She left just as Avery and Wyatt entered the room. Wyatt plopped onto a chair and gestured to one at his side. "Sit next to me, Uncle Rafe."

Avery pouted. "But he sat next to you last time. It's my turn."

Katie—who sat next to Nolan—laughed and said, "How about if he sits between the pair of you? That would make everything easier."

The twins grumbled, and Avery sat one seat away from her brother. I'd wanted to sit next to Abby, but as the kids looked at me expectantly, I slid into the empty chair. Nolan was across the table from me and asked, "Want some wine?"

I nodded. "White, please."

As he poured, I hated how fucking tense and silent the room was. Because of me, the outsider.

It reminded me of just how much Abby was sacrificing to see our deal through—more awkward dinners and get-togethers as people tried to figure me out.

That's your own fault, asshole. So fix it.

It'd been easier to charm in the UK, where no one

had known about my past or my parents, let alone how I'd pretty much abandoned my sister as a kid.

As I tried to think of what to say, Emmy asked, "How's work going at the training facility?"

I sipped my wine and replied, "We're on schedule, which is good. And..." Even though Abby had said it was fine to share, I hesitated before continuing, "Abby's going to head up the tutoring center."

Katie clapped her hands. "That's amazing! She'll be great at it, the best. Some people are just meant to be teachers, and she is one. She definitely has more patience than me."

Zach chuckled. "And me. I'd probably get distracted and turn the classroom into some kind of playground instead."

Avery chimed in. "You'd be a fun teacher, Uncle Zach. But you should probably stick to being a substitute one. That way, you won't get into too much trouble."

Everyone laughed, even Zane and West. Zach nodded. "You're wise beyond your years, Avery. At least now I have a backup plan, if I ever need it."

Abby's voice came from behind him. "Why do you need a backup plan?"

I turned, and for a second I forgot about everyone else in the room. Even though she was in jeans and a nice top, she'd piled her hair atop her head, revealing the soft skin of her neck. Her shirt also dipped just low enough to show a hint of cleavage, but not too much.

And then she walked by me and gave me a view of her ass, hips, and soft thighs encased in form-fitting jeans.

Fuck, what I wouldn't give to have them wrapped around me as she cried out my name as she came.

"Uncle Rafe? Uncle Rafe? Are you going to answer?"

Avery's voice snapped me back to the present.

Everyone stared at me, including Abby, clearly waiting for my reply. "Er, sorry. I was lost in thought about a problem at work."

West narrowed his eyes before glancing at Abby and back at me again. If anyone would notice my gawking at Abby, he would. Damn former best friend and his perception skills.

Emmy, thankfully, came to my rescue. "We were just curious if the tutoring center would open at the same time as your training programs or not."

Abby leaned over between me and Avery to lay something on the table, her scent of warm female and vanilla driving me crazy.

Focus, Mendoza. I cleared my throat and replied, "I'm not sure. I only hired Abby a couple days ago, and she has a lot of work to do still. Plus, there's the construction and getting the supplies and spreading the word. I don't want to rush it. Abby will have the final say about when she's ready to open."

And there I went, rambling.

Beck, Sabrina, and Aunt Lori entered the room with the rest of the food. Before anyone else could speak, Abby did. "This is going to be an awkward dinner if I don't share something." She glanced down at me. "Ready?"

Well, leave it to Abby to get straight to the point.

I nodded, and she placed her hand on my shoulder. I quickly covered hers with my own and squeezed.

The room was so quiet you could hear a pin drop.

Abby had convinced me earlier to let her share the news, and so I waited. She took a deep breath and said, "Rafe and I are more than co-workers. In fact, he's my husband."

After a few seconds of silence, all hell broke loose.

Chapter Fourteen

Abby

Me: I wish you could be at dinner to help and give me support.

Amber: I know, and I totally would. But if you want Zach there, then I can't come.

Me (typed but deleted): Is it really that bad? What happened? Because I know something did.

Me (actual reply instead): Am I crazy for even agreeing to this plan?

Amber: We already went through all the pros and cons! Rafe can not only give you some big favor, he'll take care of Travis once and for all. And I know he will, too.

Me: How can you be so sure?

Amber: Because I remember the teenage boy who

carried you back home after you twisted your ankle without complaint. He may have grown up, but I can't believe Rafe changed that much.

Me: Well, in for a penny, in for a pound, I guess. No turning back now. Wish me luck!

Amber: Good luck! Even if West gets pissed, your family will accept it. I know they will. And I'll always be here for you. Love you. <heart emoji>

Me: You're the best, Amber. And right back at you. <heart emoji>

When I walked into the dining room and saw West glaring daggers at Rafe, I knew I needed to share the news and settle everything as soon as possible. My eldest brother was going to be the hardest one to win over, but at least with his kids and wife in the room, he wouldn't kill Rafe.

Probably.

Plus, if Rafe kept staring at me as if he were stripping the clothes from my body, everyone would guess anyway. Better to have the truth out now than later be asked why I kept it secret even longer than I had.

So when Rafe stopped rambling, I placed my hand on his shoulder, asked if he was ready, and willed my racing heart to calm down a little. When Rafe squeezed my hand, I got the courage to say, "Rafe and I are more than co-workers. In fact, he's my husband."

After a few beats, the room erupted. West demanded to know what the fuck was going on as he charged toward Rafe. Katie and Emmy blinked at me as Avery and Wyatt cheered. Beck and Zane frowned while Zach grinned, winked at me, and gave a thumbs up.

As I tried to figure out how to calm the room and stop West from killing Rafe, Aunt Lori tapped her wineglass with a fork and said, "Calm down and sit your butts back in your chairs. Now."

She didn't even need to shout. We knew from growing up with her that you obeyed *before* Aunt Lori got angry. It was better for everyone that way.

Aunt Lori pointed to West's empty chair. "I mean it, West. Sit your butt down or I'll make you sit down. I may be older, but I'm strong enough to still twist your ear like the best of them."

West pointed at Rafe. "Why the fuck are you on his side? You know what he did to Emmy."

Aunt Lori clicked her tongue. "Watch your tone, lad. You're not too old for me to put you in time out."

West blinked, and I nearly laughed. Glancing down, I saw Rafe's bewildered expression and I wished I could explain things to him. But in our family, Aunt Lori was the Queen. Her diminutive size meant nothing.

West stared but eventually sighed and threw up his hands. "Fine, I'll sit." He glared at Rafe. "But we're going to have words, Mendoza. So don't even think of running away."

Rafe's muscles tensed under my hand, and I knew he was restraining himself. For me.

Emmy moved to West's side and took one of his hands. "Come on, West. Let's listen to their story before jumping to conclusions. I, more than anyone, know not to do that again."

She'd assumed for years that Rafe had blamed her for their parents' death—and West knew that—my brother sighed, kissed her, and followed her back to his seat.

Once everyone was seated and quiet—even Avery and Wyatt, which was quite the miracle—Aunt Lori sipped her wine and gestured toward me and Rafe. "Tell us what happened, dears."

Especially since you told me you'd never marry, Abby, was left unsaid.

Rafe whispered something to Wyatt, and he left his seat to sit on the far side of the table. I slid next to Rafe, and under the table, he took my hand and squeezed. I glanced at him, and he raised his eyebrows in question, offering to explain and take the heat. But I gave a nearly imperceptible shake of my head. If I didn't explain myself now, my family would interrogate me later anyway.

So I focused on killing two birds with one stone. "Well, I think everyone knows I had a crush on Rafe as a kid. And while it faded over time, when he came back, I started talking with him again. And despite our arguments, my crush sort of came back."

It wasn't a complete lie, although Emmy raised her brows, which said she'd be asking me more questions in private later.

I quickly continued, "At any rate, I was struggling to figure out my life, and I decided an impromptu trip to Vegas might help. I had a friend from college I wanted to see who'd moved there, and I headed out. Except my car broke down before I'd even left Starry Hills."

This much was true, and something I'd remembered in the days since waking up married to Rafe.

I looked at my husband. "Rafe saw me on the side of the road and..."

My throat tightened. I still couldn't remember exactly what we'd said or why I'd gone with him, and I hated lying to my family. Could I really do it?

Rafe searched my gaze, must've seen something there, and picked up the story. "She'd been crying, and I asked her what was wrong." I blinked, but Rafe didn't give me a chance to ask if that was true as he barreled on. "I won't break her confidence, but I offered to take her to Vegas and get her car fixed while she was away. She argued but eventually got into my car, and I drove her there. She offered to buy me dinner as a thank you, and we argued again." He chuckled. "We do that a lot, but I don't mind."

Amusement danced in his gaze, and I rolled my eyes. Rafe merely shrugged and said, "Eventually the argument turned heated, we kissed, and well...we ended up in a chapel and got hitched."

West frowned and opened his mouth, but I beat him to it. "When I woke up and remembered what we'd done, it was definitely a surprise. However, there's something between Rafe and me, and we decided to give this marriage a shot." I glanced around the table. "But I want to figure out if our marriage can work without any meddling." I peered hard at Aunt Lori. "I mean it."

She put up her hands. "I wouldn't dream of it, child."

I narrowed my eyes, but my aunt had the most innocent expression on her face.

Oh no. She would meddle, no question.

Emmy spoke up, her voice quiet. "Why didn't you tell me?"

Since she'd lived with my family after her parents had died, we were a little closer than the rest of the BFF circle. Emmy had been my sister long before West had married her.

And right now, the hurt in her eyes was like a stab to my heart.

I wasn't a coward, though, and spoke the truth. "I didn't want to ruin your honeymoon period with West. Besides, it was still new, and Rafe and I needed to figure out our future. But I'm telling everyone now." I moved my gaze to West. "And I hope you'll at least try to be happy for us."

West and I stared at each other for what felt like an hour but couldn't have been more than thirty seconds. His gaze darted to Rafe and then back to me. "I'll tolerate him, but that's the best I can do right now, Abby."

As I struggled to respond, Katie—bless her—raised her wine glass and said, "I think congratulations are in order. To Abby and Rafe!"

She smiled warmly at me, and it helped to settle my nerves a little.

Everyone—even West, once Emmy elbowed him in the side—raised their glasses and cheered.

Once I'd sipped, or more like gulped, my wine, Rafe spoke up again. "I'd like to have a big party with family and friends soon, to celebrate our marriage. I hope you all will come."

Zach spoke up. "Have karaoke and beer, and I'm there."

My brother winked at me and mouthed, "Nice catch." I couldn't help but laugh and shake my head.

Avery said, "Can we do karaoke and try some wine? I'm eleven now."

West snorted. "Nice try, but no. You're not trying wine yet. Maybe in a few years, since my parents let me try some at fourteen."

Beck snorted. "Let you? More like you stole a bottle and got pissed-face drunk."

West replied, "Not as bad as you. I swear you threw up for days."

Avery scrunched her nose. "I don't want to throw up for days."

Aunt Lori spoke up. "That's only if you have too much, and a sip or two won't do that to you, child. Keep at your dad, and he'll let you try it, at least. Whether you'll like it or not, we'll see."

West grunted. "Don't encourage her."

Aunt Lori shrugged. "Your family runs a winery. I can't see the harm. And if we don't let her try it, she'll do it on her own and might end up like her father, passed out in the barn, using a pile of horse crap as a pillow."

Zach laughed. "I barely remember that. Weren't you also mostly naked? I always felt bad for the horses."

West growled. "I didn't touch the horses, asshole."

Zach whinnied, and West threatened him again. As they bickered, Rafe leaned over and whispered, "I think it's going be okay."

The heat of his breath on my skin nearly made me shiver. Once his hand squeezed mine under the table, I decided to ask quietly, "Did you really find me crying when my car broke down?"

He paused and then said, "Yes. I remembered a little more from that day, but not all of it. We can share what we each remember once we're alone."

I nodded, and a tendril of hair escaped the bunch settled at the top of my head. Rafe's eyes traveled to where it lay against the top of my breast. Even though he wasn't touching me, my nipple beaded and my heart raced. What would it feel like to have him take me into his mouth? Torture me with his teeth and tongue? Make me squirm, and then repeat it all over again on the other side.

I made a small noise before I could stop myself, and Rafe's gaze met mine again. At the heat there, I leaned forward a little and parted my lips.

Zach's shout prevented me from replying. "Do you two need a room for some newlywed alone time? Because there's an empty guesthouse out back you can use. Much closer than racing home or trying to make it work in a car—it's not as easy as it sounds."

West sighed. "My children are here, Zach."

"What? I didn't swear or anything."

West shook his head, but before he could speak, Emmy pulled his head down and gave him a kiss.

Katie said, "Oh, good idea," before kissing Nolan.

To my surprise, Beck kissed Sabrina, and Katie kissed Nolan again. Before I could debate whether to follow suit, Rafe gently turned my head, lowered his lips, and pressed his mouth to mine.

It was soft, gentle, and not the all-consuming type of kiss from earlier. And yet, heat rushed through me and the urge to climb onto his lap again was strong.

Wyatt made gagging sounds and said loudly, "Ew, stop it! No kissing at dinner! I don't want to puke."

It snapped me back to the present, and I pulled away. However, I caught Rafe's eyes, unguarded for a second, and noticed they were filled with longing. But what for?

His expression quickly shuttered, and he answered Wyatt, "One day, you'll probably have your own person to kiss."

He made gagging sounds again. "No, thank you. I'd rather play soccer."

I bit my lip to keep from laughing, which became even harder when Avery sighed dramatically and blurted, "I want to be kissed again soon."

Her father's brows went up. "Who the fuck are you kissing now?"

Avery waggled a finger. "Language, Daddy."

As he argued with his daughter about not kissing anyone until she was at least thirteen, my phone vibrated, and then again. Usually I tried not to look at it during dinner, but it kept going off and I debated what to do. Then a piece of roll landed in my lap from Aunt Lori's direction. After I lifted my head and met her gaze, she held up her phone and gave me an expectant look.

Since she'd probably keep throwing food at me until I saw her texts, I discreetly pulled it from my pocket and read her messages:

Aunt Lori: I knew you two would end up together. <heart-eye emoji>
Aunt Lori: His gaze always turns hungry when he looks at you and he thought no one was looking. <over-heated emoji>
Aunt Lori: And don't worry, I'll work on West. He and Rafe were close once, and I think they could be friends again. <hugging emoji>
Aunt Lori: But no matter what, I'll hug your new piece of man meat every chance I get and make him feel welcome. That lad needs a family to love him, no matter what he might say. <heart emoji>

The words blurred a little as I reread her final text. And just like that, my aunt welcomed and accepted Rafe, no questions asked.

Finally meeting her eyes again, I mouthed, "Thank you."

She nodded, and then Zach tossed a pea at Zane, and Sabrina laughed as Zane dumped his water glass over his twin's head.

Wyatt tried to do the same to his sister, but Emmy stopped him and laid out why someone shouldn't pour water on another person's head at the dinner table.

Amidst the chaos, I glanced at Rafe. He must've felt

me watching him because he looked at me and whispered, "Is this normal?"

I smiled. "This is what it's like when it's just family. They were putting on more of a show in front of you before."

He grumbled, "I'm not sure which is better."

I lightly swatted his arm. "Be nice."

His lips twitched. "But being bad can feel so good."

He waggled his eyebrows, and I snorted. "So now you're spouting corny lines?"

"How can I think properly in the face of such beauty?"

I rolled my eyes, but he continued, "You must've dropped from heaven because you look like an angel."

I batted my eyelashes, pretending to be a big flirt. "And you must be the devil, tempting me to sin."

After he moved my hand to his chest, he leaned down and murmured, "No, you're the witch who's entranced me."

Avery sighed and said in a loud whisper right next to me, "You're so lucky, Aunt Abby. I can't wait until you have a baby and then I can be like a big sister to him or her, even though I know I'm just a cousin."

Her words were like dumping cold water over my head. "Baby?"

She nodded. "Kissing can lead to being naked and sex. Sex makes babies. So have lots of sex."

Nolan choked on his wine, and West's voice boomed, "Why are you talking about sex and babies?"

Avery answered matter-of-factly. "I'm not a little girl any longer, Daddy. Besides, I've seen bulls go at it for as long as I can remember. Although taking the cow from behind didn't look very comfortable. Do humans do it that way too?"

Zach, devil that he was, said, "Maybe you should write down all your questions for your dad, Avery, and he can answer them. Knowledge is power, after all."

West glared at Zach, but I couldn't help but snort. Which also earned me a glare from my oldest brother.

Beck sighed. "Can we maybe not talk about sex at the dinner table? Do we really need to make that a new rule?"

Katie said, "Ah, you're no fun, Beck."

West looked to be at the edge of his patience, but Emmy whispered something into his ear and he visibly relaxed.

Jealousy rushed through me because I'd never have that kind of relationship—where one person knew you better than you knew yourself and could help when needed, be it surviving a disaster or just a few words to ease your worries.

No, I'd never have that because my marriage to Rafe was just pretend.

And after Travis, I wasn't sure I could trust a man ever again.

Aunt Lori clapped her hands and said, "No more talk of sex at the dinner table. Now, let's dig in before the food gets cold. And while we eat, we can plan Rafe and Abby's celebration party. Or, a belated wedding reception? Hmm, maybe we can call it the Vegas Marriage Bash. We should make it unforgettable and then we can turn their story into a book!"

I glanced at my aunt. "You're a writer now?"

She winked. "You don't know what I have on my laptop."

My siblings and I all groaned. But Katie asked Aunt Lori what she wrote and if she could read it, until eventually Nolan murmured something into Katie's ear and the conversation turned back to Rafe's and my party.

As I ate, I watched Beck, West, and Nolan with their partners, and tears pricked my eyes. It was petty and childish, but it was unfair how they'd all found love despite scoffing at it most of their lives.

Life is unfair. Travis taught you that. However, don't let that dickhead's actions ruin the rest of your life.

And if that meant being friends with benefits—and having a fake marriage—for a year to figure out my future on my terms, I'd take it. Because one thing I'd finally admitted to myself this evening was that I wanted Rafe naked and inside me. And if I couldn't get my happily ever after with love and marriage and children like I'd wanted for so long, then I'd take what I could get.

Once we were living together, it was game on.

Chapter Fifteen

Abby

Rafe: I know you're moving in soon, but we need to meet and talk about what you remember from that night.
Me: I only remember driving to Vegas. You can just text me now.
Rafe: Fine. You were crying when I found you, something about never getting happiness, and you collapsed against me. Still want to do this via text?
Me (typed but deleted): OMG, what the hell did I say?
Me (actual reply instead): Yes. Anything else?
Rafe: Maybe. But I'm going to tell you in person. My voice might trigger a memory.
Me: Now you're a therapist?
Rafe: Hey, I'm just trying to figure out how we went

from you crying on the side of the road to us waking up married and mostly naked.

Me: Ah, so you haven't remembered everything, either.

Rafe: No.

Me: We'll talk later. For now, I have a lot of packing to do.

Rafe: Fine. But just remember, I'll be working long hours until the training facility opens. So it might be a few days until our paths cross and we can talk properly.

Me (typed but deleted): So you're going to avoid me. Well, we'll see about that.

Me (actual reply instead): That works. I'll let you know when you can help move my boxes.

T he next day, as I was packing up my stuff, someone knocked on my door. I'd basically avoided my family since dinner had ended, and had barely murmured a goodbye to Rafe when I left, only talking to him via text.

However, I couldn't be a coward forever. So with a sigh, I trudged over and opened the door, only to blink at finding Emmy there.

She smiled. "Can I come in?"

Frowning, I stepped aside. "Why are you even asking that? You usually just barge inside."

She entered, turned around, and I hated the uncertainty in her eyes. In that moment, I realized how much I'd hurt her by not telling her about my marriage to Rafe.

I crossed the room and hugged her. "I'm sorry,

Emmy. I just needed time alone to process and figure out what to do."

She hugged me back before leaning away and meeting my gaze. "Rationally, I know that. But you know you can tell me anything, Abby, and I'll always love and support you."

"I know, and it wasn't you I was worried about, but West. And I can't keep putting you in a position where you have to hide things from him."

"Just because I'm married now doesn't mean all my friendships instantly melt away. He and I both have some secrets we keep for friends and family, ones that they don't want to share with the world."

I was tempted to blurt out the truth, that my marriage was fake, but I couldn't break my promise to Rafe.

So I'd just have to be as truthful as I could and see if Rafe would be okay telling Emmy about our arrangement before the year was up. Because Emmy was my best friend and sister, and knew more about me than anyone else in the world. And the thought of deceiving her for an entire year made my stomach churn.

Worry about that later. Tilting my head, I asked, "So how's West taking it?"

Emmy sighed and rubbed her forehead. "Not as well as I'd like. He's protective and stubborn, and thinks Rafe isn't trying hard enough to make up for all the years we were apart." She lowered her hand. "But Rafe *has* tried to do better. He's not an open book by any means, but until he finally accepts that our parents' death wasn't his fault, he's always going to keep his distance." She smiled.

"But even so, I'm happy for you, Abby! We're sisters now, so many times over!"

I chuckled, embracing the moment and forgetting about the future. "There's no getting rid of me now."

She rolled her eyes. "And why would I?"

"Because I've been gloomy and temperamental and reclusive ever since returning to Starry Hills after my student teaching internship. And before you ask, yes, I told Rafe about Travis. I think he's hell-bent on some kind of revenge, although I haven't wheedled out his plans yet."

"Good. I hope he teaches that asshole a lesson because even only knowing some of what happened, I know that dickhead needs a good ass-kicking."

While I hadn't told Emmy about the deep fake porn-like video, she knew enough and had always encouraged me to report Travis's threats to the police.

But I'd been afraid and hadn't wanted it to blow up any more than it already had, so I'd resisted. Especially since I'd either be villainized as a slut or as a stupid, naïve girl who should've known better.

Pushing aside thoughts of Travis, I took Emmy's hand and squeezed. "Just don't get your hopes up about me and your brother yet, okay? Rafe and I are married but still dating, if that makes sense? And if we don't truly fit, we'll get a divorce."

"I know that. But in a strange way, I think Rafe suits you more now than when he was a carefree teenager."

I frowned. "What do you mean?"

Emmy gestured toward my boxes. "Let's pack while we talk."

Since Emmy was a master at packing—she had to pack and unpack stuff all the time for weddings and receptions as a wedding planner—I wasn't about to turn down her help. As she put books into a box, I folded some clothes and asked, "Why do you think Rafe suits me better now?"

"Well, he was a cocky, charming teenager who was forever getting into trouble with West and Mark. But now, he's more cautious, rarely laughs or smiles, and keeps mostly to himself. I think you could help him have fun again."

Curious now, I asked, "You say that despite everything he did in the UK?"

Emmy taped up a box as she replied, "Having spent some time with my brother in recent months, I start to wonder if that was all an act. Nolan and Katie have to portray themselves a certain way to the world because of his fame, and I suspect it was the same for my brother." She glanced at me. "Plus, you married him and you never would've done that if he'd spent the night in Vegas flirting with random women the whole time."

I nearly said that I didn't remember that day, but held back. However, she was right—even drunk, I never would've stayed with Rafe if he'd been constantly hitting on other women.

Although, even just a few weeks ago, I had been against marrying anyone at all. So why had I done it?

If only I could remember that night.

Emmy's voice snapped me back to the present. "Not to mention I think you can bring back some of teenager

Rafe's charm again, and maybe even help him open up a bit. And not just to me, but to his old friends as well."

"I don't know about getting anyone to open up when I still have trouble doing it myself." Emmy opened her mouth, but I continued, "As for bringing back his charm and having fun, I'm not the same person I was a few years ago, Emmy."

She came over and took my hand. "I know you aren't. But fun-loving Abby still comes out sometimes. All it takes is a drink and a good song on the jukebox at The Watering Hole, and you become the life of the party."

I snorted. "More like entertainment for everyone watching since I'm not a good dancer."

"You're more than that, and you know it. Hell, you can get Amber to dance, and that takes some doing."

Amber hated being the center of attention, or being noticed by a large group of people. "True."

She released my hand. "Plus, I think with Rafe at your side, having your back, you'll feel safe again." I opened my mouth to protest, but she beat me to it. "I know you're still worried about Travis showing up in Starry Hills. You showed me a few of his threats that one time, when you were drunk and confessed some of what happened. I still think you should report that asshole and maybe get a restraining order."

If only I could. But I wasn't about to tell Emmy about the videos he could release to the world. She'd probably keep my secret from my brother, but I didn't want to put her in that position. "I just want to move on from him and focus on getting to know Rafe better, get used to living with him, and maybe think of the future."

"Well, if you need any help, just let me know."

"I may need your help with my family, and not just with West. Aunt Lori will meddle, no matter what she might say."

Emmy nodded. "Aunt Lori will, but only to a point. She's far more strategic than many people give her credit for."

"Oh, I learned that a long time ago. Maybe it's because I'm the youngest, and I lived with her for the longest. But Aunt Lori's outrageous words hide her cleverness and how lonely she is, too."

"Well, she likes Fernando Morales, and more than she says out loud. I was with her one time when we went into his antiques shop, and she couldn't stop staring at him."

I bobbed my head. "He steals looks at her, too. I sometimes wonder if she holds back to help us all settle down and find happiness before going after her own."

"Then maybe it's our turn to meddle and help her because she's sacrificed so much to take care of us. It's high time she had someone to care and look after her. Not that we don't, but you know what I mean."

"Yes, although it's going to be tricky, since most of the single people in town seem to flock to him. Even though he's in his sixties, he's definitely a sexy silver fox."

"Hmm, I think we need to visit and welcome him to Starry Hills. We can give him some Starry Wolfe wine and interrogate him at the same time to see if Aunt Lori really has a chance or not."

Glad to have someone else's life to focus on, I nodded. "Yes! We can include a card, sign Aunt Lori's name, and set things in motion."

And so Emmy helped me forget about Rafe, Travis, and my rough year ahead. Instead, we planned how to help Aunt Lori find some love of her own, or at least a way for her to nab a hot date.

Although, given how my aunt talked about Fernando, I suspected it was more than her finding him attractive. The story of her falling fast for my late uncle was legendary, and I wondered if she'd already started falling for the town's newcomer.

Because while I may not end up with my happy ending, I could sure as hell help my friends and family get theirs. That would help me face what was to come with Rafe, the conversations we'd have, and my year of maybe getting to sleep with him but never allowing him close to my heart.

Chapter Sixteen

Rafe

West: This is West. You and I need to talk.
Me: Wait, how did you get my number?
West: Emmy. But don't change the topic.
Me (typed but deleted): It's none of your fucking business. I'm trying to help your sister.
Me (actual reply instead): Fine. But not until after I finish helping your sister move.
West: Then a warning: Make her so much as shed one tear, and I'll fucking destroy you.
Me: I'm not like that bastard who broke her heart. He's on my shitlist, and I'm going to find him and teach him a lesson in fucking manners.
West: Wait, what?

Me: I'll tell you about it later. For now, let's just call a truce? For Abby's sake?

West: I guess. But don't expect me to smile and hug you anytime soon. I'm still pissed you hurt Emmy.

Me (typed but deleted): You can't punish me for that more than I'm punishing myself.

Me (actual reply instead): <thumbs up emoji>

I t was three days after the dinner when I finally moved the last of Abby's boxes from my truck into the garage and went looking for my wife.

Earlier, she'd looked exhausted, with dark circles under her eyes, and I hadn't liked it. So I'd offered to finish with the boxes while she rested.

But as I went upstairs, I heard singing. Once I reached the landing, it was louder and coming from the hallway bathroom.

The bathroom with a mostly open door.

The shower was on, mingled with the singing, and the urge to peek inside and listen to Abby was strong.

No. She wasn't really my wife, wasn't mine to claim. No matter how much I'd like to shuck my clothes and climb into the hot water with her.

Just as I reached the door to shut it, the singing stopped, and Abby screamed.

Without thinking, I raced inside and drew back the shower curtain. "What's wrong?"

"Spider! There! Kill it!"

Normally spiders and I had a rule—stay away from me and I left them alone.

But a big-ass spider crawled along the side of the tub, and Abby backed away and slipped.

I caught her, and her wet, naked ass pressed against my groin. She was so warm and soft and so very, very wet.

Before my gaze could look down, she shouted, "Rafe! Please, I'm terrified of spiders. Get rid of it."

Her words broke the spell and snapped me back to the present. I helped her out of the shower, tossed a towel at her, and found the eight-legged creature chilling in the corner. It wasn't a poisonous type, so I maneuvered it into my hands and cupped them together.

I turned, and Abby moved away. "You're crazy."

Unable to help myself, I thrust my cupped hands toward her. She screamed and promptly kicked me—right in the balls.

Grunting, I barely managed to keep the spider in my hands and crouched down, trying to breathe through the throbbing pain. "What the fuck, Abigail?"

"Oh, sorry! I didn't mean to kick you there. But what did you expect when you put that spider in my face? It was a reflex."

I bit out, "Who the hell kicks spiders to get rid of them?"

"Usually it's not because of spiders. It's just a reflex from dealing with unwanted male attention."

The pain in my balls eased a little as I registered her words. "Who the fuck have you been kicking away?"

She bit her lip, debating whether to answer me.

Cursing, I rose—slowly—and muttered, "I'll be right back."

Maybe some would think I was crazy, but I didn't like killing spiders if I could help it. So I rushed to the balcony attached to my bedroom, put it down, and turned back around, only to find a towel-clad Abby standing in the doorway. "Why didn't you just squish it?"

"Because spiders are useful and get rid of bugs. But that's not important. Tell me who the hell couldn't keep their hands to themselves, to the point you had to knee them in the balls?"

Irritation flared in her eyes, and I knew it wouldn't take much more to provoke her temper. And yet, I couldn't help but state, "Tell me, wife. Who dared try and lay a hand on you?"

Narrowing her eyes, she strode toward me. And despite only wearing a towel, she could've been a warrior marching toward battle, what with her head held high as anger glinted in her eyes.

The towel slipped a little, and she didn't try to read-just it. For a split second, I willed for it to fall to the floor.

But then Abby poked my chest and had my full attention again as she said, "Don't try to pull that posses-sive bullshit on me, Rafael. We're not married, not really, and our bargain doesn't mean you get to growl at me and demand anything."

I leaned closer, until my face was only six inches from hers, close enough I could see the water trailing down her neck. What I wouldn't give to be able to lick the droplets off, one by one, and nibble right where her shoulder met her neck.

Focus, Mendoza. I replied, "I promised to protect you, Abigail. And if there's anyone local I need to tell to keep their fucking hands to themselves, I will. You're mine to claim, at least for the next year."

"I'm not yours beyond a piece of paper, any more than you are mine."

I dared to raise a hand and trace her jaw. She sucked in a breath, and all the days of watching her and dreaming of her and desiring her came rushing back. Warning bells blared inside my head, but I ignored them. The heat and scent and full force of Abigail Wolfe —no, Abigail *Mendoza*—was too delicious to resist. "If you only knew, Abby. If you only knew."

And then I leaned down and took her lips.

I half-expected her to knee me in the balls again, but she moaned, wrapped her arms around my neck, and pressed her soft body against me.

My restraint snapped, and I placed a possessive hand on her ass and another on the back of her neck, and thrust my tongue between her parted lips. She met me stroke for stroke, a hand in my hair and the other one snaking between us. When she stroked my hard dick through my jeans, I groaned and broke the kiss. "Abigail..."

"I wasn't sure if you had recovered yet, but you have." She squeezed me and I sucked in a breath. "Which means I don't need this."

She stepped back, and I released her. And in the next second, she tugged off the towel and tossed it aside.

Holy fuck. Abigail was naked and flushed and damp from her shower. Her breasts were the perfect handful, her dark pink nipples hard and jutting. Her hips flared out in that way that drove me crazy, soft and round, with her belly begging for me to kiss and lick and tease. Then I saw her neatly trimmed pussy, and I could think of nothing but wanting to taste her.

"Rafe?"

The uncertainty in her voice snapped my eyes back to hers. At the flash of insecurity in her gaze, I crossed the distance between us, took her face between my hands, and said, "I'm tired of resisting you, Abigail. You're so fucking beautiful, and I want you. Tell me to stop, though, and I will."

"Don't stop, Rafael. Don't you dare stop."

With a growl, I kissed her again. Her arms went around my neck and mine went to her ass. I lifted, and she wrapped her legs around my waist. I held her close as I claimed her mouth, rocked her against my dick, and reveled in the way she moaned as I did it again.

I walked us to the bed and leaned over until her back hit the mattress. She tugged my shirt up, and I finally broke the kiss to stand up and strip off my clothes. The second her gaze shot to my erection, I let out a drop of precum.

When she licked her lips, I went to my knees, tugged her to the edge of the mattress, and spread her thighs. "I'm tasting you first, wife."

I paused a second to see if she'd tell me to stop, but she merely widened her legs.

Never taking my gaze from hers, I lowered my head and licked her pussy.

The taste of her sweet honey triggered something inside me, something primal that needed to make her scream my name, and I lapped and nibbled and lightly fucked her with my tongue. She tried to buck, but I kept her hips in place, wanting her to do nothing but feel me devour her.

Chapter Seventeen

Abby

Aunt Lori: Remember to leave your bed to eat once in a while, so you can keep up your strength. <blowing a kiss emoji>

Me: <eye roll emoji> There's more to life than staying in bed.

Aunt Lori: Then that man of yours isn't doing it right. I'll have to put together some romance books and give him his marching orders.

Me: Wait, what? No! That'll just embarrass him.

Aunt Lori: Nah, it'll probably make him all hot and bothered and want to try the scenes out with you. You can thank me later. <winking emoji>

Me: <sighing emoji> Remember when I said no meddling?

Aunt Lori: It's not meddling, it's an education. I've given some books to Zach and Zane already. Maybe it'll help them find women of their own.

Me: I'm surprised they didn't throw it back in your face. <sweat drop emoji>

Aunt Lori: Zach looked happy and interested, but Zane was tempted to throw it, I could see it in his eyes. Still, I highlighted passages and quotes to help.

Me: <laughing emoji> Oh, I wish I could've seen their faces!

Aunt Lori: I swear Zane blushed after reading the first one. <smiling demon emoji>

Me: I love you, Aunt Lori. But let me try handling Rafe first, okay?

Aunt Lori: Fine. But I'll put together some books for him just in case. Now, go enjoy that sexy man of yours. <overheated emoji>

I'd come up with a half-dozen plans on how to seduce my husband. Not a single one of them had included a spider.

And even though I'd screamed and kneed him in the groin, Rafe had still wanted me. As soon as he kissed me, my reservations and hesitations and insecurities faded away. The more confident version of myself before the disaster in San Jose came rushing back, and I teased his hard cock over his jeans, driving him wild, and even managing to toss aside my towel without hesitation.

The hungry look in Rafe's eyes had only made me

wetter, and before I knew it, I was on my back on his bed, Rafe kneeling between my legs, telling me he wanted to taste me first.

I'd barely blinked—no man had ever wanted to go down on me without some sort of coaxing—before Rafe was licking and lapping and nibbling. Every stroke made me crazy, and I arched my hips as he lightly fucked me with his tongue.

I wanted to move, to have his tongue on my clit, but he kept me in place, stoking my desire higher.

While close, my orgasm was just out of reach. I didn't know if I wanted to scream at him or ask for more. Then he lifted his head, and I cried out in disbelief.

"Don't worry, wife. I'm not done yet."

It was the second time he'd called me his wife while I was naked, and it sent a rush of wetness between my legs. As a teen, I'd dreamed of marrying him for years. And now? The more time I spent with him, the more I wanted it to be real.

Before I could tell myself to stop being stupid, he traced a finger around my clit without touching it, and again before lifting my hood and blowing across my aching bud.

"Rafe...please. I'm so close."

"Keep your eyes on me, Abigail. I want to watch you fall apart."

I struggled to obey, but managed to. And with a growl, he took my clit between his lips and teased me with his tongue. Slowly at first, then faster, and I tried to arch toward him but couldn't move.

Then he lightly suckled and pleasure coursed

through me, wave after wave, my pussy clenching and releasing. To the point I forgot about everything but my orgasm and Rafe's tongue as he drew it out.

I whimpered, torn between asking him to stop and riding it out longer. Eventually, he gentled his strokes, and I sighed, melting into the mattress.

He wasn't done, though, and thrust his tongue inside me and groaned. For a few seconds, he lapped like a man starved before he finally raised his head. "So fucking perfect and sweet. I'll never get enough of your taste, Abigail."

For a split second, my heart skipped a beat, wondering if maybe—just maybe—this marriage would become real at some point.

But then I quickly pushed that thought aside. I still didn't know the grown-up version of Rafe, and for all I knew, he'd eventually hurt and abandon me like so many others had in my life.

He frowned. "What's wrong? You just tensed up."

I tried to laugh, and it came out strained to my own ears. "Nothing, just coming back down from my orgasm." I put out a hand and brushed the hair from his forehead, reminding myself I could have the physical side and nothing more. "Tell me you have a condom in here so we can finish this."

Okay, that hadn't been the sexiest way to put it.

Rafe noticed, too, and backed away from me. My skin turned cool, instantly missing his furnace-like heat.

"Unless you're going to be honest with me—because something made you freeze up just now—then I think you should go to your room and get dressed."

Feeling exposed and vulnerable, my temper flared. I closed my legs and sat up, crossing my arms over my breasts. "Honest about what? That I want you to fuck me hard, every which way that you can?" I stood, walking toward him. "Because yes, I want that, Rafe. I've wanted it for a long time." I glanced at his still-hard dick. "And obviously, you want me to some degree."

"To some degree? Fuck, Abigail, I've been thinking of nothing else since the first day I saw you, back in October, after returning to Starry Hills."

My heart skipped a beat. "What?"

"You want to know why I was such a dick to you? Because that way I would turn you off and could keep my distance. But now that we're stuck together for a while, I can't resist wanting to get to know you better."

"You do?"

He leaned closer and lowered his head a fraction, making his eyes level with mine. "Yes, for many reasons." He gently traced my cheek with a finger. "And even though I think you're the sexiest woman in the world and I want nothing more than to fuck you hard like you asked, I won't do it if you're going to hide away from me and not reveal anything of yourself." He searched my gaze. "So, why did you tense up, Abigail? Tell me."

As I processed his words, I dropped my arms, uncaring about my nakedness. Part of me wanted to believe him, wanted to believe he truly wanted more from me than just my body. Maybe he even cared.

And yet, being too trusting and naïve had hurt me so many times, both with my family and, later, with Travis. People liked to say or offer things, but eventually they left or discarded me. Something about me just wasn't worth holding on to.

So I did what I probably would always do with men going forward—try to piss him off and put distance between us again. "How many other women did you also say were the sexiest? I doubt I'm the first."

With that, I turned and ran from the room, my eyes stinging with tears.

For so long, I'd dreamed of being with Rafe, of him caring for me, and maybe even finding my own happy ending.

And yet, I was so scared of him maybe doing like all the others and breaking my heart that I'd just deliberately pushed him away and probably made him mad.

If he didn't ask to end our agreement, then I didn't know how I was going to survive eleven months and two weeks more of this. Of not being strong enough to give him a chance.

At least I could get back at Travis. Although that seemed hollow when compared to a possible future with Rafe.

Chapter Eighteen

Rafe

Abby fled the room, and I stood there, stunned, trying to figure out what the hell had just happened.

She'd been warm and responsive and so fucking beautiful as she'd come on my tongue.

Then something had come into her head, some thoughts or doubts or who the hell knew what, and she'd grown cold. Well, cold and then did her damnedest to insult me and push me away.

However, she'd said she wanted me. And I'd seen the internal struggle in her eyes about what to do before throwing my words back at me.

I swore there'd been longing, too.

Something had spooked her, and my best guess was

that something from her past was messing with her head. Probably something to do with that asshole who'd hurt her.

Regardless, I was determined to find out what.

After walking down the hall, I stopped outside her door and was about to knock when I heard Abby crying. My heart clenched at the sound, and I debated what to do. The easy route would be to leave her be and hide behind my work.

However, each quiet sob tugged at my gut, and I knew I couldn't leave her like this. Even if we weren't a true couple, I remembered something my dad had told me: *"Never run away from an argument or go to bed angry with your partner, Rafael. Talk, always talk, and everything should be okay."*

I hadn't thought of my dad in years. Usually the memories were too painful and caused guilt to crash down over me, to the point I'd rush off to drink and have sex and find ways to dull the pain.

But today? His words only made me more determined to be brave and find out what was wrong with Abby. Even if she'd only agreed to be my wife for a year, part of my job as her husband was taking care of her. Orgasms were all well and good, but I wanted her smiles and laughter, too.

Taking a deep breath, I knocked. The crying stopped, and I knocked again.

Eventually, Abby's muffled voice came through the door. "Go away."

"Not until you tell me what's really going on.

Because I wasn't lying earlier, and I need to find out why you don't believe me."

She gave a strangled laugh. "Says the world-famous soccer player who's dated models and actresses and trust fund ladies."

"I don't want to have this conversation through a door, Abigail. Let me in. Please."

For a few seconds, I thought she would tell me to get lost. Eventually she said, "Come in."

I entered and found her sitting on her bed, wrapped in a light pink bathrobe dotted with cats wearing ridiculous outfits. I couldn't help but smile. "You still like cats, I see."

Frowning, she glanced down at her robe and hugged her arms around her body. "It helps me feel cute sometimes." She looked up at me, her swollen eyes stabbing my heart. "What do you want, Rafe?"

I leaned against the dresser, keeping a distance between us. "You're upset, and I want to know why. Because I don't like it."

"Right, because I should just bare my soul to you whenever you want it," she drawled.

"Of course not. But if we're to live together and play the part of a couple, then we need to be able to talk and resolve things. If you won't believe me when I say a simple truth, such as about how beautiful you are, then it doesn't bode well for when some of my past catches up to me and I have to explain it."

Fuck. Had I really mentioned my past so easily?

Abby tilted her head. "What do you think will catch up with you?"

I shook my head. "Not until you tell me why you don't believe me when I say you're the most beautiful woman in the world to me, Abigail."

She searched my gaze, huffed, and looked down at the quilt on the bed. As she traced the boxes making the design, her voice was low, so low I barely heard it, as she replied, "I've been burned so many times, Rafe. I've been too trusting, too naïve, and it culminated in me being with a man who, as soon as I fell in love with him, proceeded to change me little by little. He criticized me, made me feel inadequate, and I kept trying to please him, to change for him, only to be tossed aside and humiliated." She paused, met my gaze, and whispered, "I find it difficult to believe anyone outside of my family, and even then, it's sometimes hard."

I itched to cross the room, pull Abby close, and vow to be better than that. Hell, to treat her like she deserved.

But as she was staring at the quilt again, hunched into herself, I knew that would be the wrong approach. Probably. I didn't know what the hell I was doing, but I had to try something. I wasn't about to become a shitty husband on the first day of living together.

Not to mention I'd rather stab my own heart than see Abby with tear-swollen eyes ever again.

Memories of another time tear-filled eyes had looked at me and begged me to stay, after my parents' funeral, flashed into my head. I'd failed my sister for too long. I wouldn't fail in this, too, even if it was a marriage of convenience.

Which meant sharing some hard truths, things I'd not shared with anyone before.

After taking a deep breath, I finally spoke up. "I've done a lot of things I'm not proud of, Abby. I hurt my sister, my parents, and even the friends I had here in Starry Hills. I isolated myself for over a decade, thinking if I did that, I couldn't hurt anyone ever again. And you know what? That made everything worse, as I found out with Emmy." Her gaze met mine, full of curiosity, and I pushed on. "Part of how I isolated myself was by wearing a persona, a mask, where I pretended to be a playboy, a charmer only looking for a good time. That's how the press saw me, at any rate. But I wasn't happy. Not really."

All the years of wanting someone to confide in—to drop the act and be a little less perfect and charming and sexy—had been fucking difficult.

"Rafe..."

Abby's voice brought me back to the present, and I knew I needed to keep going before I chickened out. "I know you're probably wondering why the hell I'm unloading this on you. Well..." I rubbed the back of my neck and said in a rush, "I haven't told anyone this before. No one. I'm sharing it with you to prove that I'm not perfect, that I lived a lie for so long it became exhausting, and I just want that phase of my life to be over." I stood and crossed over to Abby, before kneeling before her. "I want to be me, Abigail. Just Rafael Charles Mendoza, the man with a dodgy knee, a sordid past, and a loneliness that I'm working on. I'm trying to be honest, especially with you. And if you won't believe me when it comes to something as simple as me thinking you're beautiful? Then I'm not sure anyone will ever believe me, the real me, instead of the fiction I lived for so long."

Her eyes searched mine, and I held my breath. Because if sharing one of my deepest secrets wouldn't convince Abby that I wanted to be truthful, then I wasn't sure what else I could do.

So I waited for her response, my heart racing, hoping that maybe, just maybe, she'd believe me and confide more in me, too.

Chapter Nineteen

Abby

I wasn't sure what I'd expected when Rafe came into my room. But him telling me about being lonely and keeping his distance so he wouldn't hurt anyone hadn't been it.

I knew his actions had something to do with his parents' car crash and feeling responsible for it. Emmy had shared her own guilt but had dealt with it by giving others happiness rather than taking it for herself. Well, at least until West had come along and helped her heal and realize it wouldn't bring her parents back. No, they would've wanted their daughter to live her life and be happy.

Rafe, on the other hand, had kept himself apart, thinking he would hurt anyone he became close to. Just thinking about him living a persona for over a decade, never being himself, made me want to hug him. Despite all my own trust issues, I knew, deep down, that my family loved me. I bet this man kneeling before me hadn't even realized that he'd had his sister's love all this time.

He'd had no family, no close friends, either, it sounded like, and no one to love him.

I itched to cup his face, pull him close, and kiss him. *Let him in a little*, my heart screamed. And yet, my brain remembered the last time I had done that.

"I want to believe you." His face fell, but I quickly added, "While I can't snap my fingers and erase all of my doubts and pain and past, I want to give you a chance. I really do. Just answer one more thing, and I'll promise to try and do it."

Rafe reached as if to take my hand, but then stopped. "Ask me, Abigail. Anything."

"Do you still feel responsible for your parents' death?"

He looked away, frowning, and I thought he wouldn't answer. Then he whispered, "Yes."

At the sadness in his voice, I couldn't help but lean over, hug him, and lay my head atop his. I wanted to tell him it wasn't his fault. That he couldn't have stopped the drunk driver who'd hit his parents' car on the way to the airport.

And yet, I sensed Rafe would close up again if I said that. I would have to bide my time and press it later. For now, I merely said, "Thank you for answering. If you ever want to talk about it, about anything, I'm here."

He wrapped his arms around me, and we stayed that way for over a minute, silent and embracing. It would be so easy to love this complicated man.

Not that I would allow myself to fall, of course. Rafe may have shared a little about himself, but we were friends, nothing more. Okay, maybe friends with benefits, considering he'd had his mouth between my thighs. But this wasn't love.

Couldn't become love.

I released him, put out my hand, and said, "Let's shake on trying to believe one another."

He took my hand, and I ignored the little thrill at the feel of his skin against mine.

As soon as he released me, I hesitated. Part of me wanted to ask him to hold me so we could give each other a little comfort. No sex, just acknowledging we'd each have someone to lean on, at least for the next year.

But I was drained and tired and probably not the best picture with swollen eyes and who knew what my hair looked like. So I wrapped my arms around myself and smiled. "I think we each need a little time to recharge. Will you be here in the morning?"

He stood and nodded. "Until the training facility opens, my schedule will be somewhat unpredictable. However, I will try my damnedest to have breakfast with you every day. Maybe lunch some days, when you're working too. But breakfast, for sure."

"As long as you don't eat at like 4 a.m."

"While I'm a morning person, even that is an ungodly hour to get up." His lips twitched. "You weren't ever a morning person, as far as I can remember.

Do I need to brew some extra strong coffee before ten a.m.?"

After sticking my tongue out at him, I replied, "I'm not that bad. I was a teacher, after all."

I waited for the shame and pain of my student teaching semester to crash over me. And yet, all I remembered was my strong morning coffees, teasing the students in class, and sometimes wanting to pull my hair out as I learned how to deal with high schoolers.

Pushing aside the past, I focused back on Rafe. "I try to eat around 7 or 7:30 a.m. But speaking of mornings and getting ready, how is your water heater?"

He blinked at the non sequitur. "My water heater?"

"Will it survive two people taking showers in the morning, at about the same time? Or is it temperamental, like the one at my family's house, where you have to schedule showers carefully with so many people or risk arctic temperatures?"

"It's tankless, so don't worry about it. Although you might want to close the door when you shower. Your singing..."

I narrowed my eyes. "What about my singing?"

"Well, let's just say you have something in common with the cats on your robe."

I grabbed a pillow and tossed it at him. Rafe caught it easily, the bastard, and lunged it right back. "Hey, you wanted honesty."

"Maybe. But you could've just asked me to close the door because I'm loud and not compare me to a howling cat."

He smiled, and my heart skipped a beat. Damn, he

was handsome. Rafe had rarely smiled since returning to Starry Hills, and now I wanted to see it all the time.

Rafe said, "Just think of it this way—it gives you the freedom to tell me the truth as well."

"Do I dare, though? Men and their egos..."

With a growl, he crossed the room and tickled my side. I laughed, trying to kick him away, and eventually I made contact with something soft.

"Abigail, fuck, my balls aren't going to survive much longer around you."

"Oh, I'm so sorry, Rafe! I didn't mean to kick you there."

I rubbed his back, and he curled onto his side, cupping himself. "I thought I was done wearing a cup, but I guess not."

I felt bad, and yet, I still couldn't help but laugh. "What, so one day you'll just show up and walk around the house in full football protective gear? American football, that is."

"If I can handle an asshole kicking me with cleats, I can handle my wife."

"Hmm, cleats. Now there's an idea..."

He growled, and I laughed again, unable to help it. Teasing him was so much fun.

"It's good to see you smile and laugh, Abigail. Your tears just about tore out my heart."

My gaze shot to his, and something electric passed between us. "Is that part of your husbandly duties now? To make me laugh?"

"One of them." He slowly sat up, wincing, and added, "I need a bag of frozen peas."

"I could go get some and help you until you recover."

"No." The word was harsh, but then his voice softened. "No, Abigail. Rest. I'm just going to watch whatever game I can find, drink a beer or two, and freeze my balls until they stop hurting." He added something under his breath that I couldn't hear.

But he stood before I could ask him about it, and he almost waddled to the door.

I bit my lip to keep from laughing again. "Good night, Rafe."

"Good night, Abigail."

He paused, as if debating about saying something else, but then he was gone.

I plopped back on my bed, smiling, and wondered about two things. One, would he truly make time for me every morning for breakfast? And two, would he ever kiss me again? Because not asking him to stay the night in my bed had been hard. Way too hard.

Time would tell just how far I'd take being honest with Rafe Mendoza.

Chapter Twenty

Abby

Katie: Have you and Rafe broken the bed yet?
Me: Er, no.
Katie: Try harder! Nolan's finally gave out last week. <overheated emoji>
Me: <puking emoji> No. Just no. He's my brother.
Katie: He's not mine, thank goodness. <winking emoji> But that's not why I texted you. Okay, not the only reason. Nolan and I want to help with the tutoring center. What can we do?
Me: I'm not sure yet. But you might want to ask Rafe. It's his place. I'm just an employee.
Katie: And his wife. Besides, he said it's up to you. So when you have a better idea, let us know. <heart emoji>
Me: Thanks, Katie. And tell Nolan the same. It'll prob-

ably be supplies, especially computers and laptops. But I'll let you know soon.

Katie: Maybe we can double date and talk about it. Nolan keeps saying he knows this amazing hidden gem in San Francisco. We could make a day of it. Especially since Rafe could use some friends, and Nolan doesn't have the history like a certain other Wolfe brother.

Me: That Wolfe brother will get pissed, though, when he finds out about it.

Katie: Maybe. But we're all going to have to get along, so if I have to knock some heads together until West recognizes Rafe is family twice over, I will. I'll send the details soon, and I won't take no for an answer. <heart emoji>

The next morning, I debated showering and getting ready before heading downstairs, but said screw it. I was going to spend the day at home, working on my computer and making plans for the tutoring center, and my pajamas were comfy.

So, a little before seven, I headed downstairs in my shirt and shorts, and heard some sports game blaring from the kitchen. After one last deep breath, I entered and stopped, watching as Rafe shouted, "What the fuck was that?"

I glanced at the tablet next to him on the counter and smiled as he continued to mutter not very nice things about the referee. I walked closer, saw it was a soccer game—probably in Europe, given how it said live and the time difference—and asked, "You still enjoy the game, even though you don't play any longer?"

He turned off the tablet screen and turned around, his mouth open, but he stood silent. My cheeks heated as he took in my pajamas, lingering on my legs, before he cleared his throat and replied, "Yes. Aren't you cold? It's February."

"No, I'm always warm when I wake up. I need lots of blankets to fall asleep, but I like cooling down in the morning." I walked over to him and peered at the stove. "You're making pancakes?"

I stood right next to him, close enough to feel his body heat and smell the purely masculine scent that was Rafael Mendoza, but somehow restrained myself from pressing up against his side.

He glanced at me and raised an eyebrow. "Pancakes aren't rocket science. If I can't stir together the pancake mix and water, then I have some issues."

I snorted. "Zach would struggle. That man can burn toast in a toaster."

"I can cook breakfast, at least. It was usually the only meal I was home for." He gestured toward the kitchen island. "Sit down and I'll make you some coffee."

"Extra strong," I said as I rubbed my eyes. I'd had trouble sleeping, my brain replaying Rafe's mouth and how he'd made me come so hard.

Not wanting to go down that train of thought again, I asked, "Are you going to start an older guy soccer league in the area?"

"Older guy?"

"You know what I mean. For men not in their teens."

"I don't know. I'm not sure I'll ever be able to play again, though, but I could maybe coach."

"Wait, what? Was your injury truly that bad?"

He fell silent, and I wondered if he'd answer. I probably should've waited until we were more comfortable around each other, but it'd just popped out.

Eventually he said, "It's not just the last injury, to be honest. I'm thirty-six years old and my body has taken a lot of abuse over the course of my career. My physical therapist says if I take it easy for at least the next six months, I might be able to play for fun. But I knew the instant I hurt my knee this last time, it was over."

"How are you coping? Are you okay? I mean, soccer was your life for nearly as long as I can remember."

He flipped the pancakes before saying, "Yes and no. I love the game, and always will. But being a professional athlete is brutal, what with all the training and games and more training. The seasons are long for soccer, especially when you include all the championships, and it'll be nice to slow down a little."

"I sense a but."

He sighed. "But I miss having a team, a purpose, and the sense of working toward a single goal." He turned around and met my gaze. "It's why I started a business instead of just retiring and living a life of leisure for the rest of my days."

"I'd never really thought about that, retiring so young. I'm not sure I could do it, either."

"Good, because that means I get to have a certain amazing teacher I know help me with the tutoring center. If I keep giving you raises, I have a chance of keeping you forever."

It was on the tip of my tongue to ask if he'd still want me around after the year was up, but he went to the espresso machine to make me a latte and I clammed up.

As soon as he finished and placed it in front of me, I noticed the chocolate cat design on top and laughed. "Did you already have that one, or did you get one for me?"

"I could be all smooth and say I went out at the crack of dawn to find it. But, no, it was part of a pack. It didn't have horses, or I would've done that for you."

At the mention of horses, my heart squeezed. As a kid, I'd loved them so much, to the point my parents had thought I might train them for a living.

But after my mom died, it'd been too painful. While my dad had been the one to teach me to ride, to show me how to pick out the best horse, and how to care for them and treat them with respect, I'd ridden the most with my mom.

Once she died, Beck had tried to get me to ride again. But I'd never been strong enough to try.

Rafe's voice interrupted my thoughts. "Why did you lose yourself in thought when I mentioned horses, Abby? Did you have a really bad accident or something that turned you off them?"

My eyes shot to his. "What?"

He shrugged one shoulder. "You're fairly easy to read sometimes." He glanced at the stove. "One second, and we'll talk more about this."

Part of me wanted to scream no, it would only remind me of my dad and bring back my grief.

And yet, I'd asked Rafe about something even more painful—losing his ability to play a game that had become his entire life.

So I could be strong and give him some honesty, too. It wasn't as if he would laugh at me or strong-arm me into riding again. I may not know everything about the grown-up version of Rafe, but enough to trust that he'd respect my wishes.

He put a plate in front of me, and I laughed. It was a stack of pancakes with link sausage as the mouth and blueberries as the eyes and nose. The hair was drawn on the plate with chocolate syrup. "It's cute."

He hesitated before saying, "I used to make this for Emmy when she was a little girl. It always made her smile. And I know you're a grown woman, but I figured I'd try it, anyway."

"I love it, truly. But you better have one for yourself, too. Because I can't wait to see the tall, sexy man eat his happy face pancake breakfast."

He raised his brows. "Of course I have one. But he's a little more manly."

After grabbing his plate, he sat it next to me and took the stool. As soon as I saw the design, I snorted.

The pancake face had a beard made of bacon, his mouth drawn with maple syrup, and his eyes were fried eggs. The hair was made of whipped cream. Before he could cut into it, I swapped our plates.

"Hey!"

"Yours is better."

"But you don't even like bacon, or so you said."

"Do you have more sausage? Because I want a sausage beard and then you can have yours back."

"Are you blackmailing me by holding my breakfast hostage?"

"Yep."

"And absolutely no remorse." He sighed dramatically. "You want me to starve, I see."

"Oh, stop it. You used to have a thing for eating peanut butter out of a jar. I'm sure you could have that for breakfast. Although giving me more sausage would be easier. A tall girl needs to eat. It's one of the benefits, at least, to being a giant."

He frowned. "You're the perfect height, Abby. I wish you'd believe me."

Not wanting to discuss this again, I moved as if to cut into his bearded pancake man, and Rafe jumped up. He came back with a plate of sausage. "Here. Just give me my pancakes back."

Grinning, I picked up a link and bit into it, moaning. "Damn, this is good. What kind is it?"

But Rafe didn't answer me. I opened my eyes and sucked in a breath at the heat in his gaze. "Rafe?"

He shook his head and dug into his breakfast. "The sausage is from my secret source."

"Secret source? Really? You act like it's something from the black market or an illegal enterprise."

He winked. "Maybe it is."

"You can be ridiculous, you know that, right?"

After swallowing his bite, he nodded. "Although the

rest of the world probably won't believe you. Speaking of the world..."

At his serious tone, my stomach churned. "What is it?"

He sipped his coffee and then answered, "The news about our marriage is out in the world now. A reporter contacted me for comment late last night, and I thought it better to get ahead of the story instead of letting them control the narrative."

"Do they know about Vegas?"

"Only that we married there. However, they believed our childhood friends-to-lovers story."

"What, exactly, did you say?"

"Just that when I came back home after my injury, I saw you all grown up and lost my heart on the spot. Not wanting my fame to ruin anything, we kept it secret and eventually married before telling anyone."

"That's not so bad." I paused and then asked, "Will it be a big story here, too, do you think?"

"Maybe on the sports channels, and possibly the local news. You're thinking of that asshole, aren't you?"

I nodded, suddenly losing my appetite and pushing the plate away.

Rafe took one of my hands and squeezed. "I already have some trusted people looking into him and his life. If there's a way to shut him up for good—and no, I don't mean by killing him, no matter how tempting it is— they'll find it. I promise to do all that I can to protect you, Abby."

I met his gaze again, finding concern and sincerity. "I know. But that doesn't mean I won't worry. He's a fragile, vindictive piece of shit. And the fact I married someone richer and arguably more powerful than him? He'll hate it, and who knows how he'll act. He could do anything, uncaring of the consequences to his own life if it means I lose and he wins."

"Maybe, maybe not. But no matter what happens, I'm here for you, Abigail. I know I can't guarantee anything, but if he does lash out, he'll pay. I vow it."

His vehement tone made me blink. "I believe you."

"Good." He waved toward the pancakes. "Won't you eat a little more? Otherwise, I'll have to eat it, and then I'll have to waddle out the door."

Smiling, I tugged the plate back. "At least you wouldn't be waddling because I kneed you in the balls this time."

He narrowed his eyes. "I didn't waddle."

"You totally did last night. It was hard not to laugh."

He swiped whipped cream off his plate and dabbed my nose.

"Hey!"

I lunged for his plate, but he moved it out of the way. "Now, now, no food fights. This isn't a Wolfe family dinner, after all."

"Just for that..."

I lunged across the counter, grabbed his plate, scooped all the whipped cream off, and rubbed it all over his face.

He blinked at me, looking adorable, and I grinned. "There. Now we're even."

"Not even close, Abigail. Come here."

I squeaked and dodged his hands. He chased me out

of the kitchen, down the hallway, and I turned into a dead end. "Damn it."

He slowed down, stalking toward me, his lips twitching even as the whipped cream slid down his face. "Now, come give your husband a kiss."

He made loud kissing noises and leaned toward me.

"You're being ridiculous."

His tongue darted out, licking the whipped cream off my nose, and heat shot through my body. His hot breath danced across my skin as he said, "Maybe you wanted an excuse to lick my skin? Or maybe to suggest you want me to do it to you?"

He ran a finger down his cheek, and then lightly rubbed the whipped cream on my lips.

My heart thudded in my chest and time stilled as I waited to see what he'd do.

He murmured, "Do you want me to lick you clean, wife?"

"Yes."

Leaning closer, his breath danced across my lips as he said, "Then I suppose I need to fulfill my husbandly duty and listen to you."

His tongue flicked out, swiping across my bottom lip, before retreating, and he hummed. "Delicious, but not as good as the sweet honey I found between your thighs."

Before any memories could flash in my head, Rafe licked my top lip and then took my mouth in a hot, lingering kiss. I melted against him, uncaring that we were both a little bit sticky, and moaned as his tongue stroked mine.

I was just about to press my body against his when

he broke the kiss. His eyes searched mine, and the heat and yearning I saw there made me suck in a breath.

His voice was low as he said, "I have a contractor appointment in half an hour. I need to clean up and go, Abigail. No matter how much I want to stay here with you."

My heart thudded in my chest. Part of me wanted to be selfish and ask him to stay. And yet, his earlier confession about needing something to keep him from feeling adrift came back to me. I couldn't be responsible for derailing his plans, especially since I wasn't really his wife.

So I patted his chest and smiled. "I know. Besides, I have to finalize any construction changes soon myself, so I should probably get to work too. And it'll be easier to concentrate with you gone."

Rafe looked about ready to say something else, but instead he stepped away and nodded. "I'll see you at breakfast tomorrow, Abigail, if not sooner."

I nodded. "And I'll cook tomorrow."

He smiled. "Will you wear a frilly apron for me? Combined with those tiny shorts, it will almost look like you're naked from the front under it."

I snorted. "You'll just have to wait and see. Now, go, before I make you late and your business partner regrets you hiring me."

"Mark never would." I opened my mouth to protest, but he put up a hand. "But I do need to get ready and go. I hope you have a good day, Abby. Let me know if you need anything, anything at all."

With that, he headed upstairs to clean up, and I

leaned against the wall, closed my eyes, and tried to calm my heart.

I needed to be careful, really careful, because at this rate, I'd lower my walls, let Rafe into my heart, and then I'd fall to pieces all over again when we divorced in a year.

No, I needed to be strong. *Remember, enjoy the physical but keep your heart separate.*

With that, I went to wash my face and get ready for work. Just like Rafe could throw himself into something new and find a purpose, I'd do the same with the tutoring center.

That way I wouldn't have much time to fawn over Rafael Mendoza and do something stupid, like fall in love with him.

Chapter Twenty-One

Rafe

Aunt Lori: Everyone told me to wait before texting you, but you've had enough time with Abby. I want some of you to myself. This is Aunt Lori. <waving emoji> <heart emoji>

Me: Er, okay.

Aunt Lori: You need to make things up with your sister and West. And soon. When are you going to do it? <raised eyebrow emoji>

Me: Excuse me?

Aunt Lori: Oh, come on. You know you're going to be BFFs with West again eventually. But the clock's ticking, and you're not getting any younger. <alarm clock emoji> <old man emoji>

Me: Did you just call me old?

Aunt Lori: Don't you remember the time you both tried to build a tree fort, only for a bobcat to decide they liked the spot and chased you away? <hands on face scared emoji>

Me: We were nine. That was a long time ago.

Aunt Lori: He misses you, you know. But don't tell him I said that.

Me (typed but deleted): I wish we could at least be civil again, if not friends. But I'm not hopeful.

Me (actual reply instead): We'll see what happens. Now, I have to get back to work. Enjoy your day.

Aunt Lori: Hmm. Bye. For now. But you'll hear from me again soon. I need to learn about your favorites, so we can invite you to dinner and spoil you. <blowing a kiss emoji>

Three days later, I tried to concentrate on the branding and website designs on my computer screen. And even though I had to pick something by the end of the day or risk a delay, I kept thinking about Abby's behavior this morning.

Like yesterday, she'd been a little more distant—teasing me less, trying to keep the conversation to work and world events, and scurrying away the one time I'd tried to kiss her again.

After so many years of keeping people at arm's length, it was hard to get a glimpse of closeness and then have it ripped away again.

But this is what you agreed to.

True. But I hadn't expected to want to know everything about Abby so quickly, to enjoy teasing her, and maybe want to woo her for real.

With a sigh, I ran a hand over my hair and tried to concentrate on the designs again. But I'd barely scrolled a few inches before a familiar voice reached my ears.

The growly voice of my brother-in-law, Weston Wolfe.

"What did you do to my sister?"

Frowning, I glanced up. At West's thunderous expression, I raised my brows, refusing to be intimidated. "What the fuck are you talking about?"

He strode in. "Abby's withdrawn, more so than normal. What the hell did you do to her? I warned you what would happen if you hurt her."

I rose slowly and couldn't resist poking the bear a little. "I made her breakfast a couple of times. Maybe the food didn't settle right?"

"Why you..."

He stalked around the desk. But even with my knee still healing, I was quicker than West's big, stocky form.

I stopped at the other side of the desk and turned to face him. My knee throbbed, and I wouldn't be able to run or fight. So I decided what the hell, and blurted, "I don't know what's wrong with her, West. And that's the truth. She's withdrawn from me too, and I've been trying to figure out why."

He blinked, obviously not expecting honesty from me.

While I could bark for him to get out, or maybe ask

Mark to convince West to leave, an idea sparked. We were each married to the other's sister, and we needed to find a way to get along.

And while I could probably figure out Abby eventually, I was impatient and could use any help I could get.

I gestured toward the chair and couch on the far side of my office. "How about we sit and talk? We both care about Abby and want to make her happy. Why not work together on this?" He studied me and I added, "We don't need to become best friends, but for fuck's sake, we can have a few civil and honest conversations. Besides, you know I can keep secrets. Your brothers still don't know that it was you who wrecked your dad's motorbike when we were kids."

West's lips twitched. "I'd forgotten about that." As if realizing I was still there, he frowned and grunted. "Fine."

He sat on the sofa, and I took the chair. Next to me was a mini-fridge full of soda, iced tea, and water. I took out a water and raised my brows at West. He muttered, "Coke."

I handed him a can and after we both sipped our drinks, I decided to get the ball rolling. I was desperate to get the teasing version of Abby back from a few days ago. "Sometimes she seems happy, and other times, it's as if she's a million miles away. And before you ask, we didn't fight or anything."

West sighed. "She's been like this ever since I returned to Starry Hills last year. Something happened during her student teaching internship, something that devastated her. But I don't know much beyond that. And yes, Emmy does, but she won't share it." He peered at me closely. "Do you know?"

"Some, but I won't share her secrets, West. So don't ask."

For a few seconds, he stared at me. Then he nodded. "Good. She could use someone at her back."

"What do you mean?"

He shifted in his seat, looking uncomfortable. For a few minutes, I'd forgotten about our strained relationship and all the years I'd been away. At one time, West had been like a brother to me, and we'd shared nearly everything with one another.

But those days were long gone. And for the first time, I thought about Aunt Lori's text message about us being friends again, and kind of wished it could happen.

I leaned forward and propped my elbows on my thighs, the water bottle dangling from my fingers. "I know this isn't easy for either of us, West. But I promise you, I'm trying to make your sister happy. I'm trying to repair things with Emmy, and I'm trying to mend fences with everyone I abandoned when I left Starry Hills. Can't we start over?"

He gulped the rest of his soda before staring at the empty can. As I tried to think of what else I could say—something that I hadn't said a dozen times already since my return—West spoke up. "Abby is the youngest. She was only seven when our dad died, and sixteen when our mother passed. I left her not long after Dad died, Nolan a few years later. And within months of our mom's death, Zane joined the Navy SEALs."

He paused, and I could tell West had more to say. I didn't want to break the spell, so I kept quiet.

Eventually, he cleared his throat and continued, "I was too consumed with my grief, and then later my disastrous first marriage, to think much about my little sister back then. But she had the hardest time out of us all, with the least amount of support to deal with her own grief." He slightly crushed the can and continued, "Despite all that, she remained strong and happy, at least on the outside, and always had her group of friends at her back." He met my gaze and added, "But whatever happened to her in San Jose was the final straw. It broke her. And I wish I could help her heal, even just a little. But in some ways, I'm still a stranger to her. And while my kids and her friends are good at cheering her up, she needs more than that—she needs someone to always be there for her, to love her and never let her down, to be a better man than me and two of my brothers ever were for her. So can you be that man, Rafe? Because if not, then you need to divorce my sister and let her find the person who will treasure and love her as she deserves."

I tried to process everything West had told me. I knew, in a general sense, about three of her brothers leaving at some point, as well as her parents' deaths. And yet, I hadn't really put together how much loss that was. Especially for one person, and starting so damn young.

And then add her finally trusting her heart with that asshole Travis, and I could see how she might lose hope of anyone putting her first, let alone loving her and staying around.

Oh, Abigail.

West's voice interrupted my thoughts. "I think you're starting to understand just how much my sister has gone through. I played a small part in it, and I regret it so fucking much. But you still haven't answered my question—are you going to treat her as she deserves? Or will you let her go so she can find someone who will always stand by her?"

The thought of letting some other man hold Abby close, love her, make her laugh one moment and moan the next, made me crush the water bottle in my hands. The top flew off and water splashed all over me. "Fuck."

I quickly grabbed a towel from a cupboard along the wall and dried off. Tossing it aside, I turned toward West and stated, "I will be that man for her, West. I can't make her trust me, but I'm going to try my damnedest to win her over and be there for her."

Love her, too. Because it wouldn't take much more for me to fall for her.

Her humor, her wit, her ability to survive so much loss and still work toward her childhood goal of being a teacher—there was so much to admire about her.

And that was before I even remembered her kisses or how soft and warm she felt in my arms.

West stood and put out a hand to shake. I took it, and as he shook, he said, "Then I think we need more than a truce—let's start over. If you need my help with Abby, let me know." His grip tightened on my hand and he pulled me close. "But my threat still stands—hurt her, and I'm going to kick your ass into next week, brother-in-law or not."

I rolled my eyes. "I'm not going to hurt her, at least

not on purpose." West growled, and I added quickly, "Your threat is noted. Now, if you'd let me go, I have a few questions about Abby. I want to surprise her and could use your help."

West released me and sat back on the couch. "I'll try my best. Although you should visit your sister and ask her, too."

I plopped into the chair. "Will you growl the entire time, like during my previous visits? It's hard to have an honest conversation with a guard dog."

West narrowed his eyes, and I couldn't help but laugh. "Hey, it's true." I sobered. "Although I'm glad Emmy has you, West. I've never seen her as happy as she is with you and your kids."

His face softened. "I am definitely a lucky man." West cleared his throat. "Now, what did you have in mind?"

As we discussed my plans, a little of our childhood camaraderie returned. Oh, we weren't suddenly best friends or anything. But there was a chance, albeit a small one, that we could be friends in truth one day.

But for now, I focused on Abby. Because as much as I would like to get along with West for my sister's sake, the clock was ticking. The longer Abby kept her distance from me, the harder it would be to break through.

Especially once her ex reared his ugly head—which my gut said would happen at some point—she might shut down completely if I hadn't earned her trust a little by then.

However, when West finally left and I had a plan in place, I started to feel a little optimistic.

Chapter Twenty-Two

Abby

Aunt Lori: Make sure to leave the hotel room once in a while, for food and fresh air. <winking emoji>

Me: I told you, it's a business trip. Rafe and I need to buy furniture and supplies for the training center. That's all.

Aunt Lori: I remember what it's like to be a newlywed, Abby. If he's not making you sore from all the sex, then you've got problems.

Me: Aunt Lori!

Aunt Lori: Those dark eyes of his and the tattoos on his upper arms...rawr. Makes me wish I was twenty years younger.

Me: What about Fernando? I thought you liked him?

Aunt Lori: That man doesn't seem to know that I exist.

But enough about me. Enjoy your trip, child. And make sure to get me an ugly mug for my collection.

Me: Of course. And I know Fernando will come around. You're quite the catch, Aunt Lori.

Aunt Lori: Give Rafe a kiss from me and enjoy yourself, Abby. You deserve it.

Me: I'll try. <heart emoji>

A little over a week after Rafe had kissed the whipped cream from my lips, I was on my brother Nolan's private plane, wishing it wasn't dark outside so I could look out the window.

Rafe sat across from me, asleep. He was one of those annoying people who could sleep anywhere, I'd discovered.

Me, on the other hand, well, I had never been able to sleep on anything that moved. No matter if this plane had a small bedroom and I could've tried lying down, my mind buzzed trying to decipher Rafe's clues about where we were going.

As soon as I'd turned in my construction needs for the tutoring center, Rafe had declared we were going on a business trip. All he'd said was that I needed my passport, warm clothes, and that the flight would be a long one.

I'd tried asking the flight attendant about our destination, but he'd smiled and replied that it was a surprise.

And now, after far too many cookies and cups of coffee, all I wanted to do was jump up, dash back and forth, and get rid of some of my pent-up energy. But I settled on tapping my fingers against the table.

A sleepy voice interrupted my thoughts. "You never were patient when it came to secrets. You and Emmy searched our house from top to bottom each Christmas, looking for the presents. But you never found them."

"No. Because you hid them too well."

He smiled. "I like surprises. Besides, I had to irritate Emmy. It's every big brother's duty, especially when their little sister trails behind their every move."

I huffed, too irritated to reminisce about the past. "It's been hours, Rafe. *Hours.* Can't you tell me where we're going?"

He glanced at his watch. "We're nearly there. Have you slept at all?"

"No. I can't."

He yawned and stretched his arms overhead, and I couldn't help but drool over his broad shoulders and big hands.

Hands I'd dreamed about far too often in recent days.

Stop it. Until you securely lock your heart away, you can look but not touch. You need to protect the both of you.

It'd been hard pulling away from Rafe, and I'd nearly caved the first time hurt had flashed in his eyes. But it was better this way. As soon as Travis tried to blackmail me again or who the hell knew what, Rafe would recognize how much trouble I was and wish he'd never met me.

Yes, he'd said he would protect me. And I mostly believed him.

But when things turned bad, really bad, I'd be the liability. So, keeping him at arm's length was better.

It was.

The flight attendant returned to say we were about to land. Once he left, I looked out the window. It was still dark, but there were lots of lights below. As the minutes passed, the lights grew in number, to the point I knew we flew over some kind of city.

But what city was more than ten hours away by plane?

Still, I'd always loved watching as a plane descended into an airport. While I couldn't see the houses or roads or businesses, the lights grew brighter and eventually I saw the straight lights of a runway. Within minutes, the plane touched down and made its way across the tarmac. I noted the planes and companies as we went, and there were a lot of British Airways, Ryanair, Air France, and a number of other European and American companies.

"Are we in Europe?"

"Yes."

I turned to meet his gaze. "Are we in Manchester?"

He smiled. "How did you guess?"

For a second, I nearly squealed and danced in my seat. I'd never been to England, but had always wanted to go. Not just because Rafe had played soccer here, either. I loved old buildings, and they were everywhere in the UK.

I finally replied, "Well, the time it took to fly, combined

with the fact you mentioned needing to go to Manchester a few times back when we discussed whether or not to stay married, made it my first guess. But why am I here?"

"I didn't lie when I said we were going on a business trip. I have some former teammates who might be interested in donating to the tutoring center, and I need to finalize a few things myself. But I thought you might like to take a break and have some fun. We can go anywhere you like, do anything, and I have a townhouse here we can stay at, too."

I should be grateful and say thank you. But I couldn't help but blurt, "Why did you really bring me here, Rafe? I could've handled things via video conferences." Then it hit me. "It's your image. You want them to see us together as a happy couple."

"Abby, that's not why—"

The fact it was such a practical reason made me mentally sigh in relief. "No, I get it. Don't worry, I know our marriage isn't real, we're not in love, and there's no need to pretend otherwise when we're alone. But you should've just told me, Rafe. I didn't pack clothes worthy of a famous soccer star."

He took my hand and stilled my tapping fingers. "I brought you here because I wanted to, because I thought you might enjoy seeing where I lived and played soccer, because I thought you might like visiting another country. But if not, we can hide out the entire time in my townhouse, or we can travel incognito and avoid the paparazzi." He leaned forward and gently squeezed my fingers. "But I brought you here because I thought you'd like it. And I wanted to show you a little of my life. That's it, Abigail. Do you believe me?"

My first impulse was to say no. And yet, we'd agree to try and believe each other. "You'd really do that? Hide away the entire time, if I asked?"

"Yes. I don't ever want you to feel like a prop, Abigail. Because you're more than that to me."

At the intense look in his eyes, I sucked in a breath and my heart thumped harder inside my chest. His words sounded so sincere.

But then again, so had Travis's.

Biting my bottom lip, I searched Rafe's eyes. *At least try to trust him. You're not handing over your heart. You can be friends.*

After a long pause, I placed my other hand over Rafe's. "I don't want to hide out the whole time. But seriously, I don't have anything fancy to wear."

"You could wear yoga pants, for all I care, Abby. But if you want fancier clothes, there are plenty of shops. Manchester might not be London, but it's not a small town, either."

"Well, maybe we can get a few things. High heels aren't my jam, but I'd like to look a little fancier than a former schoolteacher turned winery worker."

He lifted one of my hands to his mouth and kissed it. The soft brush of his lips sent a rush of heat through my body.

Who knew that such a small touch could suddenly make the cabin way too hot?

How easy it would be to go to him, sit in his lap, and kiss him again.

But the flight attendant returned, and Rafe released me. Apparently, we'd disembark momentarily to go through customs.

Rafe said, "Technically, I still hold a visa until the end of the season. But we'll go through the foreign customs section together."

"Oh yes, the amazing experience of a longer line," I drawled and then smiled. "You must like me at least a little if you're willing to go through that."

"I like you more than a little, wife."

At his growly words, a shiver ran down my spine. And then something hit me. "As your wife, don't I get included in your visa?"

"I would need to file some paperwork, and the visa would probably expire before it went through. But it's okay. Standing in a regular line won't break me." He lowered his voice and humor danced in his eyes. "If I can handle my wife kneeing me in the balls all the time, I can handle a longer line."

"Hey, I haven't done it again since that one disastrous day."

"I brought a cup, just in case."

He winked, and I laughed. Even though I should change the subject and put some formality back between us, bantering with Rafe was too tempting. So I lifted my leg and patted my knee. "If you need someone to test how effective the cup is, then I'm your woman."

"I'd rather not have to walk hunched over in public. I don't want to be the playboy any longer, but a guy still has his pride."

His words hit me. "Oh, so you're going to be yourself this time?" He nodded, and I asked, "Are you nervous?"

He shrugged. "Yes and no. Not because I miss that life—because it was fucking exhausting—but I don't want the press to tear you apart."

I reached over and took his hand again. "Don't worry about me, Rafe. I'm made of stronger stuff."

"I know you are. And yet, you shouldn't have to suffer because of me."

Maybe his words were a throwaway comment. Or maybe he was trying to play the nice husband, to practice for when we were in public.

And yet, at the sincerity blazing in his gaze, I swallowed the tightness in my throat.

If only I could truly believe he would be there for me, wanted the best for me, and wouldn't leave me at the first sign of trouble.

Don't ruin the trip. He went to a lot of trouble, and you are excited to see Manchester and maybe do a little sightseeing.

So I pushed aside my doubt, at least for now, and said, "Thank you, Rafe. But I knew you were famous, especially here, when I agreed to our bargain. I'll just be the charming American, not the annoying type, and it'll be fine."

"Oh no, you're not going to buy a cowboy hat and suddenly develop a southern twang, are you? Not that I have anything against either one, but it's not you. And the world deserves to see the real you."

I nearly asked why he kept saying such nice things, but resisted and shook my head. "No, I plan to be me.

Well, mostly me. I'm not sure if dancing in public will go over well for either of our images."

He grinned. "I'd love to see it. Especially if you want to go to a match while we're here."

I squealed. "Really? We can see a Dragons' game?"

"Yes, if you want. Although it'll have to be in a private area as being in the stands could be dangerous. Some people will love me, and others will still blame me for that one championship match we lost five years ago."

"That wasn't your fault! That French player tripped you and the ref was blind. I still can't believe he missed it!"

Rafe smiled. "You really did follow my games, didn't you?"

I should say no, but I nodded. "When I was younger, it was because of that childhood crush. However, it only took a few games before I saw how fast-paced and interesting soccer was, and soon became a fan. It was hard to watch some of the matches because of the time difference, though. The internet helps with replays, but I always wanted to watch you live. It got me into trouble a few times when I stayed up late, but once Aunt Lori learned about it, she would stay up to cheer you on with me." I dramatically lowered my voice. "Although she's always had a thing for the Dragons' goalie in recent years instead of you. But don't tell her I told you that."

Rafe laughed. "Your secret is safe with me. And James has a lot of admirers, for sure. Probably because of that perfect smile of his."

"Don't sound so grumpy. I never noticed his smile."

Damn. Had I really said that?

Before Rafe could reply, the flight attendant returned, and we were soon ushered off the plane and had to deal with customs.

Thankfully, it was one in the morning and very few people were arriving at the same time as us, and we went through quickly.

I kept staring at the Manchester stamp as we collected our luggage. Eventually Rafe whispered, "I wish we had time to visit some more countries, but I can only be away from the training facility for a few days right now. However, we can come back, if you want to, Abigail. Just say the word, and as soon as my schedule clears up a little, we'll go wherever you want."

Looking up, I saw the truth in Rafe's gaze. "Thank you."

He leaned down, and I thought he might kiss me. However, he cleared his throat and gestured. "This way. A car will take us to my home and we need to go to sleep soon so we can get used to the time difference. In the late morning, we'll go shopping and then I'll take you on a tour of Prestwich Stadium afterward, if you like."

Prestwich was the home of the Manchester Dragons. "Can we? I've always wanted to walk on the pitch. Maybe even kick a soccer ball around. Oh, but your knee."

"It's fine. I can handle a few friendly kicks. Just don't expect me to make a mad dash down the field and do some kind of dramatic goal score."

Part of me was sad he couldn't do that any longer. And not just because watching him play live would've been one of my fantasies come to life. Well, when you included him finishing the game, all sweaty and in need of a shower, and we headed to the locker room...

Stop it, Abby. Not going to happen.

Instead, I smiled at him. "Thanks, Rafe. I can't wait! I just hope I can fall asleep."

"I'm sure once you're in bed, you'll be fine."

An image of the pair of us in bed, naked and cuddling, flashed into my mind.

But I barely had time to think of how nice that would be, or if Rafe only had one bed or not in his home, before we were in the car and heading toward town.

Within minutes, I leaned against Rafe's side and surprisingly fell asleep, dreaming of him whisking me around Europe, showing me off as his wife, and loving me for real.

Chapter Twenty-Three

Rafe

Giles: I'm doing my best to distract the paparazzi this morning. But you might want to leave through the back garden.
Me: I thought they'd give up now that I'm no longer playing football.
Giles: You've sold a lot of papers over the years, Rafe. They'll always want news and gossip. Use the back exit.
Me: Fine. As long as everything is ready for later today?
Giles: It was tricky, but yes. Private shopping times, the pitch to yourself, and the last surprise I'm nearly done with. I'll update you ASAP.
Me: Once this dies down, you can retire, I promise.
Giles: So you said. Don't worry about it. My little place

in Spain needs some upgrades. Your bonus will pay for them.

Me: Just have your contacts in the US keep digging for me and I'll pay for all your remodeling.

Giles: Done! (And I would've done it without the bonus.)

Me: I know. But after putting up with my bullshit all these years, you deserve it.

The next morning, after finalizing a few things with my soon-to-retire assistant in the UK, I fiddled with the fruit plate, yogurt, and granola spread I'd laid out and waited for Abby to wake up. Would she still be the teasing, lighter version from the night before? Or, would she retreat back behind the wall of formality?

Hearing her laugh and tease me again had nearly made my heart burst. And when she'd fallen asleep against me in the car on the ride home from the airport and snuggled into my side? I'd treasured every moment, hating that I'd had to wake her up once we got to my townhouse. I wish I could've carried her, but my knee might've given out, and I wasn't going to risk dropping her.

I'd given Abby my room, and I'd slept in my home office. My UK place only had two bedrooms, and I'd never needed a guest one before. And given how this was the UK and not the US, everything was smaller—the home, the rooms, and even the couch. So I'd opted to sleep on the floor, and my neck was far from happy.

Especially when all I'd wanted to do was to curl up behind Abby, hold her close, and sleep with her in my arms.

Then I remembered West's words from our conversation in my office: *"You have to find the right balance of pushing her and giving her space. She's stubborn—hell, we all are—but she'll dig in more than most if she's trying to protect herself."*

As I tried to think of how to accomplish that balance, Abby entered the kitchen wearing her tiny shorts. I stared at her legs as she rubbed her eyes. "Morning. I think."

My gaze shot to hers again. "Yes, it's nearly ten. If you didn't wake up soon on your own, I would've done it. Because if you want to beat jet lag, you need to force yourself to follow the new schedule as quickly as possible."

"I know. Somehow, the eight-hour difference is easier than the three hours when flying across the US."

Her gaze roamed the kitchen, which was small, with an L-shaped counter and a small area for a two-person table.

Abby frowned. "Is that a washing machine in your kitchen?"

"Yes. That's pretty normal here, to be honest, to have one in the kitchen."

"I guess it'd be nice to toss in some laundry while making dinner. But it's so tiny!"

I chuckled, went to the espresso machine, and

turned it on. "Things here are usually on a smaller scale, which makes sense when you consider how much less land there is in the UK compared to the US."

"True." She spotted the breakfast spread. "Is that a flower made out of fruit?"

"Kind of. I tried my best. I know sunflowers are your favorite, but it looks more like a daisy or something."

She clicked her tongue. "And here I thought you were a breakfast artist extraordinaire!"

I made a face at her. "Better than you."

She snorted. "Maybe I should be offended, but it's true. I can't draw or paint or sculpt anything to save my life, apart from stick people. Oh, I know! I should make a stick person breakfast out of sausage and bacon."

"I can't wait to see it." I put her latte in front of her.

She smiled as she looked at the design on top. "It's a chocolate unicorn."

"Well, you did have those things everywhere as a kid. I still remember trying to remove all the stickers you put on my bike."

"I forgot about that. It was like twenty of them. Emmy and I thought to make your boring bike a little prettier."

"A sixteen-year-old boy doesn't want a pretty bike," I grumbled.

"Hey, I was six or seven? I didn't exactly understand the coolness factor for teenage boys. Although, to be fair, I still didn't understand it when I was a teenager myself."

"Why? What happened?"

At the thought of some boy trying to take advantage of her, my fingers curled into a fist.

Then I remembered how she'd knee me in the balls, and I relaxed a little. I'd still go after any fucker who hurt her, but she wasn't completely helpless. Far from it.

"Let me get some food first and then I'll tell you." Abby sipped her coffee and then took a plate, dishing out what she wanted.

Once we both had our breakfast, she finally answered, "When I was fifteen, guys started talking to me, flirting with me, and asking me out. I didn't know why they'd all started paying attention to me at the same time, but I merely enjoyed it. Until..."

"Until what?"

She speared a grape with her fork before she said, "Until I discovered they were trying to see who was the bravest."

"Bravest? What the fuck does that mean?"

She shrugged. "It wasn't about me, but my brothers. Even if they weren't all there when I was in high school, the Wolfe brothers were infamous. And so the guys at my school started a betting pool to see who would try to date me and stand up to my brothers, proving they were the manliest, or some such bullshit."

Rage shot through me. "What?"

Abby peered at me. "It's okay. It was over a decade ago. Although high school me wasn't so nonchalant about it. I mean, it's not exactly flattering when someone will only dance with you because they want to win some money."

I nearly asked for some names, but held back. My focus needed to be on her ex in San Jose, not some sad high school boys. "Well, none of the guys at your high school were worthy. You were too good for their lame asses."

Her lips smirked. "Lame asses?"

I replied solemnly, "Super lame asses."

She snorted and shook her head. "Are you next going to shout, 'Psych!'?"

"I'm not that old."

I tossed a grape at her, but she smacked it back at me and it bounced off my leg. I reached for another, but she moved my plate away. "What was it you criticized my family for? Oh, that's right, food fights. Pot, meet kettle."

The urge to stick out my tongue was strong, but I restrained myself. "I'm just trying to make you feel more at home, that's all."

She shook her head. "I think it's more that your life revolved around soccer for so long and you missed out on being a kid. But feel free to let out your inner child with me." She pointed her fork at me. "Well, mostly. Put gum in my hair, and it's war."

"Duly noted." I smiled, she did the same, and something shifted inside me.

Abby had been so fucking strong, survived so much, and still had her sense of humor and used it to try and make me relax.

A guy could get addicted to that. Addicted to her.

An image of us old and gray, still teasing and laughing, flashed into my mind. Yearning blazed inside me.

More and more, I started to think I wanted Abby as my wife for real.

Scratch that. I didn't think, I knew that I wanted her in my life.

Because I was falling fast and hard for her.

Abby cleared her throat, ate a little more yogurt and granola before asking, "Did you even go to dances during high school? I know soccer practice and extra coaching took up all your time."

"It did. And no, I didn't have time for much of a social life. And it was kind of funny going from being the tall, skinny kid to the pro athlete with women all wanting to hook up."

She raised an eyebrow. "If you want me to feel bad about you getting too much attention from women, then you're going to be waiting a long-ass time, Rafael."

I searched her gaze. Was she jealous?

It shouldn't make me happy, and yet it sent a small thrill through me. For all her protestations of having a crush on me as a kid and feeling nothing later, she might actually feel something for me.

Which gave me hope. And given how well the morning had gone, I wasn't about to change the subject anytime soon and risk making her dig in again. So I said, "Hey, try having people throw bras at you and see how comfortable you feel."

"Oh, that's happened to me before."

I blinked. "What?"

Amusement danced in her eyes. "A night out in San Francisco with the BFF Circle ended up with us in a hotel, drunk, and flinging bras at each other. You'd be surprised how far they can go, if you do it just right."

The image of a naked Abby, breasts bouncing as she flung her bra across the room, flashed into my mind.

A strawberry bounced off my cheek, and Abby said, "Get your mind out of the gutter. I love my friends, but I don't want to make love to my friends. Leave it to a guy to turn everything into a dirty fantasy."

I should stay quiet, and yet I blurted, "The only woman I want to see without a bra is you."

Electricity sizzled in the air, and Abby's cheeks flushed.

Shit. Had I just ruined our trip?

Chapter Twenty-Four

Abby

Katie: So when are you going to invite us over to England? It's not fair you get to see Mr. Darcy's place without us.

Amber: I wish I could see that house, the one they used for the *Pride and Prejudice* mini-series. It's not that far from Manchester.

Emmy: Maybe I can convince West to walk out of a pond. <hearts for eyes emoji>

Me: I somehow think they don't allow that. Or they'd have a line of people watching their partners walk out of the pond in a shirt like Mr. Darcy did.

Katie: Maybe Nolan could pull some strings and set up a mini-shoot. Then we'd be allowed that way!

Amber: Wait, you're really going to have him create some fake short movie just so you can watch him walk out of a pond in a mostly see-through white shirt?

Katie: Hell, yes.

Emmy: Now, finding a way to get West to do it, though. That's going to be hard...

Me: What about you, Amber? Will you convince your boyfriend to do that?

Amber: Er, I'm not sure Jay would. It's a little over-the-top for him.

Me (typed but deleted): Are you sure he's really what you want? Because you need a little fun and silliness in your life, and Jay doesn't have a sense of humor.

Me (actual reply instead): You all can have your Mr. Darcy fantasies. I'd rather watch Rafe on the soccer pitch. Without a shirt, all sweaty and...

Emmy: Ew. Okay, now I understand how you feel when I talk about West and sexy times.

Katie: I'm not related to either, so I'm always available and open to finding new ideas to try with Nolan.

Me: <puking emoji> Okay, that's my cue to leave. I have a city to explore!

Katie: With a sexy husband on your arm. Not too shabby. Take lots of pics. <heart emoji>

hen I'd first woken up in Rafe's place, I dreaded leaving my room. Rafe had been so...nice on the plane. It'd felt so easy and

natural to tease and talk, and I'd wanted nothing more than for him to kiss me.

But being separated overnight had restored some of my self-preservation skills, and I knew I'd have to find the balance of not completely being cold to Rafe while also not allowing him to burrow further into my heart.

Because each time he made me laugh or shared another part of his life with me, or even surprised me—like with this entire trip—I yearned for the naïve woman I'd once been. The one who'd trusted so easily. The one who'd loved so easily.

Thankfully, my friends' group chat had cheered me up. I'd long ago learned that Lyme Park, used for Mr. Darcy's house in the 1995 version of *Pride and Prejudice*, wasn't far from Manchester. My friends and I had watched that show more than we should've as teens, and I'd always dreamed of seeing Rafe play a game and then visiting Lyme the next day.

I hadn't asked him yet if I could go, but I hoped he'd let me.

I just had to get through today first—facing the public, the possible paparazzi, and constantly wondering if someone would mention my ex.

Or if my ex would sell our story and embarrass Rafe.

Don't allow what-ifs to control your day. You knew Rafe was famous, especially in Manchester. And you can't do anything about Travis. So, buck up and try to enjoy yourself.

Once I finally got my ass out of bed and brushed my hair, I headed downstairs and found Rafe in the kitchen. After some banter and eating some food, he eventually said, "The only woman I want to see without a bra is you."

My cheeks heated at the intensity of his gaze.

It was on the tip of my tongue to call bullshit. And yet, as regret and worry flashed in his eyes, I paused another second.

For all his chiseled jaw and hard muscles, in this moment, he looked almost...vulnerable. As if he thought he'd fucked up, or hurt me, or somehow had let me down.

And I hated it. Fucking hated it. He shouldn't have to keep tiptoeing around me. Especially since Rafe had only tried to accommodate me, to make me happy, to ensure I didn't feel awkward or out of place.

And what had I done in return? How had I compromised?

By giving him almost nothing. Not much at all.

He's not Travis. Don't make him suffer for someone else's actions.

For the first time in a long time, that fun-loving girl I'd been surfaced, and an idea struck. One that I wouldn't have dared do a few weeks ago.

But now? Oh, I wanted to do it. Badly.

So I lifted my tank top and flashed Rafe.

His eyes darted to my breasts, and my nipples tightened. He growled, reached out as if to touch me, and then stopped.

No. Don't stop.

I must've said it out loud because Rafe's eyes met mine again. "Are you sure?"

My heart raced, and my nipples throbbed. If I let

him do this, there would be no keeping him at arm's length to protect my heart.

And yet, I was tired of being cautious. Tired of punishing myself for something Travis had done to me. Tired of longing to be touched again, to experience the intimacy of sex that would temporarily make me forget about being lonely.

"I want you, Rafe. Touch me."

He put out his hand, palm up, and I dropped my shirt to place mine in his. He tugged, and I went to him until I stood between his legs. I could feel his hot breath through my shirt, my nipples begging for his touch as wetness rushed between my thighs.

He lightly traced me through the material of my top, and I sucked in a breath. His dark brown eyes met mine. "Last chance—do you want me to suck these hard little nipples before I make you come?"

I squeezed my thighs together and licked my lips. "Yes."

His hands went to the hem of my shirt and lifted. Inch by inch, the material brushed over my sensitive skin, until finally he reached my breasts. Instead of tugging the shirt off, he moved the material up and down, snagging my nipples, and I cried out.

"I've dreamed of this, Abigail. Every night since I returned to Starry Hills."

Before I could think too much about that revelation, he tugged off my top and took a nipple into his mouth.

He lightly nibbled and suckled, and I had to put my hands on his shoulders to stay standing. Each tug or pull or lick made my knees even weaker. And once he repeated it all over again with the other side, I was nearly whimpering.

He finally released me, kissed the top of my breast tenderly, and then ran his hands down my side, up again, and then to the waist of my shorts. "Let me see all of you, Abigail. Let me taste you again."

I nodded, and he said, "Tell me with words. I don't want you to regret this later."

My temper sparked, and I raised my chin. "You'd better eat my pussy now, Rafe, or I may knee you in the balls again."

He chuckled before taking my lips in a rough, demanding kiss. Then he murmured, "As my lady wishes."

After standing, he slowly tugged off my shorts, until I had to step out of them. Since I didn't wear underwear to bed, I stood naked in front of him.

His hands went to my waist, lifted, and he set me on the tall chair. His fingers caressed my cheek, so softly that I could barely feel it. Combined with the awestruck look in his eyes, my own heated with tears.

No man had ever looked at me like that before—as if I were the most precious thing in the world, the person they wanted to treasure and keep forever.

It's not for forever, Abby. Remember that.

His brows drew together, but then his expression cleared and he ran his hands down my neck, my shoulders, and then cupped my breasts.

Leaning down, he kissed one and then the other. "You're so fucking perfect, Abigail, so beautiful."

Memories threatened to return, ones of my ex saying

I was too small-chested or that my hips were too wide or that my thighs were too thick.

But I quickly shoved them aside. Right here, right now, I wanted Rafe to help me make new memories to replace the old. Even if it wasn't forever, it would help. I knew it would.

His hands cupped my face before he kissed me. Slowly, tenderly, taking his time to sample and nibble and caress.

Part of me wanted to tell him to hurry up. And yet, another part of me reveled in feeling treasured, special, and desired.

I widened my legs and pulled him closer. Needing to feel more of him, I ran my hands under his shirt and moaned at how hot and hard his chest was.

His hands traveled down my body until he pressed my legs even wider. One hand moved along my inner thigh, stopping to caress the crease where my leg met my torso, and my pussy throbbed.

He was so close, and yet in no hurry.

I growled with impatience.

Rafe chuckled, kissed the tip of my nose, and said, "The anticipation will only make it better, love. Trust me."

I may not be able to trust him with my heart. But when it came to orgasms, he'd already given me a mind-blowing one. So I replied, "I will. But no edging me for hours. I still want to see the stadium."

His hand moved from the crease of my leg to lightly brush my entrance. The touch was featherlight, barely there, and yet I cried out at the sensation.

His husky voice rolled over me as he said, "Not this time, love. I'm too greedy to watch you fall apart on my tongue again."

Before I could think too much about his use of "love," Rafe slowly kneeled in front of me. It was awkward to watch, as he had to be careful with his injured leg, and I tried to tug him up. "No, Rafe. Don't hurt yourself."

He ignored me and finished kneeling. "I'm fine, love. The pain goes away as soon as I do this."

Lowering his head, he licked my pussy.

As he continued to tease and lap and nibble, I forgot about everything but the man between my legs and the building tension in my lower belly. My fingers went to his hair to hold him in place, and I arched my hips. But Rafe moved away from my clit to my entrance instead, fucking me with his tongue, and I tried to guide his head back up.

With a chuckle, he stopped and met my gaze again, his lips glistening with my arousal. "I'll make you come, love, I promise. But let me stay in control this time. You can tease me all you want later, if you ever want to suck my dick."

At the thought of Rafe naked and standing, his cock jutting out long and hard as I licked and teased and finally took him into my mouth, even more wetness rushed between my thighs.

He gently traced my opening. "You want that, don't you? You're getting wetter just thinking about my dick between those perfect lips of yours."

His words were ambiguous and could mean my

mouth or pussy. And yet, suddenly, I wanted to know what it was like to have him inside me both places.

He lightly thrust his finger into my pussy, and I arched toward him. "Please, Rafe. Stop talking and use your mouth on me instead."

He snorted, but lowered his head and continued fingering me as his mouth suckled my clit. The more he teased me with his mouth and tongue, the harder it became to breathe until lights danced before my eyes and pleasure rushed through me.

Wave after wave made more intense as Rafe continued to lap at my clit with his tongue.

Eventually I slumped in the chair, feeling relaxed and sleepy, and looked down to meet Rafe's eyes again. He looked smug, and yet I couldn't fault him for it. Before I could think better of it, I said, "You're good with your mouth."

He grinned, and my heart skipped a beat.

He said, "Just wait until you see what I can do with my dick."

He waggled his eyebrows dramatically, and I laughed. "Someone's confident."

After kissing my inner thigh, and then the other, he stood awkwardly and wiped his mouth with the back of his hand. His finger trailed gently down my cheek. Combined with the tender look in his eyes, I stopped breathing.

He murmured, "Say the word, and I'll show you it's more than being cocky."

As we stared at one another, my heart raced and my

cheeks heated as I struggled to reply. A few words from me, and I could have one of my most desired fantasies.

And yet, the thought of merely sleeping with Rafe and walking away squeezed my heart.

At one time, that would've been enough. And now? Now I wanted the impossible—to date Rafe for real and maybe keep him forever.

Eventually, Rafe stepped back and smiled at me. "Think about it. For now, if we don't get a move on, we won't have time for everything on today's schedule. I'll shower while you finish eating, and then you can get ready."

Part of me screamed to say screw it and ask Rafe to take me to bed.

However, I needed time to think about what I wanted. Because taking a leap of faith with Rafe would mean no going back.

And I wasn't sure if I was quite ready for that yet. Yes, I wanted it. But there was still so much in the air when it came to my ex, that I needed to fix some of that first.

Since he looked at me expectantly, I replied, "Um, okay. Sure."

He nodded. "I'll be quick."

With that, he raced up the stairs, and I heard the bathroom door close.

After quickly tossing on my tank top and shorts, I headed back to my room, closed the door, and leaned against it. Part of me was confused, another part angry, and another part just sad.

Because for a split second, Rafe's eyes had said he cared about me and wanted me for real.

And I'd chickened out.

So why did getting exactly what I wanted make me feel so sad?

Chapter Twenty-Five

Rafe

West: Does Abby like the surprise?

Me: So far, so good.

Emmy: Offer to take her to Lyme Park and she'll love you forever.

Me: Wait, is this a group chat now?

Emmy: Of course. West hates texting. So I'm here to help.

Me: More like you're just nosey.

Emmy: <tongue out emoji> See if I offer any more advice.

Me: Sorry, sorry. I could use all the help I can get.

Emmy: Just update us later, okay?

West: Only if it's good news. If it's not, then I may have to meet you at the airport and have a little talk.

Emmy: West! Be nice. He's trying.
West: Hmph.
Me: I'll let you two know how she reacts later. For now, I'm turning off my phone for a bit.

E ver since I'd run away from Abby to take a shower, an apology had burned on my tongue.

I'd rushed things and offered myself to her, and she'd hesitated. Long enough to make me feel like a dick for even suggesting it.

Did she think I expected it in order to keep helping her?

Because no, I wasn't that asshole.

For the moment, though, I couldn't even attempt to say I was sorry. We were in the second store I'd booked a private session with—to try and avoid the paparazzi—and I currently sat waiting while Abby tried on some clothes.

The fact she'd stated explicitly that she wanted to do it alone had squeezed my heart. But I hadn't fought her, and so I'd resorted to answering emails and texts. I was just composing a message to one of my former teammates to see if they'd come to the stadium during Abby's tour when my sister's name flashed on the screen.

Since Emmy would only call if it were an emergency, I picked up. "Emmy? What's wrong?"

"Oh, Rafe. Has Abby seen it?"

"Seen what?"

She paused, the two seconds of silence pure agony

before she whispered, "The interview her ex gave to Celeb Gossip and News."

CGN was famous for scandal and borderline unethical practices. They were also effective at blasting their videos all over social media and streaming sites to get the word out quickly.

And yet, despite some of their illegal practices, they always managed to avoid being shut down.

"What the fuck did they say?"

Emmy gave a quick summary, and I cursed. Eventually, Emmy said, "You need to watch the video yourself and then determine if Abby should see it. But she needs to know what her ex did, Rafe. Everyone will soon be talking about it."

Because even if soccer wasn't as popular in the US as other sports, CGN had hundreds of millions of followers across all social media platforms. Abby's pain would spread like wildfire.

I gripped my phone tighter. "I'm going to fucking kill him."

Abby's voice came from behind me. "Kill who?"

"I'll call you back later, Emmy."

I pressed End, took a breath, and then stood to face Abby. "If there's anything you want to buy, get it first and then we'll talk in the car."

She frowned. "Okay, now I'm worried."

"I know, but I'll tell you everything once we're alone."

"I already had them ring it up. You just need to pay and we can go."

I went through the motions, trying my best to be

polite and nice. The store manager had done me a huge favor—even if it'd been for free tickets—and I didn't want to take out my anger on a near-stranger.

By the time we both slid into the rear of the SUV and the window partition between the front and back was up, I was clenching my fingers so hard that my nails might draw blood.

"Rafe? You're scaring me. What's going on?"

Taking a deep breath, I scanned her face. I hated the confusion in her eyes and the fact her expression was going to get worse. A lot worse.

Still, I couldn't keep this from her, nor would I watch and decide if she could handle it. The world was probably already talking about Abby, and she needed to prepare herself for what was to come.

"Emmy called to let me know that your ex gave an interview. And not just any interview, but one to Celeb Gossip and News."

Her face paled. "What?"

"I only know the basics but haven't watched it yet."

I tried to take her hand, but she swatted me away. Her voice was hoarse as she said, "I need to see it."

It was on the tip of my tongue to ask if she was sure. And yet, no matter how much I wanted to protect her from this, I couldn't.

However, even without knowing what that asshole had said, Travis Doucey was a dead man.

"Rafe, please. I-I can't set it up myself. Let's watch it and then you can close it right away so I don't see the comments."

Fuck. I hated this. The internet could be hateful and

downright mean. I'd learned to brush trolls aside out of self-preservation, but Abby hadn't.

And the only reason she had to endure any of this was because she was my wife. I didn't have proof, but I was pretty fucking sure it was my fault, given what my sister had told me.

Still, as Abby hugged herself and opened her mouth to ask again, I pulled myself together. "Just a second, love. I'll get it going."

I pulled up their channel, found the video—which already had two million views—and hit Play.

Chapter Twenty-Six

Abby

While I normally didn't like shopping because of my height, there was something about going to stores where they would alter anything to flatter you that was nice. Oh, I still wouldn't spend this much money on my own. Ever. But to help Rafe's image, I'd given in and enjoyed being pampered.

However, after I exited the dressing room area and headed Rafe's way, I overhead him say, "I'm going to fucking kill him."

As Rafe explained what was going on, my stomach dropped the second I heard the name Celeb Gossip and News. They could be vicious when it came to sharing highly personal stuff about celebs, their families, and spouses. They'd been sued more times than I could count. However, since they were located in some small country with few laws regarding slander or libel, they kept getting away with it.

And now they'd set their sights on me.

Eventually we got into Rafe's SUV, and I asked him to play their video. As I waited for him to load it, I couldn't stop shaking. This was everything I'd feared would happen.

Rafe gave me one last look before hitting Play, and I tried my best to concentrate.

After the intro, the most famous host of CGN—the blonde-haired, blue-eyed Blair Montgomery—smiled on the screen. "Hello everyone. Today we have a bombshell, one I never saw coming. For those who don't know, Rafael Mendoza is one of the top soccer players in the world. You may have seen him play for the Manchester Dragons in the UK, or for Team USA. However, he recently retired from soccer and returned to his hometown of Starry Hills in California, where he plans to launch a training facility for talented teens. Seems rather boring, doesn't it? But just wait, it gets better, I promise." She gave her trademark wink and leaned in closer. "He recently married a woman from his hometown named Abigail Wolfe." My picture flashed on the screen. "And on the surface, she seems ordinary. But here at CGN, we don't let that stop us from digging. And sure enough, within a week, our team found something scandalous!"

A graphic flashed on the screen with the word "Scandalous" surrounded by stills of former breaking scandals.

My stomach churned as I recognized a few of them, including the one about a pro football coach impregnating all the girls on his daughter's high school volleyball team. Emotion choked my throat, and I did my best not to shout at the screen. I didn't deserve to be on the same level as that bastard, not even close.

Which meant Travis had definitely embellished and lied. Otherwise, CGN never would've touched the story.

The video returned to Blair. "Now, as much as I like to spill the tea with you all, wouldn't you rather hear it from the source himself? To get all the sordid details, let's welcome Mr. Travis Doucey, Abigail's former mentor teacher from her student teaching internship."

As Blair greeted Travis, I struggled to breathe. Both because it was the first time I'd seen him since the day he'd threatened me with blackmail, and also because I knew he'd say whatever it took so he could play the victim.

My eyes heated with tears as I remembered the deep fake video he'd shown me, where I looked like I was sleeping with a student. Had he shared that with CGN, too? Did they believe it?

Rafe paused the video. "Abby?"

My gaze moved to his and before I could think about why it was a horrible idea, I launched at him and he hugged me close.

I breathed heavily, trying my best to get myself together. And the more Rafe stroked my back and murmured sweet nothings, the easier it got, until I could finally talk again. "Thank you."

"Do you want to stop for now, love? Say the word, and I'll take you anywhere you want, do anything, to make you forget about that dickhead."

I hugged Rafe even tighter and breathed in the scent of male and something woodsy. "No, I need to see what he says before I can think of how to handle anything."

Because I didn't want to just hide away forever.

Searching Rafe's gaze, I saw the concern and worry in his eyes. Not pity or regret. Nothing to suggest he blamed me for all of this, or would run away the second I looked away.

How I wanted to trust he'd stay by my side.

I might not be completely there yet, but I needed him with me right now. To face this video together. To lend me a little strength until I could be with my family and friends again.

Those were the only reasons. It definitely wasn't because everything felt a little less daunting and horrible in his arms.

Stop lying to yourself. For whatever reason, Rafe makes all of this hurt less.

I blurted, "Can you hold me while we watch the rest? Normally I'd ask my friends, but they're an ocean away, and—"

He kissed the top of my head. "Of course. But if it gets to be too much, tell me to stop, okay?"

At his gentle tone, my throat tightened again. "Okay."

After hugging me closer, he positioned his phone. "Ready?"

"Yes. Let's get it over with."

He hit Play, and I steeled myself for what was to come.

In the video, the CGN host asked, "So when did Abby, as you call her, start seducing you?"

I blurted, "Motherfucker!"

Rafe squeezed my shoulders, and I managed to focus on the video again.

Travis replied, "Within the first couple of weeks. She's a nice girl, and pretty. However, I make it a rule to never get involved with someone at work. But I was on a break from my now wife—we all have those rough patches at some point—and vulnerable. Abby must've seen that and jumped at her chance."

Blair asked, "Why would she 'jump at the chance' to seduce you?"

"Well, I learned later that she wanted two things from me—a glowing recommendation for a permanent teaching job and to help cover up her indiscretion with a student. He was just 18, so he was of age. But still, if that news ever came out, she would never teach again. Oops." He looked abashed. "I guess the cat is out of the bag now."

I barely restrained myself from punching the screen and his smug-ass face before he lowered his voice dramatically and said, "And I believe she also slept with a few who weren't yet 18. Some students confided in me, and I'd never break that confidence. However, if they ever want to prosecute Abby Wolfe, I'm ready to testify."

Rafe growled, and his screen cracked and went blank.

My head reeled as I vaguely heard Rafe shout, "That fucking bastard! I'll kill him."

But I barely paid attention to Rafe. No, Travis's words hinting that I'd slept with a minor kept repeating inside my head.

He thought nothing of ruining my life and putting innocent students in the spotlight, all to play the victim and get back at me.

How the fuck had I ever believed myself in love with him?

But as much as it hurt to know I'd been that stupid, this was all bigger than me. Bigger than maybe a few students he would use against me.

Travis had just destroyed Rafe's chance of a successful training facility launch. Destroyed any hope of showing he had turned a corner and was leading a better life.

No, now he was just married to a woman alleged to have seduced minors.

All of a sudden, the car felt too small, too stifling. And even just looking at Rafe hurt my heart. My stomach roiled, and I was on the verge of breaking down.

And I definitely didn't deserve to have Rafe hold me and calm me and be nice to me again.

Needing to get some fresh air, and thankful the car hadn't gone anywhere yet, I grabbed my purse, opened the car door, and ran. I didn't know where, and barely managed to weave around people on the sidewalk. But I ran and ran, tears streaming down my face, wondering how I could disappear and somehow still fix things for Rafe.

Chapter Twenty-Seven

Rafe

Emmy: Is Abby okay? She won't answer my texts or calls and I'm worried.
Emmy: Rafe? Are you there? Please answer me. I'm out of my mind over here.
Emmy: Rafe, please. At least tell me you're with her.
Me: I'm working on it.
Emmy: Wait, what does that mean?
Me: Emmy, I love you. But right now, I need to help Abby. I'll update you later. Okay?
Emmy: Okay. Tell her we love her and that Amber is plotting how to kill Travis and get away with it.
Me: I will.
Emmy: Love you. <heart emoji>
Me: Back at you.

. . .

I barely had time to tamp down my murderous plans for Abby's ex before she bolted from the car and took off down the street. I exited and tried my best to follow her. But with my injured knee, I struggled to keep up and soon I couldn't see her dark hair anywhere. We were in the city center, with people milling about, crowding the sidewalks. Plus, there were dozens of alleys she could've ducked into.

Since blindly looking for her would be pointless, I darted into one of the side streets so I could come up with a plan.

First and foremost, I needed to try contacting Abby. And since my phone was broken, I could either find a new one or ask to borrow someone else's.

The latter would probably end up with someone wanting a selfie. Normally I didn't mind, but given how that horrible video about my wife had just dropped, it'd look like I didn't care.

I scanned the shops and dashed to one that sold phones. It took far too long for me to buy one and set it up. But as soon as I did, I tried calling Abby. However, it went to voicemail. So I left an encouraging message, asking her to come home, and then called my sister.

She answered. "Rafe? Abby sent me a voice text, saying she was going into hiding. What's going on?"

"Fuck, she did what?"

"Is she not with you?"

After I explained the situation, I finished with, "I'm

going to find her. But let me know if she contacts you again. And try telling her that I want to help her."

"Of course. I just hate that she's alone right now."

"Me, too, Emmy. Especially since it's probably my fault she ran."

"What the hell are you talking about? It's her ex's fault, not yours."

"She probably blames herself for ruining my life. She hasn't, not at all. Like you said, it's that asshole's fault. But..."

"But what?" Emmy asked.

"We can talk about it later. Right now, Abby needs someone standing by her to fight at her side, which means I have to find her."

"I believe in you. And let her know that we're all here for her, too, Rafe. The sooner she comes home, the sooner we can all stand by her side. She's probably afraid of what her family will think, but they only want to support her. Somehow, you have to convince her of that."

"She probably needs to hear it from them to truly believe it. But don't worry, I'll find a way to get her home. I promise."

"You know, I had my doubts about the two of you at first, but I can see now that you love her. Take care of her, Rafe. I'll see what I can do here."

I mumbled some sort of reply, but Emmy's words kept coming back to me: *I can see now that you love her.*

At the thought of never seeing Abby again, never holding her, never making her laugh, my heart clenched.

In a short amount of time, she'd become precious and necessary and...mine.

Even just imagining her divorcing me at the end of the year and finding someone else made me want to punch the mystery guy in the face.

I loved her. And maybe if I'd been more honest with myself and opened up to her, she would've trusted me to stay by her side and not run away. Instead, keeping my feelings to myself and maintaining some distance had ended up hurting her, not protecting her.

Well, I was done fighting my feelings.

Abby was my wife.

Mine.

I would do whatever was necessary to win her heart and trust, and find a way to destroy the asshole ruining her life.

But first, I needed to find her. Where would she go?

Then it hit me—both she and Emmy had talked about some old fancy house she'd always wanted to visit in Lyme Park. Since Piccadilly Station was nearby, she could've easily taken a train. No doubt, she'd walk around the grounds to get some peace and quiet since not many people would visit in March.

It was the best lead I had for now. So after buying some sunglasses, I went back to my car and headed toward Lyme Park.

Chapter Twenty-Eight

Abby

Emmy: Abby, please text me back. Or call me. Call any of us.

Katie: That asshole is going down, Abby. Nolan has people who can dig up everything. His secrets will come out.

Nolan: I already have one possible secret. Trust me, no matter what, this asshole will eventually be alone, jobless, and humiliated.

Amber: That will take too long. But I have a plan to make him disappear. And we'll never get caught. Say the word, and I'll put it into motion.

Aunt Lori: Abby, dear, are you all right? Of course you aren't. But I have lots of hugs waiting for you. Come home and let us stand with you, love.

Beck: Anyone who so much as breathes a word of that video will be kicked out of the winery and banned for life. I don't care how much business we lose. We have your back, Abby.

Sabrina: Same for anyone coming to my office. I'm sure most of Starry Hills would ban them, too. A lot of people love you here, Abby. More than just us.

Zach: Zane knows people. Former SEALs and green berets who can take care of your ex-asshole problem. Ones who'll let us beat his ass first, before they make him disappear. Just say the word.

Zane: They won't kill him, but there are worse things. And he deserves it.

West: I would've gone after him already, but Emmy says you need to decide what to do. But I'm up for helping Zane's friends.

Emmy: Or even just ask Rafe for help, Abby. Please don't face this alone. We love you. <heart emoji>

A s I walked the grounds of Lyme Park, I took in the big house in the distance and wished I could enjoy the view. And yet, I kept readjusting my sunglasses and looking over my shoulder, afraid someone would rush toward me and say, "You're the woman from that CGN video!"

I still hadn't been able to watch the rest of it. At some point, yes, I needed to know what Travis had said. But right now, I just wanted to forget about everything but the surrounding nature and historical buildings. Oh, and walking briskly to keep warm.

March in Northern England wasn't exactly balmy.

Zipping my coat up to the very top, I put my hands in my coat pockets and walked toward the building known as the Cage. It was a tall, square building with turret-type towers at each of the corners. There were supposed to be breathtaking views from near the building.

Once I reached it and removed my sunglasses, I looked over the rolling hills of the Peak District. My eyes stopped on the sprawl of Manchester in the distance.

How many people were there watching that video and thinking the worst of me?

The worst of Rafe?

Was he even still there? Or had he rushed home to try and mitigate the worst of the damage? Damage I'd caused.

I'd known this would happen. I'd warned him, too. And yet, I'd wanted so badly to see if Rafe the man was anything like the boy I'd loved.

And now? Because of me, his training facility was in jeopardy, he'd be humiliated, and my ex would win in the end.

If only I could go back in time and warn myself about Travis and his charm.

I had no idea how long I stood there, staring at the city in the distance, before I heard something faint in the wind.

"Abby!"

I frowned, but turned around. A man rushed toward

me, slightly limping. He wore sunglasses, but I'd recognize him anywhere.

It was Rafe.

My first instinct was to run away again. And yet, when he removed his glasses and I watched him struggle to reach me, I just couldn't. Instead, my feet moved, and I walked toward him. When I was close enough, Rafe pulled me into a hug and said, "Thank fuck I found you."

I should push him away, tell him to leave me alone. And yet, he was warm and comforting and before I could stop it, I clung to him and started crying.

The cries turned into sobs and soon Rafe was holding me close, murmuring words I didn't hear, and rubbing my back, my arms, my side.

Eventually, I quieted, and embarrassment rushed through me. Why was I always crying around this man?

I tried to pull away, but Rafe only held me tighter. "No. You're not running away again, Abigail. We need to talk."

He was right. After raising my head, I steeled myself for Rafe's rejection and his ending our marriage.

But when he cupped my cheek, I blinked. His voice was soft as he said, "I can tell from your face that you expected me to toss you aside and abandon you. But no, I'm not going anywhere, Abby. You're my wife. And we're going to face this together."

"What? Why?"

His thumb stroked my cheek. "Did you really think I'd abandon you because of some bastard's lies?"

Hurt flashed in his gaze, and my stomach dropped.

"You're honorable, Rafe, as well as kind and caring. I know you're nothing like him, I do. But staying by my side will destroy your dream and ruin everything."

"I wouldn't be the first person to have my dream change."

"What are you talking about?"

He shook his head. "We'll get to that later. Right now, I need you to do something extremely difficult, Abby. I need you to trust me. Trust me to stay at your side and to help fight back. Trust me not to run away and abandon you. Can you do that?"

I nearly blurted no just to protect him. However, searching his gaze, all I saw was sincerity. He *wanted* to help me.

But could I trust my judgment? After all, it'd gotten me into this mess in the first place.

And yet, I was so tired of it all. Tired of worrying about what Travis would say or do. Tired of giving up my dreams out of fear. Tired of protecting myself from possible pain and abandonment by hiding away and keeping new people at arm's length.

Yes, my parents had died, but neither would've done so by choice. And my siblings had probably been so overwhelmed with grief that they hadn't realized how their leaving would affect anyone else.

Plus, all the messages from the group chat proved they wanted to stand with me.

Travis's shitstorm could hurt the winery, Emmy's wedding business, West's new cattle ranch, Amber's bakery, Sabrina's PR firm, or even Nolan's acting career.

And yet, they still all offered to do whatever they could to squash my ex and help me fight his lies.

Lies they hadn't even needed me to deny.

Because they knew me, trusted me. It was time for me to put my faith in others in return. Because if I couldn't even believe in my friends and family a little, then I'd never be able to trust anyone.

And I wanted to trust. Not just them, but Rafe as well.

The question was whether I was strong enough to risk getting hurt again?

Yes rushed through my head. It was time to stop walling off my heart.

Tears threatened to fall again, but I cleared my throat and pushed down my emotions to reply, "I'm going to try and trust you. I can't promise I won't try to run again, or if things get worse, try to fight things on my own. I've been doing it a long time, Rafe. So long that I almost forgot what it was like not to handle this huge secret on my own. And yet, I'm so damn tired of it all." I raised a hand and traced his jaw. "Just promise me you won't resent me later if things get worse. This thing with Travis could affect the opening and reputation of your training facility, your image, the new start you've been working so hard on."

He continued to stroke my cheek. "The training facility will survive, one way or the other. And if it struggles at first, I'll make sure Mark and his wife don't suffer because of my actions. Nor will any of the staff." He raised his other hand to cup my cheek before laying his forehead against mine. "Let me help you, Abby. Please."

As I stared into his dark brown eyes, seeing how much he yearned for me to say yes, I leaned forward and kissed him gently. "Yes, you can help me. Thank you, Rafe. For not thinking the worst of me."

"You're my wife, Abigail. I told you I'd protect you, and I meant it."

The word "wife" kept repeating inside my head. What would it be like to truly be his wife, in more than name only?

Don't hope for the stars. Take his friendship and deal with Travis. Then think about the future.

Wanting to lighten the mood a little, I said, "Too bad it's so windy and cold. I would've loved to see you come up the hill shirtless, like this was some sort of movie."

"Is that what you were doing up here? Imagining me shirtless?"

I smiled, loving how he knew I needed some lightness right now. Oh, shit would hit the fan and the world might come crashing down, eventually. But right here, right now, I wanted to be a little ridiculous before facing reality.

"Well, wouldn't you like to know?"

In one quick motion, Rafe scooped me into his arms and held me close.

"Rafe! Your knee!"

"I can hold you for a few minutes. Just don't ask me to walk down that hill. Or slay a dragon. That kind of thing."

Laughing, I looped my arms around his neck. "At least I know you won't be able to carry me off to your evil lair and have your way with me."

"I may just have to try that. Having my way with you sounds more like fun than evil, though."

"Are we really getting into the semantics?"

"Have you met your family?"

I rolled my eyes. "Are you going to start flinging peas at the dinner table now?"

"Peas aren't the best choice. I'd go for mini-potatoes. Or rolls. Maybe I could use napkins to make my own projectiles. Now, there's an idea..."

He winked at me, and I snorted. "Who are you and what have you done with Rafael Mendoza?"

"He's right here, being himself. With you."

"Oh, Rafe." I kissed him gently, and said, "I like real Rafe better than the fake playboy. Even more than the teenager I couldn't stop staring at."

"Do you, now?"

His gaze turned heated, and my belly flipped. "I always had a thing for hot yet silly guys."

"Silly, huh?" He cleared his throat. "What should we do now, my lady? Shall I serenade you? Maybe summon a unicorn to take us on a ride? Or how about if I use rocks to spell out your name on the hillside?"

I snorted. "None of that." I sobered a fraction. "Put me down and just hold me as we look at the scenery. I want to remember this moment forever."

He slowly put me back on the ground, spun me away from him, and pulled my back against his front. Once he wrapped his arms around my waist, he laid his cheek against mine and whispered, "I want to remember it forever, too, Abigail. To remember this perfect moment with my wife."

As he tightened his hold around me and the wind whipped around us, I simply lived in the moment, needing happy memories to help ground me for what was to come.

Chapter Twenty-Nine

Abby

Amber: Are you going to tell everyone the truth about you and Rafe?

Me: I don't know. I want to, but the last thing I need is for West to hate Rafe again.

Amber: Maybe just tell Emmy and Katie first, and then we can figure out how to tell the guys at the right time.

Me: Will there ever be a right time, though? What with the Douchebag's latest stunt.

Amber: There will be. Once you get to Starry Hills, you'll see how much this town has your back, Abby. Even old Mrs. Gunner is putting people in their place who try to badmouth you, and she loves gossip.

Me (typed but deleted): For now. But as it gets
worse, if the deepfake releases, fewer will stand with me.
Me (actually reply instead): I'll think about telling
Emmy and Katie. But first, I need to face you all and set
the facts straight about what happened in San Jose.
Amber: We already know that Travis is full of shit.
How much you want to tell us is up to you, but we won't
judge you. We love you, Abby.
Me: Thanks, Amber. I love you all, too. See you soon.
<heart emoji>

After I finished walking around the grounds at
Lyme Park with Rafe, everything became a
blur.

We returned to Manchester, packed, and boarded
Nolan's private plane, all without facing the paparazzi.
Something about Rafe's UK assistant leaking false infor-
mation to get them to gather elsewhere.

And after drinking copious amounts of vodka on the
plane—trying and failing to get the courage needed to
watch the rest of the video—I passed out for the
remainder of the flight.

Once we reached the airport near Starry Hills, Rafe
managed to get me into his car and then into his house,
all with me barely awake.

Eventually morning came, and I lingered in bed.
Both because my head pounded and because I didn't
want to leave the safety of my room.

However, Rafe eventually knocked on the door and

his voice came through the door. "Abby, you need to eat something before we go over to your family's place. You know you get grumpy when you get hungry."

I flung my arms to the side and stared at the ceiling. "Can't we put off seeing my family until tomorrow? I have a hangover and I'm still getting used to the time difference."

"Can I come in so I don't have to talk through a door?"

It would be easy to say no, stay right where I was, and be a coward for a little longer.

But I missed my family, my friends, and part of me yearned to finally be free of the secrets I'd been carrying.

Well, most of them. The one about Rafe and my marriage could wait for another day.

After sighing and rubbing my face, I replied, "Fine, come in."

Rafe entered, carrying a tray. The smell of pancakes and sausage made my stomach growl.

I sat up against the headboard, and he placed the food in front of me. The rose lying at the top of the tray warmed my heart.

Rafe was such a good guy, so sweet, and so different from his playboy image. I was starting to understand just how lonely he must've been overseas.

Stop pushing him away. If nothing else, he's your friend. A sexy friend you dream about riding, but still a friend.

I scooted over a little with the tray and gestured for him to sit next to me. Once he'd settled and leaned against the headboard, his heat and scent wrapped around me, familiar and calming.

He said, "Don't put off seeing your family, Abby. I did that for nearly ten years with my sister, trying to avoid a much-needed conversation, and it only hurt us both. And yes, I know you wouldn't wait ten years, but the longer you delay, the longer you have to carry the burden on your shoulders."

He looked over to meet my gaze, and I took his hand closest to mine and threaded my fingers through his. "I don't really want to wait. But I'm also afraid of what they'll think."

"Don't be. Like I told you, Emmy said they all can't wait to see you. And I'm sure they have some sort of group text, like always."

I'd been putting off reading them, but I wouldn't any longer, once I was alone again.

He gestured. "Eat, Abigail. It'll help with your hangover."

I released his hand and cut into my pancakes. "Thank you, Rafe. For everything."

"Of course, Abigail. I'll always be there for you. Always."

I focused on chewing my food and not looking at Rafe. Because it wouldn't take much for me to toss the tray to the floor, kiss him, and ask him to make love to me.

Today's not about your attraction. Get your life straightened out first.

I decided to change the topic. "I just wanted to let you know that I'll help any way I can with the training center. I'm already thinking of people who might replace me."

"Replace you?"

"Well, yes. You can't want me working there now."

He gently took my chin and turned my head until I looked at him. He said, "The job is still yours. And yes, I talked with Mark about it. He, like most of the town, knows you, Abby, and doesn't believe some questionable, gossipy content creator. We want the best working for us, which means we want you."

My eyes heated, and I laughed awkwardly. "How is it that you're so nice that I want to cry all the time?"

His thumb brushed the tears off my cheek. "I don't know. I don't want you to cry. But I cared for you, Abigail Mendoza, even before you became my wife."

I searched his gaze. "What are you talking about?"

He shrugged one shoulder. "You were my sister's best friend. And despite how annoying you were back in the day, you had your own kind of charm."

"Oh, right." Realizing how disappointed I sounded, I quickly added, "Well, if I'm to eat, shower, and get ready in the next hour and a half, I'd better get started. I'm sure you have some work to do."

He looked about ready to say something else, but then nodded and slid off the bed. "I need to answer some emails for the training facility, as well as talk to my assistant. I'll be in my home office, if you need me."

As soon as the door closed behind him, I mentally scolded myself for chasing him away.

But I pushed that aside. I was going to have to face

my family and friends soon, and I need to be ready to answer any questions they asked.

Oh, and think of contingency plans in case my five brothers decided to hop in the pickup truck and go hunting for my bastard ex.

Two hours later, Rafe opened my car door and once I stood, he took my hand in his. He asked, "Ready?"

"Ready as I'll ever be."

He walked and tugged me along. But we'd only made it a few steps before the front door opened and Avery came racing toward us.

I barely registered my niece flying toward me before she engulfed me in a hug. I hugged her back and said, "It's nice to see you too, Avery."

She replied, "Daddy said you needed a hug."

I held her tighter. "Thank you. You give the best hugs, after all."

Wyatt had walked up to us, and after hesitating, joined in the hug.

As I held my niece and nephew, I looked up and saw Aunt Lori standing in the doorway, beckoning us to come in. However, I enjoyed the group embrace a little longer before I found my voice. "Thanks, both of you. I feel much better now."

They finally released me, and Avery tilted her head. "Daddy said you might be sad, or angry, or both. Although we're not allowed to ask what's wrong yet, but you can always tell me. I won't tell anyone."

"Thanks, Avery. Maybe later. But first, I need to talk with the adults."

Avery sighed. "Adults have all the fun."

Wyatt muttered, "Let's go, Avery. I want to ride Thunder."

Avery said, "For now, Wyatt and I are going over to the King's place to see and ride the horses. But I made cookies for you! And don't leave before we get back. I want to hear about your trip to England. Do they really all talk funny over there?"

I smiled. "They have accents, yes." I lowered my voice dramatically. "But some of them are pretty sexy."

Wyatt rolled his eyes. "I don't want to hear about sexy anything. Avery already talks too much about Diego at school."

Avery's cheeks heated. "I do not!"

"Do too!"

With that, Wyatt raced down the path to the King's place on the other side of the winery, and Avery chased after him. When we were alone again, Rafe whispered, "I'm glad we can take them out for the day and give them back to my sister and your brother."

It was on the tip of my tongue to joke about our future kids, but then I remembered we weren't married for real.

So I grabbed his hand, tugged, and shouted, "Aunt Lori! Rafe would love to answer your questions about James the Goalie."

Rafe muttered curses, and I bit my lip to keep from laughing.

But Aunt Lori replied, "Maybe later, child. Right now, come in and tell us what's going on."

At Aunt Lori's look, I knew she wouldn't be distracted. She was determined to find out what had happened, no matter what.

Still, as soon as I reached her, she pulled both Rafe and me into a hug. "Welcome home, you two." She released us and looked first at Rafe and then me before adding, "Yes, things changed on the trip. I see it."

I frowned, but Rafe spoke first. "What are you talking about?"

My aunt patted his cheek. "Later. Now, come on. Everyone's in the living room. We added some more furniture since you were here last, to make sure there are enough seats for everyone." She lowered her voice. "Including an extra spot for when Zane finds his special someone."

"What about Zach?"

"Oh, he already knows his and just needs to do something about it."

Before I could tell her not to meddle—which would fall on deaf ears, but I owed it to Zach to try—we reached the doorway to the living room, and my words died on my tongue.

Everyone was there—all my brothers, plus Sabrina, Emmy, Katie, and Amber. The room erupted into chaos, a mixture of hugs and questions and hands gesticulating wildly.

Aunt Lori's voice cut through it all. "Quiet down and let Abby talk."

The room fell silent, and my aunt signaled for

everyone to take a seat. I was too worked up to sit, so I paced back and forth as Rafe leaned against the wall. I met his gaze. He nodded at me in encouragement, and I took one last steadying breath before I said, "All of you guessed that something happened to me in San Jose during my student teaching internship. Well, let me start at the beginning..."

Little by little I shared what had happened between Travis and me, from his first flirtations to him asking me to be his girlfriend to him eventually dropping hints about what I should do to please him—with a few things left out since I didn't want to talk about sex with my brothers.

The more I shared, the more my family and friends clenched their jaws. And once I finally finished telling them about his blackmailing and deepfake videos, the room stayed silent for exactly two seconds before Beck asked, "Why didn't you tell us about this earlier, Abby? We could've helped you. I know I was busy with the business, but I would've made time for my little sister."

I met my second-oldest brother's gaze. "I was worried about what it might do to the winery. Plus, you were shouldering everything and barely sleeping enough most days. I didn't want to burden you."

Zach asked, "And what about me, Abby? You, me, and Zane were a little group growing up. We helped with those assholes in high school, when needed. We could've dealt with this little shit, too."

I went to my brother and took his hand. Zach was the sibling who'd stayed around and been there for me. And yet, I still hadn't wanted to burden him with it all.

Especially since he often acted without thinking, and no matter how good his intentions, I didn't want him to get arrested because of me. "I didn't tell anyone, Zach. I'd gotten myself into the mess with Travis, and I'd wanted to get out of it alone. And..."

"And what?" Zach asked.

I looked down. "I was somewhat ashamed of being so stupid."

Zach shook his head. "You're one of the smartest people I know, Abby. But sometimes, we don't see what's right in front of us until it's too late."

I noticed Amber frowning at Zach from the corner of my eye, and I sensed there was a double-meaning there. However, Aunt Lori came to my side and gave me a one-armed hug. She spoke before I could ask Zach any more questions. "We're here for you, child. When I promised your mother I'd look after you like you were my own, I meant it. We might not share blood, but you're like a daughter to me, Abby. And I would do anything to help you. I love you, we all do."

My eyes heated with tears at my aunt's words. "I know. And I can't change the past. But that interview is probably only the beginning. Things will get uglier, especially with me now being married to a world-famous soccer player. However, if it ever becomes too much, I'll understand if you want to step back and distance yourself from me."

Zach stood up. "No fucking way that's going to happen."

West followed suit. "I'm not about to let that asshole win."

Beck stood too. "The winery is important, but you're far more important, Abby. And I'm not going anywhere."

Nolan walked over to me. "I already have people looking into that dick's background. I'll do more, whatever you need, just ask."

Zane managed to get out of his chair, slowly, and nodded. "I still have a lot of contacts in the SEALs and the Navy. I'll also ask around for anything else he might be hiding."

Emmy came over and hugged me. "You're my sister twice over, and I will grab and twist his balls if he ever shows his face in town."

Katie pumped her fist before saying, "Exactly. I still think we should find him in San Jose, when he least expects it, and show him no one messes with the BFF Circle."

Amber shook her head. "Let's not make it obvious. I'm still thinking of how to teach him a lesson without anyone realizing it was us."

As everyone started talking about plans and who could help, my eyes met Rafe's. He was still across the room, leaning against the wall, and he smiled and winked at me. I smiled back and gestured for him to come over.

He did, and as he took my hand, I squeezed his and mouthed, "Thank you."

Confusion flashed in his gaze, and I nearly explained that without his support, his trust, him simply being there for me, I might never have had the courage to face my family this way.

But before I could say anything to him, Aunt Lori produced a whiteboard from who knew where and proceeded to write down everyone in town that was on our side, the allies my family had, and ways we could fight back. Everything from Sabrina's take on messaging for PR to when Nolan would have background information, to even Zane's tactical predictions of what might happen next was talked about.

The more they talked, the lighter I felt. Oh, I still had an uphill battle to face, but my friends and family had my back. And just knowing that made it all a little less awful.

Chapter Thirty

Rafe

West: Keep me updated on anything new.

Me: As long as Abby says yes, then I will.

West: Good answer. And...

Me: And what?

West: And let's meet for drinks soon. I have things to say.

Me (typed but deleted): Will we both need ice packs by the end of it?

Me (actual reply instead): Sure. I'll text you tomorrow with some times. I haven't been to The Watering Hole in a while.

West: This time I'm going to kick your ass at pool.

Me: Keep talking. We know I'm the town champ.

West: <middle finger emoji> I look forward to your loss.

. . .

It was hours later when I finally drove us home. Abby sat staring out the window, and I remained quiet. The last few days had been overwhelming for her, and she probably needed some downtime.

Even if I burned to ask why she'd thanked me earlier, right after she'd explained everything to her family.

It'd been strange to be a part of the chaos, yet still a little apart. That was on me, of course. Abby's family had tried to include me when possible. And yet, my guilt about not being married for real had kept me from truly enjoying myself or joining the group.

And when Aunt Lori had suggested our trip had changed things between us? I'd wanted to shout, "Yes!" Because for me, it had.

While holding my wife on the hill overlooking the Peak District, it'd become crystal clear what I wanted for the next stage of my life—Abby. To love her and treasure her and always be there for her. To finally have a family and start living the life my parents would've wanted.

Months of my sister suggesting I needed to realize our parents would want us to be happy and not forever grieving had started to sink in.

However, while I might be ready to pursue Abby, she'd only just started to trust me. And only a little.

We were a long way from being a couple in love.

Not that I was giving up. Watching Abby share everything with her family, afraid but confident, had shifted my feelings even more. And by the end of the night, when she'd laughed with her friends at dinner as her brothers tossed rolls at each other? I'd all but fallen for her.

It wouldn't take much more to push me over the edge.

I was deep in thought about how to take down her ex as quickly as possible so I could focus on making her happy when Abby asked, "Was my family too much for you?"

I glanced at her and then back to the road. "Hmm? Why do you ask that?"

"Well, you were pretty quiet tonight. I wanted to rescue you, but people kept talking to me."

The corner of my mouth kicked up. "I needed to be rescued?"

"Hey, pretty much anyone new to my family needs rescued at some point. Sabrina took a little while to feel comfortable, more than Katie and Emmy, who were already used to us all. But Sabrina was even more of an outsider in the beginning than you. And now look at her —secretly tossing green beans at Zach when he wasn't looking."

I chuckled. "Seeing it land in his hair and staying there, without him ever noticing, was pretty funny."

Her hand rested on my knee, and her touch sent a rush of heat through my body. It took everything I had to keep my dick from hardening.

She said, "None of tonight would've been possible without you, Rafe. I hope you know that."

"I think you would've gotten there by yourself. Maybe it would've taken a few more days, but your family would never sit by while some asshole badmouths you to the world."

"Maybe, maybe not. Without you, I might've run away. It's something I've thought about doing on and off since returning to Starry Hills."

I was never so glad to see the entry to my property so I could talk to Abby properly. After pulling up the drive and parking, I turned to face her. "I don't think you would've run." I hesitated, not wanting to reveal even more of my flaws. But if I ever wanted to win Abby for real, I had to be honest. More so than I'd ever been in my life. So I took a deep breath and added, "You are braver than me, in that regard." She opened her mouth to protest, but I beat her to it. "No, you are. Yes, you had a setback. But you still came home and tried to deal with it. You didn't pretend to be someone else in public, distracting yourself with parties and women and booze. You might've kept a secret, but you still returned home."

"You did too, eventually."

"Only because I was forced into retirement and had nowhere else to go."

She shook her head. "No, you knew exactly where you belonged, even if you hadn't realized yourself." She smiled. "Starry Hills is your home, Rafael. Family and friendship and even supporting the community—you want and need all of that."

Before I could think better of it, I blurted, "What I need is you."

She sucked in a breath, and I wondered if I'd fucked up. Then she leaned forward and whispered, "Then come and get me."

After exiting the car, she rushed to the front door and opened it. I turned off the car and followed, doing my best not to limp—rushing after Abby at Lyme Park hadn't done me any favors—and saw her at the top of the stairs. She smiled at me and then went into a bedroom.

My bedroom.

I hurried as much as I could until I finally stopped at the doorway of my room. Abby was only in her bra and panties, lying on my bed, with her hand propping up her head. "I'm cold, Rafael. Come warm me up."

Striding toward her, I tugged off my jacket and then my shirt. "Are you sure?"

She laid back and arched her back. "I'm sure."

I unbuttoned my jeans. "You don't owe me anything, Abby. If you want this, I'll fucking make it so good, love. But there are zero strings attached to me helping you."

She slid down her bra straps. "I know. I've wanted this for a long time, Rafe. Now, come make me forget about the outside world for a little while."

As soon as she unhooked her bra and tossed it aside, my mouth watered at her hard little nipples.

She sat up, gently batted my hands away, and slowly unzipped my fly. I was so hard, even just the brush of her fingers against me made me hiss.

After pushing my jeans and boxers down, she lightly traced the top of my cock, back and forth, so gently I almost didn't feel it.

Her eyes finally met mine. "Take your pants all the way off, Rafe."

My hesitation vanished, and I quickly shucked my shoes and remaining clothes. As I stroked my dick,

Abby's gaze zeroed in on me and she licked her lips. I groaned as I let out a drop of precum.

She rose from the bed, knelt before me, and pushed my hand away. Her hot breath danced across the head of my cock, and it took every bit of strength I possessed not to fuck her mouth right then and there.

We'd long ago discussed recent tests and being clean, so she didn't hesitate to lick the drop of wetness from my cock. I threaded the fingers of one hand into her hair and groaned. As her tongue lightly lapped me, my balls tightened further.

No woman's touch had ever affected me like this before.

And if I had my way, this woman would be my forever.

Then Abby took me into her hot, wet mouth. Her eyes never left mine as she bobbed and used her hand to stroke in time to her movements. The sight of her, the feel of her, the scent of her made me even harder. "Fuck, yes. Just like that. You feel so fucking good, so perfect, love."

Hesitation flashed in her eyes, and I tugged her head back until she released me. "I'm not saying it just because, Abigail. I promised to be honest with my wife, and I am. Your mouth feels so fucking good, love. So much so that it wouldn't take much more to make me come."

I helped her up, pulled her flush against me, and lightly caressed her cheek. "Do you believe me?"

She searched my gaze, and then smiled. "I think I do."

"Well, then it's time for me to convince you of how fucking beautiful you are."

And I kissed her.

Her lips parted instantly, and I devoured her. Every lick and lap and twirl made me groan.

She whimpered before murmuring, "Please, Rafe. I need more. Much more."

I cupped her cheek. "What do you want, wife?"

The word had slipped out, but Abby didn't bat an eye as she replied, "For my husband to fuck me. Hard. Like he promised."

With a growl, I pushed her back toward the bed, and she sat. "Take off your panties, lie down, and show me what's mine."

Abby didn't hesitate to do as I said, reclining back as she spread her legs wide.

I drank her in for a second, eager to touch every inch of her. Abby's voice brought me back to the present when she asked, "Why are you staring at me?"

Looking at her eyes again, I replied, "Because you're the most beautiful woman I've ever seen in my life." Before she could protest, I knelt between her thighs on the mattress and rubbed her inner thighs. "I love your long legs, your curves, your pert little nipples." Leaning down, I took one into my mouth and suckled. At Abby's cry, I gently bit her.

"Rafe, yes. That feels so good."

I released her and blew over her wet flesh. I loved how goosebumps rose on her skin. "Let's see if the other one tastes just as good."

I repeated my torture with her other nipple, and

Abby's hand went to my head. Wanting to drive my wife even more out of her mind, I ran a hand down her belly, slowly, stopping just above her clit.

As I continued to caress her skin just above where she wanted, Abby growled, "Stop teasing me."

With a smile, I released her nipple and met her gaze again. "What, you want a guy who pumps a few times, rolls over, and leaves you frustrated?"

"Of course not. But I'm impatient. I've wanted this..."

I moved my hands to her hips, stroking them, as I asked, "Wanted this, what?"

Her cheeks heated. "For a long time."

"How long?"

"You're really going to make me say it?"

I moved my hands to her breasts and gently fondled them. "Tell me, love. I want to know."

She glanced away. "Since I was sixteen."

After releasing her breasts, I gently cupped her face and made her look at me again. "I wasn't even here."

"I know that! But that's the thing about dreams and fantasies—they don't require real people. I can do whatever I want, with whomever I want."

I leaned down, propping myself up on my forearms. But the second my cock laid against her pussy, we both made low sounds in our throats.

Abby's voice was strained as she asked, "Do we really need to talk about this now?"

I moved my hips, my dick running through her pussy lips, and I let out another drop of precum. "You're so fucking wet, Abigail. For me?"

She bit her lip and nodded.

I kissed her, taking my time to nibble and lick and explore every inch of her mouth. My cock ached, and I wanted nothing more than to be inside her. And yet, I had to kiss her. I needed to.

This was more than just sex to me. It was the first time I'd ever be making love to a woman.

My woman.

After breaking the kiss, I brushed the hair from her face and murmured, "I want to be inside you, love. Tell me I can."

She nodded. I gave her one quick kiss and then retrieved a condom from the nightstand and put it on in record time.

Abby didn't need me to say a word as she spread her legs wider and arched toward me. I ran a finger up through her center, stopping just short of her clit.

"Rafe."

I lightly circled her clit, wanting her ready to come because I wasn't going to last long this first time. And I wouldn't be an ass and leave her wanting.

As her breathing quickened, I positioned my cock and slid inside her, slowly. Inch by inch. Loving how hot and tight she was.

When I finally was in to the hilt, I leaned down and kissed her quickly before saying, "I love how you feel, Abby." I rubbed her clit a few times, and she moaned. "Tell me you're close, love, because I'm already there."

I quickened my thumb, and she struggled to reply, "I'm close, Rafe. Move. Please."

After pulling out slowly, I slammed back in. Abby

reached up and grabbed my shoulders. "Kiss me again while you do that."

"As my wife wishes."

I took her lips in a brutal kiss as my hips moved faster and faster, loving how she would clench around me sometimes, making it harder to hold on.

I used my thumb to increase the pace and find the pressure she liked, all while kissing her and doing my best not to orgasm.

When Abby finally cried out and spasmed around me, I pumped a few more times and stilled as pleasure coursed through me. Each pulse of my cock took me higher until I finally stilled and collapsed on top of my wife.

Her arms went around me, and she nuzzled my neck as she said, "That was amazing, Rafe. I didn't know it could be like that."

Her voice was soft, and I sensed an emotion in it I couldn't define. So I rolled over, taking her with me, until she rested against my chest. I gently raised her face until I could see her eyes, and at the mixture of disbelief and pleasure, I frowned. "Could be like what?"

She bit her lip and looked away. "That a guy could make me come too during sex."

A thread of anger shot through me. It wasn't hard to guess that her ex had been selfish in bed, too. "Any guy who doesn't make you orgasm too isn't worthy of you."

Her eyes met mine again. "I should know that. But after weeks of..."

I sat up against the headboard and settled Abby next

to me, covering us with the blanket. I stroked her arm with my thumb as I said, "Tell me, love."

"Promise you won't go and murder anyone afterward?"

"I guess I can agree to that. Although I can't promise I won't punch the guy if he hurts you."

Her fingers trailed across my chest, and she played with my nipple. I focused on her words and not on how her touch made me want to have her all over again.

"When I first fell for Travis, he was charming and sweet and did little things to make me smile. But once we started sleeping together, his behavior changed."

I already regretted my promise to not murder anyone, but nodded, not wanting to break the spell.

Abby continued, "In retrospect, I can see it was a sort of manipulation to lure me in. But he knew just what to say to make me want to please him, not disappoint him, and because I so wanted someone to love me and not leave me, I did whatever he wanted.

"The changes were small at first, like wearing my hair down instead of up. Or wearing skirts instead of pants. But eventually he struggled to get hard enough for me and told me what I could do to fix that. To make him happy. And I believed I was so in love with him, so determined to please him, that I forgot about myself and orgasms and anything but getting him hard and coming. And eventually, after weeks of it, I thought nothing of him fucking me, coming, and rolling over to sleep or going home. He always praised me for putting his needs first, showing how much I cared for him."

I clenched the sheets with my free hand, doing my

best to tamp down my anger. I'd learned that Travis was nearly twenty years older than Abby and had probably known exactly how to manipulate her—by pouncing on her desire to be loved and wanted.

Given how smoothly and quickly he'd changed Abby, he probably had experience manipulating other young, vulnerable women.

But I pushed aside my anger to focus on Abby, who'd remained quiet.

"Hey, look at me." Her lovely green eyes met mine again. Right then and there, I knew that if Abby ever loved me, I would treasure the gift and not take advantage of it.

But that meant first trying to win her over and earn her trust.

I continued, "I'm not an expert on relationships, but based on my parents' marriage, it was about taking care of and loving each other. If something becomes all about one person and what they want or need or demand, then it's not really a true relationship. Sure, my parents fought sometimes, but they'd talk and make compromises. And I never, ever want to know about their sex lives." I shuddered. "But for me, at least, giving you pleasure makes me happy. And when we come together? It makes it all the more intense."

Her hand cupped my cheek as she searched my gaze. "You're a good man, Rafael Mendoza. And I'm glad you came back to Starry Hills."

I placed my hand over hers. "Me, too."

I love you, was on the tip of my tongue. Because, yes, it was true. Abby was kind yet strong, funny yet determined, and the only person in the world I felt okay to be myself around.

But she was still hurting, still healing. And until she could live her life without fear of her ex fucking things up, I wouldn't say the words.

However, now that Abby held my heart, I wanted to know every little thing about her. And so I held her tight, laid my head atop hers, and asked about her life during the years I was away.

Chapter Thirty-One

Abby

Aunt Lori: We haven't seen you in days. When are you guys coming over?

Me: Er, soon. I promise.

Aunt Lori: Too busy heating up the sheets, huh? <winking emoji> No hurry. Enjoy that sexy man as long as you want. Maybe you two will give me a new grand-nephew or grandniece. Maybe they can just call me Nana Lori. That'd be easier.

Me: Aunt Lori!

Aunt Lori: What?

Me: Could you not plan out my life? Rafe and I have only been married about a month.

Aunt Lori: True, true. You need at least six months of constant sex before you think about adding a little one.

Me: <sighing emoji> Your life rules don't always make sense.

Aunt Lori: They make perfect sense. I should write a book. Oooh, or start a Dear Aunt Lori video series! Yes. That would be amazing. Then I could help so many more people.

Me: <sweat drop emoji> I don't even know what to say to that.

Aunt Lori: Enjoy your husband. Maybe by the time we finally see you again, I'll have my first video posted! Before you know it, I'll be the super cool, older influencer with advice to die for. <winking and blowing a kiss emoji>

Three days later, as I tried to think of how to dissuade my aunt from becoming some kind of advice influencer—I wasn't sure she could handle the hate that would come with it—Rafe walked into the home office we were sharing until I was ready to face the public. He handed me a latte and sat down.

I smiled at the dragon made out of chocolate powder. "It's almost like the Dragons FC logo."

"I'm working on my art skills." He paused and tilted his head. "I came to see if you're ready for your surprise or not."

As I sipped my coffee, I kept my gaze on the floor. Rafe wanted to take me off his property for a surprise. However, I was still struggling to leave our little bubble of happiness.

And not just because of the sex—which had been amazing and taken up a lot of our time over the last few days—but I'd also loved just chatting with Rafe about everything and nothing. Like learning how he loved sushi but hated cooked fish. Or how he always had to sip his water twice before going to bed or he felt uneasy. Or even that he missed helping his parents with the cattle, especially during the calving season.

Little by little, I better understood Rafe the man instead of the little boy I'd known, or even the superstar soccer player he'd shown to the world.

I also recognized more and more just how lonely he'd been in Manchester. And whether he'd realized it or not, he loved Starry Hills and had missed this community.

Rafe's voice interrupted my thoughts. "I promise you it's a place where the people support you, Abigail. The sheriff has also been good about keeping the lookie-loos away, and Nolan's assistant is a miracle worker at finding out when the press are here."

Rafe had been nothing but supportive, always discussing what he learned about my ex or CGN with me. He never held back, even if the news was less than great—like the mean headlines that had surfaced in the UK about us.

He'd gone out of his way to make me trust him. And I did, to some degree.

Then prove it. Let him take you to his surprise. Because if you never risk anything, you'll always be stuck inside the prison Travis created for you.

Just thinking about how my ex was still making my

life miserable, I decided, fuck it. After meeting his gaze again, I replied, "Okay, then let's go."

Happiness flashed in his eyes, and I smiled. As much as I liked Rafe trying to be there for me and cheering me up, I also liked making him happy.

I'd been doing a good job of that in bed, but I wanted to do more. Although I often worried that I might go too far, like before, and lose myself in the process.

Not this time. You're not the same naïve woman as before.

Rafe nodded. "Right, then make sure you wear jeans and something comfortable on top, because you might get dirty or muddy."

"Now I'm curious."

He stood. "And it's only going to get worse since you'll be wearing a blindfold the entire way there."

My brows came together. "Is that really necessary?"

"Yes." He hesitated before adding, "However, if it's too much for you, then be honest and you don't have to do it."

Sometimes Rafe acted this way—one minute he was being fun and flirty, only to worry if he was pushing me too far in the next.

And for some reason, I didn't like him always tiptoeing around me.

Why was that?

Oh, that's right—I was teetering on falling for him for real.

Not wanting to think about how if I wasn't careful, my heart would break in eleven months' time, I stood.

"The blindfold is fine. Just give me fifteen minutes to get ready."

He smiled. "Then I'll be ready in fourteen minutes."

I gently shoved his arm. "You always say you'll be ready a minute before me."

"Hey, most of the time, I could be ready in four minutes. But I like to put in some extra effort for my wife."

He winked, and I couldn't help but laugh before replying, "Your hair is really short and you don't wear guyliner, so what are you doing all that time? Manscaping?"

Waggling his eyebrows, he leaned in and said, "Wouldn't you like to know?"

Doing my best not to laugh, I rolled my eyes. "Is that supposed to be sexy? Because if you think I want to shave your balls, then you don't know me at all."

"I'd trust you to do it, but no, it's way too itchy when the hair grows back."

"TMI, Rafe. TMI."

"What, you don't want to know how fast the hair grows back on my balls?"

"Er, no thank you."

He placed a hand over his heart and shook his head. "And here I thought you wanted to know everything about me."

"To a degree. But we all have a few secrets. And your ball-hair growth should be one of them."

Snorting, he moved closer. "Maybe not that kind of hair. But I think you're fond of my second-day face stubble." He nuzzled his cheek against mine, and I nearly moaned. "That little sound tells me you like it."

"What sound? I didn't make any."

"Oh, yes, you did. It's a little hum in your throat."

He nuzzled me again, and I noticed what he was talking about.

After kissing my neck, he said, "Now you hear it."

"Maybe." He playfully slapped my ass, and I said, "Fine. Yes, I heard it."

For a second, he stayed close, and I wondered if maybe we'd delay leaving for an hour and head for the bedroom.

However, he soon sighed and moved away from me. "If not for your surprise, I'd rub my stubble over all the sensitive parts of your body. But I'm too excited to see how you'll react. So, your fifteen minutes start now."

He made a big show of starting the timer on his phone.

While I could keep him waiting just because, I was too curious. So I raced up the stairs and briefly forgot about how reality could come crashing down as soon as I set one foot off Rafe's property.

Chapter Thirty-Two

Abby

Amber: I have a new scone recipe I'd like to try out, and I need my taste tester. Will you come to the bakery today?

Me: I can't. <sad face emoji>

Amber: Can't, or won't? I promise if anyone says anything to you, I'll kick their butts to the curb. <strong arm emoji>

Me: I know you would. But I can't. Rafe is taking me somewhere. And no, I don't know where.

Amber: Ooh, maybe it's someplace romantic! <smiley with hearts for eyes emoji> Tell me about it as soon as you can. Maybe you two can stop by afterward for some scones. You can take them home and try them there. <heart emoji>

Me: Thanks, Amber. I might do that.

Amber: And since you're venturing out into the world, does this mean we can talk to Katie and Emmy soon, too?

Me: Maybe we can meet at your apartment and I can tell them. I'll talk to you after my surprise with Rafe.

Amber: I'll be here. <heart emoji>

D uring the entire drive to Rafe's mystery location, I couldn't stop tapping my foot and drumming my fingers on my thigh. Part of me loved the waiting and anticipation. And yet, part of me still worried. "Are you sure no one will look at me with contempt at this place?"

"No, Abby. I promise you, it won't happen."

"But what if there are strangers who walk by? You can't control every person's movement in town."

"I can where we're going. It's not in town proper." His hand gently squeezed my knee before he removed it. "I'd rather stab my own heart than see you hurt, Abby."

I bit my bottom lip and held my tongue. Rafe kept saying things that made me think he had feelings for me, beyond being a friend. Feelings I wanted to be true and was starting to share.

And yet, I still had trouble trusting my judgment.

Will I ever be able to throw off my past? Oh, how I wanted it. Maybe once Travis was no longer a threat and spewing lies, I could finally move on.

The car stilled, and I heard the engine turn off. "Can I take my blindfold off yet?"

"No, let me come around and I'll guide you."

"Okay."

It wasn't long before the door opened, and I felt the cool air on my skin. Rafe took my hand. "Just a little longer, Abigail. Come with me."

After sliding out of the car, I followed his directions and walked toward something. His hands were on my shoulders, helping to guide me. Then the wind blew and a familiar scent filled my nose—manure.

Then I heard a whinny in the distance, and I stopped walking. "Where are we?"

"Let me take off your blindfold and you can see."

It seemed to take forever as my heart pounded.

Another whinny probably meant horses. And I was torn between wanting to rush toward one and stroke its side, and running away to avoid my painful memories.

When the material finally dropped away, I blinked my eyes against the light and took in the scenery.

I stood in front of a wooden fence. Inside the field were several different horses, ranging in color from all black to a chestnut with a white blaze to even an all-white horse.

For a second, I merely watched them graze and walk around, flicking their tails or ears, and a deep sense of longing rushed forth.

At one time, I'd been horse crazy and had spent as much time as possible in the saddle. I'd even thought about training them for a living at one point.

But then my mother had died. While my dad had first stoked my love of horses, she and I had ridden together the most. And once she'd passed, it'd been too painful to follow along the same paths and trails that we'd taken together.

And so I hadn't ridden a horse again since I was sixteen.

However, as one walked closer toward us, it wasn't sadness that filled my heart but a flicker of joy. My eyes heated as the chestnut came to the fence. I offered my palm, and she sniffed. The flutter of her lips and breath on my skin made me smile. "Hello there, beautiful."

When she offered her head, I rubbed and scratched and murmured nothings. Eventually, the horse walked away. It was then I noticed the stables and buildings and recognized where we were. "Why are we at the Sakamoto place?"

Rafe leaned against the fence next to me and watched the animals in the distance. "I miss having horses, like when I was a kid. So I'm looking to buy a pair. Especially since on a horse, I'd have more freedom than I do with my injured knee." He glanced over at me. "And I thought you could help me pick them out."

"Me? Why me?"

He looked back out at the landscape. "I remember you as a kid, riding hellbent and scaring the shit out of your brothers. You loved horses and knew everything about them. You definitely have more knowledge than me."

"But I haven't been around horses in a long time, Rafe. And I wouldn't want to make a mistake."

He shook his head. "You won't. Emmy told me you gave Beck advice not that long ago about what to look for." He met my gaze again. "But if you don't want to help, I understand. Say the word and we can leave."

Rafe was tiptoeing around me. Again.

Looking back at the chestnut who'd come up to the fence, I remembered buying my first pony with my dad. He'd taught me a lot about what to look for, how to determine the best fit. It was his encouragement that had led me to learning everything I could and training hard.

Dad. For a long time, thinking about my parents had been too painful. But maybe, just maybe, it was time to honor their memories and remember their love instead of trying to forget it and avoid any pain.

Besides, Rafe revealing how his knee held him back must've been difficult. He probably couldn't run like he used to, might never be able to again.

You could help him with that. Stop being afraid.

After everything he'd done for me, I wanted to help him, to make him happy, even if it meant facing something difficult. "Okay, I'll give you what advice I can."

Smiling, he turned his head toward me. "Thanks, Abby."

He reached over, took my hand, and kissed the back of it, lingering a second before releasing me.

My heart thundered so loud I didn't hear one of the owners, Star Sakamoto, make her way toward us. So when she greeted us from behind, I jumped.

Rafe squeezed my hand in reassurance before he talked with Star about what he was looking for.

It wasn't long before she went inside the paddock to retrieve the first animal. As she approached the black gelding, I focused on helping Rafe and said, "Watch how the horse reacts to her and also how she interacts with him. That will tell you a lot."

"What, do some kick their owners and run away?"

"I doubt that would happen with this family since the Sakamotos are renowned in Sonoma—throughout all of California—for their animals. But yes, there are some sketchy-ass people who will drug a horse right before you visit to hide their temperament."

"Kind of like people who will sell you puppies with Parvo or other life-threatening diseases without telling you to make a quick buck?"

"Yes, kind of like that. But don't worry, if all goes well, my brother Beck has a vet he trusts with his horses and he can do the pre-purchase exam." I glanced over at Rafe. "Did you not research any of this?"

"I could have and would have, if you hadn't agreed to help me."

Which meant he completely trusted my opinion.

That only made me more determined than ever to pair him with the right horses.

I gestured toward Star and the gelding. "Watch them."

The woman and horse were at ease around each other, as she patted his flank, walked around his back, and came around to the other side.

She brought him over, tied him to a post not too far away from us, and came back. "Midnight's ready whenever you are. We'll see how you do with him first."

I nodded. "Thank you." I looked up at Rafe. "Now, it's your turn to approach the horse and see how he reacts to you."

"Can't you do it?"

"No, these are for you, Rafe. If you're not comfortable around him, then it won't be a good match."

As he went to inspect the horse, memories of going with my father flashed into my mind. How he'd shown me the steps to assessing a horse, him smiling at me as I rode her for the first time, and the many, many times he'd helped me cool down my pony and the best way to take care of her.

It was still painful, and yet, there was also happiness. My father was gone, but the memories didn't make me as sad as they once had.

Once Rafe finished his inspection, it wasn't long before the gelding was saddled and ready to be ridden by the owner. Rafe returned to my side as Star went through the motions. He asked, "What am I looking for now?"

"When you're in the saddle, there are a lot of things you might miss but can easily spot while watching someone else. Look at his gait, how he moves, and interacts."

"Then I get to try him?"

"Yes."

We both watched in silence as Star finished her demonstration and came back in our direction. Before she reached us, Rafe asked, "Do you want to try riding him now?"

My first instinct was to say no. I wouldn't do it. I couldn't.

But as I watched the beautiful gelding come to a stop

and the owner dismount, I longed to jump back into the saddle.

Rather than focus on how much I wanted to say yes, I asked, "Why?"

"It's important for you to trust and like him too, since you're living with me. I might even have to ask for your help from time to time to exercise him." He faced me. "So? What do you say? I wouldn't want to buy a horse who hates you." I hesitated, and he asked, softly, "Please? I trust your judgment about whether he has the right temperament or not."

He trusts me. And not with something as simple as picking out what to eat for dinner, but an animal he would have for years, hopefully decades.

The image of Rafe and I riding together, maybe even racing, flashed into my mind. To feel the power of the horse between my legs, the wind on my face, and to feel the pure joy at galloping through the trails close to my family's land was tempting.

And for the first time in a long time, I wanted that. I wanted to embrace a former passion, to remember the good times with my parents, and to rediscover a little of myself.

A part of myself I'd given up for too long.

"Okay, I'll ride him first."

Once the owner discussed a few more things, I approached the gelding and let him sniff my hand. His lips tickled my palm, and I smiled. "Hello there, Midnight. It's a fine day to be outside, isn't it? A little cold, but not too bad."

The horse huffed, and I stroked him. As he relaxed, I

moved around, rubbing his flank, and finally murmured, "It's been a while for me, so help me out, okay?"

I swore he nodded his head.

Soon I was atop the horse, trotting to the opposite side of the field, and I couldn't stop smiling.

I'd missed this. So much. And as I looked up, Rafe waved at me. I waved back, and my heart warmed a little.

I wasn't sure if Rafe had done all of this solely for my benefit or not. However, without his encouragement, I'm not sure how long it would've taken for me to get back on a horse.

It was almost as if he understood what I needed, knew when I needed a push, but also when to step aside.

It was one of a million ways Rafe was different from my ex. And I came a little bit closer to believing what we had was real and more than a one-year agreement. Or, at least, that maybe I wanted to try and see if we could last.

Because if Rafe kept being so wonderful, it would be all too easy to fall for him.

Chapter Thirty-Three

Rafe

Aunt Lori: You two are coming to dinner tonight.

Me: Do we get a say in it?

Aunt Lori: No. You need to come out of your little love nest at some point. Besides, Zach has news.

Me: Abby and I do have jobs, you know.

Aunt Lori: You're the boss and can leave on time for one day. Besides, everyone has to eat.

Me: Fine. We'll come to dinner.

Aunt Lori: Good. You'll be on my team.

Me: Team for what?

Aunt Lori: Beck is making chicken parmesan, and I want the biggest piece.

Me: Can't you just ask for it?

Aunt Lori: Where's the fun in that? Besides, I have the

perfect distraction. I'll tell you my plan once you get here. Just in case someone tries to steal my phone and learn my secrets ahead of time.

Me: Um, no one is going to steal your phone. Are they?

Aunt Lori: Zach can be a sneaky bastard. Don't let his easygoing nature fool you! Now, I need to work on my branding for my new social media accounts. Dear Aunt Lori is going to be a huge hit. I can feel it. <heart emoji>

O nce Abby dismounted, I could tell something was different about her. Smiling, she excitedly told me about her first time picking out a horse. Then she went on to recall stories about competing in local competitions as a teenager and winning.

And by the time we'd picked out a pair of animals and agreed to a trial period, the somewhat reluctant, depressed version of Abby from earlier in the day had vanished.

Every time she smiled or looked at me with bright eyes, my heart raced faster. I'd never really thought about how someone's happiness could affect my own this much. Sure, I'd helped my parents and sister when I'd been younger. But that was different, more like a son and brother helping when he could.

However, with Abby, I wanted a future together where we were stronger and happier together than we were apart. One where we raised our own little family and taught our son or daughter to ride and kick a soccer ball around. One where we could be ourselves, laugh together, and be there for one another whenever things got tough.

I loved her. So much.

And I wished I could tell her. But I didn't think she was quite ready to hear it and believe me yet. Not while her ex loomed over us and she couldn't look toward the future, always worrying about how her past might ruin the present.

I would've settled for making love to her again, but her aunt had ordered us to dinner. Since it was just family, we decided not to go home and change, but just head over to her family's house from the stables.

During the drive there, I kept stealing glances at Abby as she would glance at her phone and then stare out the window. I was content not to talk and simply feel comfortable in her presence. Especially as she hummed along to the radio for most of the drive, hopefully a sign she was in a better mood.

As I pulled into her family's place, it was hard to miss the giant banner over the door that said, "Bon Voyage!"

I asked, "Is someone going somewhere?"

Abby shook her head. "I don't know. Let's find out."

As she exited the car, I thought I saw worry cross her face. However, by the time I walked to the other side and took her hand in mine, she smiled at me.

I was tempted to pull her close and kiss her, but the door opened and Emmy rushed out. She glanced at me, then Abby, and asked, "How did it go?"

Abby raised an eyebrow. "You knew about us going to the Sakamoto place?"

"Yes. Rafe told me he was thinking of buying some horses, and I thought maybe you could help him."

For a second, my sister searched Abby's gaze. But then Abby released my hand to hug Emmy. "Thanks for suggesting it." She leaned back and released her. "I spent so many years thinking that if I ever went near a horse again, I'd only remember my parents and be bombarded with grief. But I was wrong. Yes, I was a little sad at first. But then the happy memories flooded back, and once I jumped back into the saddle, I felt as if I'd regained a piece of myself."

Emmy took Abby's hand. "It was like that when West fixed up the calving barn." Her gaze moved to me. "Sometimes, we need to revisit the past to fully be able to move toward the future."

I knew what my sister was hinting at—I'd avoided visiting most of the property that had been my parents' and then mine before I'd given it to Emmy.

Maybe it was time to walk through the fields, visit my dad's office, and maybe even the calving barn. West was even bringing cattle back to the ranch for the first time in a long time.

Abby took my fingers and squeezed. "I'm up for some exploring, whenever you're ready."

She smiled at me, and I couldn't help but do the same.

West's voice ruined the moment, though. "Do you really have to make doe-eyes at each other?"

Abby stuck her tongue out at her brother. "Considering I've had to watch you and Emmy do much worse for months and months, you can't complain."

"What? Like this?"

West tugged Emmy to him and kissed her. Not a peck, but a deep kiss that definitely had tongues involved. Instead of being upset like when I'd first learned of their relationship, I tried not to laugh at the outrage on Abby's face.

Abby turned around and shook her head. "Ugh. I really don't need to see my brother and best friend pretty much having sex with clothes on."

I turned in the same direction as Abby and murmured, "If you ever want to surprise them with an even better kiss, then just say the word."

She laughed. "I'm tempted."

Just as I was about to suggest it, someone whistled before Zach's voice reached my ears. "So many free shows these days. Too bad it's with your ugly ass, West."

Turning, I saw West flip off his brother. "Better than your face."

Zach placed a hand over his heart and put on an exaggerated sad face. "You wound me, brother. So much. I may never return home now."

Abby frowned. "Where are you going, Zach?"

Zach shook his head. "Nowhere yet. Not until we deal with your asshole ex." He glanced at the sign. "Aunt Lori put that up without my knowledge."

We all walked closer toward him as Abby asked, "But based on that sign, you have a plan, right? Why didn't you mention it to me?"

I took her hand in mine and squeezed. Given how

many times people had left Abby in her life, I wanted her to know that I was here and would stay here as long as she wanted me to.

Zach replied, "I've been keeping it quiet because I wasn't sure if Beck would agree to it."

"Agree to what?" Emmy asked.

He gestured us inside, and we followed. "I've been putting together a six-month-long business trip, one that will take me to various vendors, fairs, festivals, and trade shows. While the subscription boxes are doing well, I want to expand our reach beyond mostly the west coast. And for that, I need to make the pitches in person. And since summer is the high point for fairs, festivals, and other outdoor events, it's the perfect time for a big push."

I'd learned over the last few months about how Zach had been given more responsibility, mostly to do with sales for the winery.

In some ways, it'd help mature him a little. He and his twin had been mischief-makers as kids, and from everything I'd heard around town, Zach still was, even in his late twenties. At least until the last six months or so, when he'd focused on helping to grow the winery's revenue while Beck handled the day-to-day operations.

Zach opened his mouth, as if to say more, but Abby beat him to it. "That sounds amazing, Zach. Out of all of us, you take after Dad the most when it comes to charming strangers."

He rubbed the back of his neck. "Maybe." He dropped his arm. "But we'll see if it happens this year or if I have to wait until next year. Because there's no way I'm leaving when you need me, Abby."

She hugged her brother and released him. "You're sweet sometimes, Zach. But you should go, no matter what."

He frowned. "No. I can't bolt and abandon you." He lowered his voice. "You, me, and Zach were always there for each other as kids, and that's not going to change now."

She replied, "As the three youngest, we kind of had to band together after dad's death. But it's okay for you to go this year, Zach. Because if it came to it, you'd come home in a pinch, wouldn't you?"

"Of course. Why would you even ask me that?"

"So you'll promise me that you'll go this year?"

Zach searched her gaze. "If you want me to."

Abby nodded. "I do."

"Well, okay then. But that only motivates me to deal with your ex as soon as possible."

Nolan's voice came from behind him. "And I might have some information that can help us on that front."

I met the middle Wolfe brother's gaze, and he nodded. Ah. So his contacts had finally found some dirt, then.

Nolan had been quieter when younger, and I hadn't known him as well as Beck and West. But over the last few days, we'd texted information and devised some strategies.

Behind his quiet self, there was a determined, protective older brother, willing to do whatever it took to help his sister.

Nolan hugged Abby and then said, "Only if you want to hear what I learned, Abby. It may help you in the long run, but it might hurt you a little to hear it."

Abby straightened. "I can handle it."

"Then come into the living room. Aunt Lori, Beck, Sabrina, and Katie are busy in the kitchen with the kids. We should have just enough time to talk before dinner."

They walked down the hall and entered the living room, leaving me alone with Abby. I hugged her close and whispered, "Are you sure you want to deal with this right now?"

"Yes. Because it's not just me the bastard's actions are affecting, but my family as well. The sooner we find a way to handle him, the better."

I cupped her cheek and searched her gaze. I asked softly, "And are you truly okay with Zach leaving?"

"Yes, I think so. It's different this time—he should be back. And..."

"And, what?"

She glanced off to the side. "You're here."

My heart swelled at her words, and I gently made her look at me again. "Yes, I am. Always."

I half-expected her to question me. But she merely kissed me quickly and tugged me into the living room.

Chapter Thirty-Four

Abby

Unknown Number #1: Watch your back, bitch.

Unknown Number #15: You're a disgusting pedophile. You deserve to die.

Unknown Number #38: I'm going to find you and make sure you never hurt a child again.

Unknown Number #76: Fucking cunt, I'm going to shove a gun up your pussy and watch you die slowly.

Me (typed but deleted): I didn't do anything! It's a lie! Please leave me alone. You're scaring me.

A s my phone vibrated in my pocket again, I willed myself to stay calm. The threatening texts had started during the drive to my family's place and had only kept coming.

I suspected Travis had leaked my number. Maybe even my address. It was exactly the petty-ass type of thing he'd do, uncaring about how dangerous it could be for me or my family.

Sometimes, I still couldn't believe I'd fallen for his act and thought myself in love with him.

I'd debated telling Rafe about the messages right away, but had decided to wait until after dinner with my family. So I'd done my best to appear happy and content in the car.

I'd nearly spilled everything when we arrived at my family's house. However, once Emmy showed up and started talking, I hadn't wanted to spoil things. Everyone was getting along so well for once.

I *would* tell Rafe. But later.

Since the texts kept arriving, I quickly took out my phone and turned it off as we reached the living room. Rafe frowned at me and asked with his eyes if anything was wrong. However, I shrugged and mouthed, "Later."

He looked as if he wanted to push, but Nolan, Zach, West, and Emmy sat down, joining Zane, who was already in the room. So I tugged Rafe to sit next to me on a loveseat and did my best to focus on Nolan. "So, what did you learn about my ex?"

I was proud of how relaxed I sounded, despite worrying about how many more messages would be on my phone when I turned it back on.

My brother leaned forward and propped his elbows on his thighs before replying. "I won't sugarcoat it—there was probably at least one other intern teacher that Doucey slept with, meaning his behavior could be a pattern."

I blinked. "What?"

"There was an HR complaint to the school a few years ago concerning sexual harassment and abuse. The woman later retracted and said it was just a misunderstanding. But while my people were able to figure out who it was and are tracking her down right now, they started looking on the internet."

"And they found things."

Nolan looked grim as he nodded. "There were vile posts on various social media sites about the woman, mostly about how much of a slut she was, and that she stole from men she'd been with. There was at least one half-naked picture the woman asked him to take down, but he didn't."

That sounded like how Travis would lash out—paint the woman as the problem and play the victim. "But you think the posts are more of his bullshit."

Nolan replied, "Yes. The accusations are from social media accounts created just before they started posting. They also went silent right after she retracted her complaint and have been inactive until recently."

My stomach dropped. "Because then they started posting about me."

"I'm so sorry, Abby. But yes."

A buzzing started in my ears as I imagined what they'd said about me.

Rafe asked, "Is there any way to get that shit taken down?"

Zane answered, "I've been helping Nolan with that, and we're trying. But sometimes when you report something, it can take a long time to get a response."

That was something I'd learned recently, when Katie had been viciously attacked online by Nolan's ex. Some of that stuff was still up. Which meant mine might be up forever. "What were the posts about?"

Nolan shared a glance with Zane before replying, "They're a lot worse than before. Some are accusations of you sleeping with a seventeen-year-old boy. But there are also pictures of you I'd rather not have seen."

My heart thundered as I imagined Travis using pictures he'd taken of me, ones he'd said would make him happy and only be for him, being shared with the world. Probably manipulated too, to make me look like the villain.

I stood and went to the window, braced my hands on either side of it, and stared out at the still-dormant grape vines in the distance.

It took everything I had not to scream at the world and ask what I'd done to deserve this. All I'd wanted was to fall in love with a kind, handsome man and get my own happily ever after.

Instead, I'd been tricked into loving a man who'd then manipulated me to get what he wanted. And probably because he enjoyed the control, too.

Not for the first time, I wished I could go back and change the past.

I was so lost in thought that when Rafe's soft voice came from right behind me, I jumped.

"Abigail. We'll get him. I promise you."

My eyes heated. I couldn't take any more of his kindness right now and something inside me snapped. And even though Rafe didn't deserve it, I turned and shouted, "How the fuck will you do that?" I waved a hand to the side. "He's already out there giving interviews, telling the world that I groomed boys to be my lovers, and soon he'll probably start sharing more pics of me dressed in scanty lingerie, just to prove his point." I shook my head. "And now that I know I'm not the first one? That he's tried to smear another woman who didn't do exactly as he wanted? It's never going to end, Rafe." The room blurred as I tried not to cry. "It's never going to end."

With a sob, I raced out of the room and through the front door. I needed air, space, to be alone and just cry and cry until I was too tired to do any more.

I had no idea what to do next. But for now, I rushed through the parking lot behind the house and dashed down the gravel road toward the place where I felt the closest to my parents—the apple orchard. Because right now, I needed to remember the happier times to face the coming shitstorm.

I could barely see as I ran, sobbing and stumbling, my heart thudding so loud I could barely hear anything else.

At least until a car revved loudly behind me, followed by Rafe screaming, "Abby!"

I turned around. A car sped right for me. Fast. Just as

I expected to be hit, something crashed against my side and I went flying off the road.

The wind was knocked out of my lungs, and it took a few seconds for me to breathe and sit up, the car nowhere in sight.

Then it hit me—I was off the road. Something had pushed me.

Or someone.

I struggled to my feet and looked around. At the sight of Rafe lying still on the ground, my stomach dropped. I cried out and dashed toward him.

No, no, no. Don't let him be dead because of me. Please, no.

When I reached his body, I knelt down. "Rafe! Rafe! Can you hear me?"

Silence.

My throat closed up, but I tamped down my panic. He was breathing. Just. And if I lost it right now, Rafe might die.

Tears streamed down my cheeks as I took out my phone, turned it on and dialed 911. As the operator asked me a series of questions, I gently took Rafe's hand in mine and willed for him to make it.

Not just so I could apologize for shouting at him. It was more than that.

He'd finally shown me the type of love I'd always wanted, the kind where I could trust him with my life, and there was no way in hell he could die on me now.

I would do whatever it took to save the man I loved.

Chapter Thirty-Five

Abby

Amber: Are you sure you don't want me to come to the hospital?

Katie: I can come, too!

Me: Thanks, but there's nothing to do except wait for Rafe to wake up. I'd rather everyone work and act normal for now. It makes me less panicky.

Amber: If you're sure. But once my shift is over, I'm going to bring you some scones and coffee.

Katie: I'll go with Amber then. In the meantime, I'll ask Nolan's PI to find that CGN woman. I could take her.

Me: As much as I'd like to see it, more important people than me have tried and failed.

Katie: Hmph. Well, I'll get an update from Nolan's

guy anyway and see if there's anything that can help stop the weirdos from going after you. Maybe the town can set up a system.

Me: Thanks. <heart emoji>

Amber: I'm not much of a security guard, but I can be that, too, whenever you want!

Me: I wouldn't want to cross you, Amber. You could probably get away with murder. <winking emoji>

Amber: Maybe. But Rafe will be okay, Abby. I refuse to think otherwise.

Katie: He'd better be. And no matter his condition, if he makes you sad again, I'll pay him a visit and kick his butt.

Me: Let's save the ass-kicking for later. The doctor should give me an update soon, so I'll let you know what she says. <heart emoji>

T he next morning, I sat in the hospital waiting room, staring into my now cold cup of coffee, and replayed the scene from the night before: The ambulance. Rafe coding on the way and them reviving him. Waiting through the surgery. My family arriving and doing their best to comfort me.

And now I sat, waiting to see if Rafe made it out of the surgery.

A surgery that should've ended two hours ago.

My throat closed up again, and I took a sip of cold coffee to get myself under control. All I wanted to do was cry. However, if I fell apart now, then I'd be a mess whenever the doctor finally came to give an update. And I needed to be strong for Rafe.

I breathed in and out a few times before checking my phone, hoping for news about the hit and run. But there was nothing from the sheriff's office.

Emmy returned with a fresh coffee. She sat down, put an arm around my shoulders, and asked, "Do you need anything else, Abby? A donut? Candy? Or something healthier, like a banana? You're pale and I don't like it."

I shook my head. "No, I couldn't eat anything if I tried. Besides, Rafe should be out of surgery at any moment, and I want to be here."

She leaned her head on my shoulder. "Rafe's too stubborn to die."

Although her voice cracked at the end, betraying her words.

I hugged her back. "He only just came home and mended things with you. He won't leave you, Emmy. I'm sure of it."

She leaned back. "He won't leave you, either."

It was on the tip of my tongue to say that while I loved him, our marriage was a sham. But then the doctor appeared, and we both stood.

I asked, "Is he out of surgery?"

The doctor nodded. "Yes. He pulled through and if he remains stable for the next twenty-four hours, he should recover. We'll be monitoring him closely for the next day."

As she went through what they'd done during the surgery, I tried to pay attention. However, all I wanted to do was see Rafe with my own eyes, maybe hold his hand, and then tell him he'd better wake up so we could talk.

So when the doctor finally finished with, "Would you like to see him?" I nodded. "Yes. Please."

"Two people at a time can visit with him, if you both want to go."

Emmy spoke up. "You can see him alone first, Abby. I'll come in when you're ready."

I turned to my friend. "Are you sure? I know you've been worried too."

"Now that he's mostly out of immediate danger, it's probably better if I wait a little longer so I don't scold him about being stupid and nearly getting himself killed."

I almost smiled. "I already scolded him while waiting for the ambulance. So maybe we should hold back on doing any more until he wakes up."

"Sounds like a plan. Now, go. I'm sure once he hears your voice, he'll start healing even faster."

Even though it wasn't exactly scientific, I nodded and followed the doctor down a hallway. She entered a room, and I followed. At seeing Rafe's unconscious form lying in the bed, attached to all kinds of wires and tubes, my heart skipped a beat.

The doctor's voice was gentle as she said, "Stay as long as you like. A nurse will be by soon to check in on him."

"Thank you." As the doctor closed the door, I walked over to Rafe and gently traced his cheek. He was pale, with circles under his eyes. But at least his chest moved up and down, in a steady rhythm, telling me he was still alive.

I pulled up a chair, sat down, and gently took his hand in mine. Once I pressed it against my cheek, a tear slipped down my face. "Rafael, you have to wake up. Please don't die because of me." I kissed his palm and continued, "I love you and want the chance to be your wife for real." A few more tears rolled down my face. "Please don't die."

A sob escaped my throat, and another. "Please don't leave me, Rafe. Please."

I started crying again, clinging to his hand for dear life.

Eventually, the nurse came in and helped calm me down. She insisted I lay on the couch in the room as she checked over Rafe, saying I needed to rest.

As I watched her, I tried to stay awake. But eventually I passed out from exhaustion, dreaming of Rafe and I riding horses through the hills, laughing and teasing each other, and never taking each other for granted again.

Someone shook my shoulder and my brother West's voice filtered through my sleep-fogged brain. "Abby, wake up. Rafe's asking for you."

At Rafe's name, I bolted upright and blinked against the lights. It made me a little lightheaded—no doubt from lack of food for nearly a day—and it took me a second to steady myself.

West frowned. "Are you okay?"

I rubbed my forehead. "Fine. Just help me up?" He did, until I could finally see Rafe in the bed.

His eyes met mine, and he gave a faint smile. "I knew you were a heavy sleeper, but you take it to the next level."

With a cry, I rushed over to him and kissed his forehead, his nose, his cheek. "Rafe! You're awake!"

"I feel as if I've been run over by a car. Oh, wait." I grimaced, and he added, "Don't you dare feel guilty, either. West said they caught the guy about an hour ago. He was some middle-aged guy from the next town over who believed in conspiracy theories and thought he was a god-appointed protector of children, or some such bullshit. He saw the CGN videos. The latest had your family's address, the fuckers, and the guy made getting rid of you his next mission."

"Wait, what? There were more videos?" I glanced at West. "When? And when did you talk to the police to learn all of this?"

"Maybe an hour or so ago?"

"And you didn't wake me!"

West crossed his arms over his chest. "You needed to sleep, Abby."

My head buzzed, and I had to sit down on the edge of Rafe's bed to keep from stumbling. "Start from the beginning and update me on everything."

Emmy entered, carrying a tray of food. My stomach growled at the smell of pizza. She stated, "Only if you eat while he does it. It's been more than a day, Abby, and you look about ready to fall over."

Rafe took my hand and said, "Please, love. Eat something."

I met his gaze. At the concern and tenderness—and I swore love—there, I nodded. "Okay. But I'm staying right here, next to you."

He squeezed my hand gently before releasing it. "Right where I want you."

West sighed. "Do we need to give you two some space?"

Emmy rolled her eyes. "Be nice. You promised."

"I am being nice."

Rafe smiled at me and then replied, "I'm not about to ravish Abby while she eats. Just tell us everything, since you said you were waiting for Abby to tell me the details."

And so West went over how CGN had released another video, this time with some altered images of Abby. They'd even discovered her phone number and address and had blasted it separately, to their social media followers.

The more West shared, the calmer I became as a plan formed in my mind. There was only one way to try to make any of this stop. And when my brother finished, I blurted, "I'm going to have to give my own interview."

West frowned. "Is that wise?"

I replied, "If I keep silent, CGN will just keep publishing their own crap, Travis will stoke the fire, and it could get dangerous for all of you. And I won't risk anyone else I care about."

Rafe searched my gaze. "Are you sure, love?"

I nodded. "I've had a lot of time to think about what Nolan shared before....before..."

Rafe laid his hand on my thigh and squeezed. "Before I was hit by a car."

"Yes. That."

"And?"

I sipped some water before I could reply, "If Travis had manipulated and threatened another woman, maybe there were several. He's a lot older than me, and the way he reeled me in, well, it was too thought out and planned to be a coincidence, I think."

Emmy nodded. "I agree. And sometimes it takes the courage of one person coming forward for others to do the same."

I replied, "Or so I hope. Even if no one does, at least my version is out there and maybe some people will pause before automatically hating me. I can't guarantee it'll ever clear me completely, but it's worth a shot."

Rafe studied me for a second, and I wondered if he'd try to talk me out of it. There were a lot of reasons—it was dangerous, it could further hurt his training center's chances, and it was possible it made everything worse.

So when he said, "I agree," I mentally breathed a sigh of relief.

Rafe really did have my back. I vowed to stop doubting him. The man had been hit by a car to save me, after all.

He yawned, and I placed my tray to the side. "You need to rest."

"I don't want to, but my body says otherwise."

West grunted. "Welcome to the old man's club."

Emmy gently slapped his arm. "You're not that old."

"You do help keep me young."

As he waggled his eyebrows, I shook my head and Rafe said, "You two should go home and get it out of your system so I don't have to see that."

Emmy's face turned serious as she went to the other side of Rafe's bed. "I'm not going anywhere."

West followed Emmy and wrapped his arms around her from behind. He said, "You heard the doctor, love. Rafe is awake and out of danger now. As long as he takes it easy, he'll be fine." She hesitated, so West whispered something I couldn't hear, and she nodded. "Okay, just for a short while." Her gaze shot back to her brother. "But I'll be back soon. So no dying on me in the meantime."

Rafe crossed his heart. "I promise, as long as you stop yelling at me."

"Then stop being stupid, and I won't yell."

As the siblings bickered for about a minute, I smiled. It made me happy seeing my best friend and the man I loved getting along more each day.

Eventually, West intervened and convinced Emmy to leave. Once we were alone, I turned toward Rafe and asked, "Are you really okay with my interview idea?"

"It's the only way, I think. The people Nolan and I hired might be able to find something eventually. But even if the truth isn't as exciting as gossip, it might be enough to get more victims to come forward. Hell, if the one we know about does, it might be enough to get your ex fired. Maybe more than that."

He yawned again, and I tried to stand. However, he

grabbed my hand. "Lie next to me, Abby. There should be just enough room."

"I don't want to hurt you."

"You won't, love. Please."

Rafe gave me his puppy dog eyes, and I sighed. "Fine. But you can't complain if I fall asleep and wake up kicking you in the balls."

"I'll just have to risk it."

As he made room for me, I was torn. But when he asked me again, I caved and slowly crawled into bed.

It wasn't long until Rafe's heat and scent comforted me and I fell asleep, wondering how I'd share the most embarrassing and difficult times of my life with the entire world.

Chapter Thirty-Six

Rafe

Aunt Lori: Are you sure you don't want me to come over and help Abby take care of you? I have some experience with lads that get hurt.

Me: No, no, I just want to rest. Besides, West and Emmy are coming over later.

Aunt Lori: Okay. But I'll pop by in the morning. The sheriff and I have a plan.

Me: Um, what?

R: He's an old friend. And the whole town wants to help you and Abby.

Me (typed but deleted): Oh no. I'm scared now.

Me (actual reply instead): How?

Aunt Lori: I'll tell you in the morning. But don't

worry, it doesn't involve torches and pitchforks. They're not as effective as flamethrowers, anyway.

Me: Um, what?

Aunt Lori: Don't worry about it. I'll tell you about it in the morning. Rest, lad. <heart emoji>

Me (typed but deleted): How the hell am I supposed to do that if I think you're running around with a flamethrower?

Me (actual reply instead): I will. See you tomorrow.

T wo weeks later, I was determined to get Abby alone so I could tell her how I felt.

Ever since I'd been released from the hospital, people had been coming and going, offering food and help and advice. While it still awed me considering how I'd abandoned Starry Hills for so long—and I was grateful—I wanted time alone with my wife.

Well, when we were both awake and not passed out in bed. Only to sleep, so far. Fingers crossed, the doctor would give me the all clear at my next appointment.

But as much as I wanted to strip Abby and worship every inch of her body, I could feel her slipping behind her inner walls more and more. To the point, I wasn't sure if she'd even want to stay married to me.

Oh, she'd been nothing but supportive—taking care of me, doing her best to keep most visitors at bay, and thinking of how her interview could help my training facility. But the ease we'd once had, the teasing, the banter, was mostly gone. I wasn't sure if it was because of guilt, or if it was her way of trying to protect me.

Regardless, I refused to give her up without a fight.

So the day I could finally walk around and not need a nap after five minutes, I waited until my sister left for her latest visit. As soon as the door closed, I said to Abby, "Come with me."

Her brows came together. "Did you do too much? Do you need to use me as a crutch to get to bed?"

I tugged her to me and wrapped my arms around her. "No, I just need you. I need this."

The last time I'd tried to hold her, she'd come up with an excuse and rushed off. This time, however, I was stronger, and I held her a little tighter. "Abby, please don't run away again."

She lifted her head. "What are you talking about?"

I risked moving a hand to cup her cheek. "Please, love. Just talk to me. You've been here, but not really. If that makes sense?"

As she bit her bottom lip, she looked off to the side. "I hate how you're getting dragged into all my crap."

I gently moved her head until she met my gaze again. "You have a plan. Plus, the town has our back, and I wouldn't want to cross your friends, let alone your aunt."

"Still, this is all my mess. No one else should have to clean it up."

My heart raced as I knew I had to be honest with her, or she might slip away from me forever. "It's our mess, Abby. You're my wife."

"But—"

"No. Don't use the excuse that it's fake. Maybe it

started that way." I took a deep breath and blurted, "But it's real to me. Or, at least I want it to be. I love you, Abigail Wolfe. And quite simply, I miss you."

Her lips parted as she searched my gaze. "What are you talking about?"

"Which part? The loving you or missing you?"

"The loving part. How...what...I don't understand."

As I rubbed my thumb over her cheek, I replied, "You're easy to love, Abby. You're kind and funny, yet still strong and determined. Not to mention beautiful and sexy. You also don't put up with my grumpy asshole self and call me out when I need it." Leaning down, I laid my forehead against hers. "I love you, Abby. I want you to stay my wife. If that means wooing you and marrying you again for real, I'll do it. Just tell me I have a chance."

Her voice was so quiet that I almost couldn't hear it. "I'm nothing but trouble, Rafe. I don't know if I'll ever be able to stop my ex."

After taking her face in my hands, I said, "We'll work on it together. No matter how long it takes, we'll get the bastard. If it means using every penny I have, I will. I won't rest until he pays and you're free. Of him, your past, of everything." I stroked her cheeks and leaned a little closer. "I love you. The rest doesn't matter."

A tear rolled down her cheek, and I wiped it away. Before I could say something else, she replied, "Oh, Rafe!" She hugged me close and her muffled voice continued, "I love you too, but I'm afraid of what that means for you." She lifted her head. "You already almost died because of me. It might happen again, especially if we stay married and I can't stop my ex."

"No, I'm not about to die now that I've found you. You're the future I didn't know I needed, Abby. You're my reason for getting up every day."

"Rafe," she murmured before she kissed me.

I took my time sampling her lips, her mouth, and caressing her tongue with mine. I eventually stopped and asked, "Is that a yes to being my wife, then?"

She ran a hand down my chest and back up again, until she could caress my jaw. I leaned into the touch as she said, "Yes. And I don't need to get married again. When this is all over, I just want a party with our friends and family, like we talked about before."

I made a face. "You still want a disco ball and a 1970s-era dance floor? With bell-bottoms and roller skates?"

She laughed, the sound warming my heart. She shook her head. "No. I just suggested that to see how far I could push you. The fact you said yes still baffles me."

I lightly slapped her ass. "I was still trying to get into your pants at that point. I probably would've agreed to anything."

"Hmm. If I'd known that, maybe I would've suggested a fairytale party, with costumes. Or maybe a giant paintball competition, with some cheating to beat my brothers."

Caressing her cheek, I said, "Anything you want, Abigail. All I need is you and your love."

She leaned against me and hooked her arms around my neck. "I love you. And I'd really like to show you how much, but the doctor still hasn't cleared you."

I kissed the side of her neck. "Maybe if I just lay there, we could try. I wouldn't usually make you do all the work, but I did get hit by a car recently."

"An excuse you won't be able to use after five years."

I raised an eyebrow and met her gaze again. "Five years?"

"We should have a rule that if it's been more than five years, we can't use the incident against each other."

I ran my thumb across her bottom lip. "While I'm not using it against you—I don't blame you for it—I like how you're thinking of our future in years."

She caressed my jaw. "You stole my heart a long time ago, Rafael Mendoza. It just took me a long time to realize that it would always be you."

With a growl, I took her lips again. Maybe later I would regret all the years we'd had apart. Or how I'd avoided Starry Hills and Abby for so long. But right here, right now, I just wanted to kiss my wife.

My wife.

Now and forever.

Chapter Thirty-Seven

Abby

Amber: I think I found another woman Travis took advantage of.

Me: What? Who?

Amber: It took some digging. And using an archival website that stores previously deleted content. But there was another intern teacher he villainized after she left the school.

Me: Now I'm just getting madder and madder about him getting away with it for so long. The bastard!

Amber: Well, at least he won't get away with it again, if we can help it. I'll send you what I have so you can look over it before the interview.

Me: Thanks, Amber. And sorry I dismissed your investigative skills. You are amazing. <heart emoji>

Amber: No worries, I kind of surprised myself. I don't think I'd want to do it as a job, but it's nice to know I can help my friends when they need it.

Me: I may not be an amateur sleuth, but I'm always here if you need anything. Even if it's venting about any of my brothers.

Amber: I'll keep that in mind. For now, I need to go. I'm training a new employee for my new catering venture, and the sooner I finish with her, the sooner I won't be shorthanded.

Me: Don't work too hard. Love you. <heart emoji>

I'd just finished looking over Amber's latest information when Emmy said her goodbyes, leaving me alone with Rafe.

It'd been so hard not plastering myself to his side ever since he'd come home. But I'd avoided any serious talks about the future. Not because I wanted to divorce Rafe. No, because it wouldn't be fair to discuss staying married, let alone share my feelings, with everything looming over us.

But then he went and told me he loved me. That my past and all my baggage didn't matter.

And all the reasons I'd come up with to keep him at a distance vanished.

Rafe *loved* me.

And after I confessed my feelings, he kissed me. Or, rather, devoured me. But it wasn't enough, not nearly enough. So I pulled him closer, needing to feel his hard body against me, and he grunted in pain. Horrified, I released him and stepped away. "I'm so sorry!"

He took my hand and gently tugged me closer. "Don't apologize. We'll just have to be creative until I heal a little more." He kissed my cheek. "You're so beautiful." His lips brushed against my jaw. "And sexy." As he nuzzled the side of my neck, I nearly moaned. "And mine."

"Yes, yours."

He raised his head. "Good." He brushed some hair from my face. "Now, wife, let's go to bed. Normally, I'd chase you. But that will have to wait a little longer."

I ran my hand down his chest, to his crotch, and stroked his already hard cock through his pants. "If you weren't injured, I think you'd just take me right here, without any chasing."

He tweaked my nipple through my shirt, and I sucked in a breath.

His husky voice rolled over me as he said, "Considering it's been over two weeks since the last time I made you scream, probably." I gently squeezed him, and he growled. "Upstairs, wife. I have plans for you, and they require a bed."

Maybe if Rafe hadn't just told me he loved me, I might've teased him and drawn it out. However, my clit throbbed, and I wanted my husband naked and doing dirty things to me.

So I released his cock and turned around, looking over my shoulder as I said, "Hurry up, husband. Or I may have to dust off the toys in my drawer."

He groaned. "Now I want to see your toys."

"Another time. Tonight, I want to make love to you. Just you."

At his intense, heated gaze, I pressed my thighs together. Damn, my husband was sexy.

Husband. Knowing he was mine, I loved being able to call him that.

Rafe took my hand. "Come. I'm impatient to taste you again, love."

As I tried to think of how he could do that, given his injuries, we hurried as much as Rafe could up the stairs to his bedroom.

Without a word, we both stripped quickly. I finished first and offered to help Rafe, but he shook his head.

Not wanting to poke his pride, I merely watched as he revealed his chest and legs and then his long, hard cock. Then my eyes focused on the healing tissue where they'd had to operate on him. "Are you sure you can do this tonight?"

He strode toward me, barely limping, until he could kiss me. His hands roamed my back, my ass, and then one stroked between my legs. I cried out as he lightly thumbed my clit.

"You're so wet, wife. There's no way I'm not tasting you tonight."

Despite Rafe's wicked fingers, I somehow made my brain work. "How? I'm not about to let you crouch down and risk hurting yourself."

He removed his hand, and a playful glint entered his eyes. "I'm going to lie on the bed and you're going to sit on my face."

I blinked. "What?"

After kissing me gently, he said, "You heard me."

Rafe went to the bed and slowly laid down. Then he motioned me closer, and my feet moved toward him. Once I reached the bed, I stared down at him. "Are you sure? I don't want to squish you."

He caressed my thigh, my hip, and then my waist. "I want to feel these beautiful legs in my hands as I drive you wild, love. Now, come here and make sure to hold on to the headboard."

At the desire and love shining in Rafe's eyes, my doubts vanished. No matter what anyone had said before about my thighs or hips or whatever, it didn't matter. Because to Rafe, I was beautiful. I was perfect.

My eyes heated with tears, but I willed them away and climbed onto the bed. Rafe helped guide me into place, and as soon as he thrust his tongue inside me, I grabbed onto the headboard and moaned.

It became a blur as Rafe caressed my thighs and hips, guiding me into a rhythm, his tongue and lips and teeth torturing me. Slowly.

And meeting his gaze as he did it only made me hotter.

As he focused on my clit, I moaned. "Rafe. Please. I'm so close."

He increased the pace of his tongue, adding his lips and teeth, and soon he suckled me hard. Lights danced before my eyes as my orgasm hit, wave after wave of pleasure coursing through me.

Rafe drew it out, lightly stroking and suckling, until I went limp and slowly rolled to the side.

After kissing my shoulder, Rafe said, "I want more, Abigail. I want to be inside you."

I cupped his cheek. "Me, too. Especially since I've been on the pill long enough to not need a condom."

He growled. "Fuck, love. Yes. I need you. Tonight. You'll help me heal faster."

I snorted. "I somehow don't think that's how it works."

Nuzzling my neck, he said, "You're partly my medicine, love. You've already helped me heal so much in such a short time."

"Rafe."

"It's true, Abby. Repairing relations with my sister, with West, and even embracing myself and allowing myself to be happy—it's all because of you."

I smiled. "I think we both would've gotten there, but we helped each other along faster. Because you helped me too, Rafael. Even without completely settling my past, I'm doing better. So much better."

"Hmm, then just think of where we'll be on our first anniversary."

"I'd like to think that we'll be waking up in some foreign country, enjoying our honeymoon for real."

He kissed me. "I promise to make that happen. But first..."

Slowly, he sat up and stood next to the bed. I raised my brows. "What do you have planned?"

"If you bend over the mattress, I can take you without hurting myself."

I rose to my knees and moved to the edge of the mattress. Running my hand down his chest, I replied,

"You do feel bigger that way." I stroked his cock and reveled in his groan. "Almost like one of my toys."

"Okay, now I'm definitely going to have to see these toys of yours. But for the moment..."

He flipped me over, and I squealed. "Rafe, don't hurt yourself!"

Grabbing my hips, he pulled me down until my legs draped over the side. "Short of passing out, nothing is going to stop me from claiming the woman I love. From claiming my wife."

Wanting to feel him as deep as possible, I moved my knees to the mattress, raised my ass and lowered my chest before wiggling my behind. "Then what are you waiting for?"

He ran a finger through my center, teasing my clit a second, before murmuring, "I love you."

Before I could reply, he thrust his cock into me, and I moaned. He was big and hard and hot. So hot.

"Tell me, Abigail. I want to hear the words again."

"I love you."

He lightly slapped my ass cheek. "Good girl."

And then he began to move. I matched his ever-increasing rhythm, lost to the feel of him, his touch, the fact he loved me and I him.

Then his fingers found my clit again, and soon I came, moaning his name as Rafe stilled and came inside me.

Eventually, his hands caressed my back, up and down, as he said, "I love you, Abby."

Turning my head to the side, I replied, "And I love you, Rafe."

He pulled out. "Stay there. I'll get a washcloth."

I knew I should've said I could do it. But there was something about this moment, between sharing our feelings and him coming inside me, that I held my tongue. And when he returned, Rafe washed me carefully with the warm cloth. Once he tossed it aside, he murmured, "Come here, love."

I rose and turned around, wrapping my arms around him. Rafe kissed the top of my head. "Now about those toys of yours..."

Laughing, I raised my head. "What? You want to see them now?"

"Considering I feel as if I'm going to keel over, yes. I need to keep my wife satisfied until I'm at full strength again."

I smiled and hooked my arms around his neck. "Oh, I think between me riding your face and my toy drawer, I'll be just fine."

"You liked that earlier, then, huh?"

"Yes. As long as you did too."

His hands moved to my ass and gripped me possessively. "I love everything about you, Abigail Mendoza. And I will never tire of you. Ever."

As Rafe kissed me, a sense of rightness and peace settled over me. At one time, I might've doubted his words. But Rafe was mine, as much as I was his, and I trusted him.

Now all I had to do was find a way to banish my past, once and for all, so we could finally live the happy ending we both deserved.

Chapter Thirty-Eight

Abby

Emmy: You're going to do a great job!

Katie: Of course she will. And if you need us at any point, we're all waiting on standby at the main Wolfe house.

Amber: And I brought all of your favorites, including some of my secret coffee beans, for when you're done.

Me: Thanks, all of you. I might end up a slobbering mess once I get back to the house, and I'll need you all. <heart emoji>

Katie: If so, we'll be here to hug you and wipe your tears.

Emmy: And we'll do our best to keep Aunt Lori from going on a rampage. She's still determined to go to San Jose and take care of that asshole herself.

Me: Still? <sighing emoji> Do your best to keep her from doing that. We talked her out of the flamethrower, but I don't know what else she has stashed away.

Emmy: Your brothers are on it now. They'll ensure she doesn't head out with murder in mind.

Amber: I do have a few ways we can make his life miserable, though, if you're interested.

Me: Maybe later. Rafe's about to park. I'll talk to you all after the interview!

Emmy, Katie, and Amber: Good luck! <heart emoji>

T he next week flew by and felt like a dream. Being completely myself with Rafe, both of us lowering our guards completely for the first time, had been far easier than I'd expected. There was something about a person accepting all your moods—from grumpy to sad to ecstatic—and never having to wear a mask that was freeing.

I'd even shared more with the BFF Circle about Travis and everything I'd gone through. That had led to Amber telling us about how her life with her stepmother hadn't been as great as she'd made us believe. And Katie, Emmy, and I all vowed to help her more once I'd finally dealt with Travis Doucey.

To that end, Nolan's assistant, Jenn Jackson, had suggested who to give my interview to. Not CGN, because they wanted to keep the gossip running and would probably edit everything to fit their agenda. No, she'd recommended a smaller but more reliable woman named Penny Rogers. Her video channel, Gossip: Facts and Fiction, broke down rumors and gossip in a funny, entertaining way, using humor to make her points. After watching a few of her videos, I'd seen how laughing made me remember things easier.

It was hard for me to see the humor in my past, but Nolan trusted his assistant's judgment completely, and I trusted my brother. So I'd just have to see how it went.

The day of the interview, Rafe drove me to my family's house. And as he finally pulled into the rear parking lot, I took a deep breath and checked my appearance one last time in the visor mirror.

He said, "You're going to nail this interview, love."

I smiled and reached out a hand, touching his cheek. "Thanks, Rafe. I hope so."

"No hoping, Abigail. You've practiced a million times about what to say, have the receipts, and Penny should be able to do the rest."

"Well, that and hoping Jenn gets the word out."

"Nolan Drake still has a big online presence, despite the whole showdown with his ex. Katie refused to let him give it up."

"She's definitely braver than me. I haven't been able to check social media for weeks now."

Rafe took my hand and gently squeezed my fingers. "I'd say agreeing to this interview is pretty fucking brave, love." He lifted my hand and kissed the back of it. "I'll be in the same room, waiting, if you need me."

We had discussed a solo versus joint interview, and I still thought a solo one would be more effective. It might give any of Travis's other victims the courage to come forward, too. "Thank you."

I tugged my hand. He released me, and we both exited the car. As we headed toward one of the guest houses where the interview would take place, I asked, "You double-checked with Mark that this is okay?"

"Yes, love. I assured him I would buy him out, if it came to it, and help him find another good position. Although, given how sign-ups from within Sonoma County have gone up, I don't think it'll come to that."

Even though Rafe had assured me that he could find another calling if his training facility failed because of the scandal and rumors, I still felt bad. "I hope the numbers keep rising, until you reach capacity." I bit my lip and added, "I also meant it when I said that if me running the tutoring center prevents kids from signing up, I'll help you find someone else."

He stopped us, pulled me close, and leaned his forehead against mine. "No matter what happens, we'll find a way to make everything work out. Together. However, today is about you getting to tell your story and finally revealing that piece of shit for who he really is." He kissed me gently. "Ready?"

Nodding, I took his hand again. "Yes. Let's not keep Penny waiting."

We walked the rest of the way in silence, and I took in the familiar scenery, doing my best to calm my racing heart and get my emotions in check.

Because this wasn't going to be easy. Not even close.

As the wind blew, I took in a deep breath, feeling a little more put together. Later, I'd have to thank my brothers for keeping Aunt Lori busy. She'd wanted to be in the room during my interview. But as much as I loved her, she could be unpredictable when it came to protecting her family.

As soon as we reached the guest house, Nolan's assistant opened the door and waved us inside. "Come in, come in. Everything's set up, and she's ready for you."

I nodded. "Thanks for all of your help in setting this up, Jenn. I really appreciate it."

The red-haired woman waved a hand in dismissal. "It was nothing. Assholes like your ex need to be held responsible for their actions. Let's hope he gets fired, shunned, and maybe even charged."

"I'd be okay with people just believing me and not his lies."

Jenn patted my arm. "I know. My wife tells me I'm a little bloodthirsty at times and swears I must've been a Viking warrior in another life."

I chuckled. "Given your height and red hair, I could see it."

Jenn was nearly as tall as me, which was pretty tall for a woman.

She winked. "We can talk about my Viking roots later. Let's get you settled. Oh, and if you ever need to stop the interview and take a break, let me know." Rafe grunted, and Jenn raised her brows. "Yes, I know you would step in and do it, but I can be more tactful, since Abby isn't my wife."

I kissed Rafe's cheek, and his muscles relaxed a fraction. "Save your growls for any trespassers."

"I guess."

After kissing his lips, I murmured, "I love you."

He relaxed even more. "I love you too, Abby."

He kissed me again, and Jenn cleared her throat before saying, "As happy as I am that yet another of Nolan's siblings has found love, we don't want to keep Penny waiting too long. Come on."

We followed Jenn down the hallway to the guesthouse's living room and kitchen area. While the hallway was enclosed, the living, dining, and kitchen were all one big open space.

While Rafe's and my place was bigger, we'd all agreed it would be better to have a neutral space for the interview, in case someone tried to locate it and go after me. Yes, it was on my family's property, but no one lived here permanently and the high tourist season wouldn't start for a few months yet.

Not wanting to think of how many people the sheriff's office had stopped from trespassing on Rafe's land, I took a deep breath and walked toward the woman in the center of the room.

Penny was a little older than me, with pale skin, gray eyes, and black hair streaked with purple. She was known for cute but quirky dresses, and today was no different—she wore a white dress with cats and balls of yarn repeated as a pattern. Her shoes were bright blue, matching the yarn on the dress.

She extended a hand, and I shook it as she said, "Nice to meet you in person, Abby."

"Same. Thanks for coming. I really appreciate it."

We both sat down and Penny asked, "Do you have any last-minute questions before we start?"

I shook my head. "I don't think so."

"If you ever need to stop, just let me know." Her gaze turned sympathetic. "I know this isn't easy. And I'm beyond grateful that you want to share your story with me. But in the end, it should hopefully be worth all the pain and nerves and possible tears."

I bobbed my head. "I've seen how you helped others before, so I'm going to be hopeful."

"Well, it's not a perfect track record, as much as I hate it. But if I can take down a liar every once in a while, I'm happy. And this guy really needs to be held accountable."

"I won't disagree, but I also wouldn't hold my breath."

She reached out and placed a hand over mine. "With Nolan Drake behind you, helping to spread the word, I'd say your odds are better than normal." She leaned back and glanced at her notecards. "Ready?"

I glanced at Rafe. He blew me a kiss, and I looked back at Penny. "I think so."

She motioned to Jenn, who was helping with the cameras. Once she finished turning them on, Penny said, "Thank you for sitting down with me to tell your story, Abby." I nodded, and she continued, "Now, tell me about Travis Doucey..."

And so the interview began. The questions were hard at first, but soon I was at ease, laughing with Penny, and feeling a little freer the more I talked.

I came close to tears a few times, but glancing at Rafe helped steady me. By the end, I was exhausted and could barely thank Penny again. Once she left, Rafe pulled me close and said, "I could sneak you home, if you need a little break."

"No. Even though I'm tired, I need to see my family, if that makes sense?"

He cupped my cheek. "I get it. Although say the word, and I'll take you home."

I laid my head on his chest, closed my eyes, and listened to his beating heart. "I will. And thank you for everything."

He hugged me tighter and laid his head atop mine. "You were amazing, Abby. When will Penny show you the video?"

"In a few days."

She'd promised to let me see it first before posting it.

Rafe said, "Good, that gives Nolan and me enough time to hire some private security."

Leaning back, I met his gaze again. "What? Why?"

"Because I don't want to risk the unhinged and delusional finding you, us, or your family." I opened my mouth to protest, but Rafe beat me to it. "No, I won't budge on this, Abigail. Let me take care of you. Please."

Running my hand back and forth across his chest, I finally nodded. "Okay. But only in the beginning. I won't be a prisoner forever. I still want that trip you promised me, once things die down."

"Of course, love. It gives me time to plan the best honeymoon ever."

"And celebration party."

"Yes, and that. As long as you stand firm against Aunt Lori and her medieval court-themed party. I am *not* going to wear a suit of armor."

I laughed. "As much as I'd like to see that, I'll find a compromise. I'd rather see you in tights. Or maybe those tight pants they wore in the Pride and Prejudice show."

"I still say jeans and jerseys would be easier."

"And start arguments and possible brawls between different diehard fans once they start drinking? No, thank you."

He traced my jaw and kissed me gently. "Well, how about people can wear anything they want as long as they have on cowboy boots? And before you say anything, I'd offer to buy a pair for any guest who doesn't have them."

"Hmm. That might work. And might even make Aunt Lori happy. Although we'll have to watch Beck and West once they have a few beers because they might go all cowboy and try to rope Zach and Zane, or something like that."

He snorted. "I'd pay to see that."

"Rafe! Not for our wedding celebration."

"Okay, okay. I'll just have to put the challenge to them later."

"Just don't expect me to bail you out, afterwards, when they tie you up and leave."

As we argued about what would or wouldn't happen with Rafe against my brothers, we walked toward my family's house. Holding Rafe's hand the entire way, I laughed and forgot about my past. At least for a little while.

Chapter Thirty-Nine

Rafe

Aunt Lori: None of you had better come home with black eyes.

Me: What are you talking about? We're just playing pool.

Aunt Lori: Zach once said that and then ended up coming home with his head shaved and no shoes.

Me: Do I want to know?

Aunt Lori: Probably not. Just play nice. I don't want any of your celebration pictures to have black eyes.

Me: Understood.

Aunt Lori: Still no on the suit of armor, then?

Me: No, Aunt Lori. But I did get you those new cowboy boots. The ones with hearts on them.

Aunt Lori: I suppose that will be good enough. But just wait until you see my outfit!

Me (typed but deleted): Oh, no. It better not be you in a skintight bodysuit with cat ears, like you joked about.

Me (actual reply instead): It's my shot at pool. We'll talk more later.

W aiting to see how people reacted to Abby's interview had been torture at first. But after a few trolls and videos filled with gaslighting, people started to stand with my wife.

While Abby had refused to show pictures or name any of Travis's past victims, she'd shared as much detail as possible before mostly discussing her own experience.

Revealing it all had made her nearly break down a few times. But she was strong and had managed to rally, later lightening as we joked with her family and ate far too many brownies and scones and cake.

And on the fourth day after Abby's interview was posted, one of the other former intern teachers posted her story to social media and later gave an interview. After that, things snowballed.

Two days ago, Travis had disappeared from social media entirely. Not long after, news broke about two other victims coming forward and the San Jose Police Department starting a formal investigation.

While they were a long way from arresting or charging Travis, the news had lifted Abby's spirits. And since fewer and fewer strangers were coming to Starry Hills now that Travis was being charged, we'd decided to come to The Watering Hole to celebrate a little. And watching her across the room, laughing with her friends over drinks, made me smile.

Then something poked my side. I frowned as West said, "Are you going to take a shot or keep staring and drooling over my sister?"

Beck snorted. "You were doing the same thing a second ago, with Emmy."

West muttered, "I didn't think you saw that."

Zane slapped him on the shoulder. "I didn't see it, but you know Beck sees everything. I swear he has eyes on the back of his head."

Beck rolled his eyes. "It's not my fault you and Zach were never as stealthy as you thought you were."

Zach jumped in. "Hey, considering we're eight years younger than you, I thought we did a pretty good job." He pointed at his brother. "After all, you never knew we took Dad's motorbike out when we were seven. It's a good thing you never wanted to be a detective."

Beck shook his head. "As if you'd be a good one. You're too impatient."

Zach shrugged. "Hey, I always had Amber to help me. She's really good at sneaking around." He paused and then chalked the tip of his cue. "Not that we needed her help or anything."

Zane said, "Should we count how many times he's brought up Amber tonight? I think he's going to get lonely on this six-month-long trip he's taking."

Zach raised his middle finger. "She has a boyfriend, and we're just friends. Kind of. I think."

Zane snorted. "You think?"

He tossed his chalk cube, and Zane ducked. Zach said, "As if you can talk. How many years has it been since you dated anyone? You must be getting tired of your hand."

I jumped in. "You don't have to date someone to sleep with them."

Zach smirked. "Ah, but I know something you don't. You see, Zane wants..."

Zane put his brother in a headlock. "Don't you fucking dare say anything, or I'll march over to the BFF Circle and spill some of your secrets, brother."

I looked at West. "Do we need to break them up? Because I don't want to be barred from this place now that I'm finally home."

West replied, "Nah. They both have secrets, and it'll end in a stalemate."

I whispered, "Do you know what they are?"

West shrugged. "We all know Zach's. Zane's I'm still trying to work out."

As Zach and Zane bickered, Beck took his shot, knocking a ball into the corner pocket. I was just about to take my turn when Abby rushed over and stopped in front of me, her cheeks flushed. "Dance with me."

West frowned. "Hey, we're in the middle of a game here."

Abby gestured toward where Zane still had Zach in a headlock. "You might want to deal with that instead. They're about to brawl."

"Are you sure?" West asked as he glanced at the twins. "They always argue."

Abby nodded. "Trust me, I've learned the signs of an oncoming explosion." She took my hand. "And while you calm them down, I can dance with my husband."

As Zach and Zane struggled more, West cursed.

Abby tugged my hand, and I followed as I said, "Sometimes your family is a lot of work."

"Only if you don't know how to handle them. The twins act out sometimes just to get attention."

We reached the open space for dancing, and I pulled Abby close. "Zach and Zane are fucking twenty-eight years old."

"Ah, but it's not for us or even my brothers. They both have women they want to notice them. Not that I think acting like children is going to help. But they won't listen to me."

I leaned my head closer and whispered, "So you know the identity of Zane's mystery woman, don't you?"

"She works at the bar sometimes and has a shift tonight. Her name is Mariah Fraser-Williams, and she's making drinks right now."

I discreetly turned my head and took notice of the short woman. She had dark brown hair, dark eyes, and light tan skin. "Wait, Fraser-Williams? Didn't she marry Zane's friend? I think Emmy mentioned it at one point."

Abby nodded. "His best friend. They enlisted together, but Darren Williams died on a mission. Before he died, Darren asked Zane to look after Mariah and their son, Asher, if anything should happen to them.

And now that he's back in Starry Hills full-time, he does."

I was about to comment on how that sounded complicated, what with Zane wanting his late best friend's wife. However, before I could utter a word, Abby frowned and asked, "Who is that woman? And why is she charging toward us?"

After turning, I saw a woman about thirty, wearing tight jeans and a strapless top, glaring at me. "I have no idea. I've never seen her before."

The woman stopped in front of us, and before I could blink, she slapped my face.

Abby moved toward the woman, but I held her back and barked, "Who the hell are you and why did you slap me?"

There was a very small chance she was a one-night stand that I didn't remember. And yet, I'd never treated anyone badly enough to have them hunt me down and assault me.

The woman spoke with a British accent. "How dare you pretend not to know me, you bastard!" She lifted her hand and flashed the ring on her finger. "I'm your wife."

Chapter Forty

Abby

My jaw dropped at the woman's words. "What?"

For a split second, I doubted everything. Rafe, my marriage, my future.

Rafe said, "That's a lie! I've only been married once, and my wife is right here."

He glanced at me, and at the certainty in his eyes, my fears melted away.

Rafe wouldn't lie about this. And given his celebrity, it wasn't far-fetched that someone would pay this woman to cause trouble.

The woman raised her chin. "You're a bigamist, is what you are."

Rafe opened his mouth, but I stepped in front of

him, nearer to the woman. I stared into her blue eyes and asked, "Then where's the marriage certificate?"

"Um, what?"

I took a step closer and noticed the woman's brows come together. "If you really came all this way to charge in here and make a grand declaration, surely you brought proof?"

"I, uh..."

I stopped right in front of her. "Well?"

She glanced away and back at me. Most of her confidence was gone. "I didn't bring it with me because I didn't want him to destroy it."

She waved at Rafe, but I never took my eyes from hers. "I call bullshit."

Amber's voice came from behind me. "I think you're right, Abby."

Emmy appeared on my side. "My brother is many things, but a bigamist isn't one of them. Especially given how much he loves my best friend."

Katie appeared at my other side and cracked her knuckles. "I'd suggest you admit you're a liar and leave town."

The woman glanced around the room, but didn't say anything. So I raised an eyebrow and said, "Well? Do you have proof, or did someone send you?"

Something flickered in her eyes. Bingo. Someone had sent her. But who?

Rafe moved to my side, took my hand, and threaded his fingers through mine before saying, "You may as well tell us the truth."

Raising her chin, she tried to look confident, but her

voice was as strong as before when she replied, "I already told you the truth."

She glanced to the side, and I noticed someone with their phone up, probably filming this entire exchange.

I looked back at the woman and said, "You have a friend over there recording something."

"So what? Everyone takes videos these days."

The owner of the bar, John Thompson, walked over to the woman with her phone pointed at us and stood in front of her. "Actually, there's a sign on the door when you come in—no filming videos without permission. So hand it over."

The other woman, who had an American accent, squeaked and jumped back. "No."

Beck shouted, "I already called the sheriff, John. He'll be here soon."

The British woman took a step back, but I followed. "Who sent you? CGN?"

"Er..."

"It was, wasn't it?" Rafe cursed, but I continued before he could say anything. "Agree to write and sign a statement, with all the details, and I'm sure John could be convinced not to confiscate the phone or tell the sheriff how you're harassing one of his patrons."

I wasn't exactly sure of the legal options, but I did my best to bluff and look confident.

Rafe spoke up. "If you do as my wife says and tell us everything, then I won't include you in my lawsuit against CGN."

While Rafe had the best lawyers working on the case, I had a feeling he was bluffing like me.

Regardless, between me, Rafe, the BFF Circle, and my brothers all staring her down, the woman started to crumble. She said, "They told me I couldn't be arrested. I just wanted the thousand pounds."

Rafe said, "So they did pay you."

She nodded. "Yes. They wanted another scandal since the one about Abby Mendoza was one of their best performing ever, and this one would bring it back into the spotlight."

Anger churned in my stomach. The CGN assholes only saw what they could make off me and didn't care if they hurt me in the process.

Rafe put an arm around my waist, his touch comforting. He replied to the woman, "Cooperate and help us, and I'll make sure you're protected."

"Protected?" she squeaked.

Rafe nodded. "CGN isn't kind to those who try to stand up to them. But until my lawsuit is over, I'll help you if you agree to share the full truth."

The woman agreed to write her statement down in exchange for Rafe's protection. Soon the sheriff arrived, and once the woman gave all the necessary details to Rafe, she and her friend left with law enforcement.

My friends and brothers all crowded around me and Rafe, asking if we were okay. Once we assured them we were fine, I said, "Sadly, I think our night of fun is over. To better prepare for what else CGN might throw at us, I need to go home and discuss a few things with Rafe."

West grunted. "As long as you keep us updated."

I bobbed my head. "Of course. I'll text you all tomorrow."

Once I said goodbye to everyone, Rafe ushered me out the door and into his car. As soon as we were inside, he turned to me and asked, "You still believe me, right?"

The uncertainty in his gaze squeezed my heart. I cupped his cheek and said, "Of course I do. For a split second, I had my doubts, but then I remembered everything you've done for me. Hell, that you're still doing for me. And most importantly, that I trust you." I kissed him. "I love you, Rafe, and for better or for worse, I'm your wife."

He smiled. "Definitely for the better, love. You're all I need or want." After kissing me, he added, "Which is funny, considering what you said that day I drove you to Vegas."

"Wait, what? You remember what happened?"

He nodded. "It came rushing back as you stood up to that woman in the bar."

"And? Don't you dare keep me in suspense any longer!"

After chuckling, he replied, "Well, that day you told me I was the absolutely last person you wanted to see."

And he went on to tell me about how I'd cried over another brother finding love, and as much as I didn't want to be, I was jealous. Also, with Rafe being back in town, it only reminded me of all the dreams I'd had as a kid and teenager. And he was the absolute last person I wanted to see during my breakdown. I just wanted to forget myself for a night or two in Vegas, but of course, my car had broken down.

In the end, Rafe had won the battle to drive me there, and we both got drunk. The proposal was a little fuzzy to him—and me, as some of my memories returned as he told his side—but I'd joked about wanting to marry him when I was a teenager, and he'd said he could give me that dream, at least.

The ceremony was a blur; the night ending with us giggling and passing out in the hotel room.

When he finished, I sighed. "I don't think I've ever been as drunk as that day. Otherwise, I never would've told you about my teenage marriage dreams."

He smiled and brushed the hair off my face. "Well, I don't think I've drunk more, either. And don't take this the wrong way, but I must've been completely shit-faced to marry anyone. Luckily, it ended up being you."

Rafe moved in to kiss me, but I leaned back. "Why did you need to be super drunk to marry anyone? I'm curious."

He sighed. "You're not going to let me kiss you or take you home and do dirty things until I tell you, are you?"

"Nope. So, spill."

He ran a hand over his hair. "Well, mostly because of what happened to my parents and the ensuing guilt. I understand now that I couldn't have controlled the drunk driver that killed them. But for a long time, I focused on how they were going to the airport to see me. And if I hadn't hounded them to come to the UK for a match, they might still be alive."

I took his hand in mind. "What-ifs are dangerous. I should know, given all the crap that happened with Travis. But hopefully now you accept that you couldn't have done anything to change the past, right? No lingering doubts?"

"I don't think so. I'm sure every once in a while the years of guilt might come rushing back. But a drunk driver could've hit them any night, and it was bad luck that it happened when they were coming to see me." He paused, traced my cheek, and added, "Besides, no matter what happened, my parents would've wanted me to be happy." He lifted my hand and kissed it. "And you make me happy, Abigail Mendoza. More than anyone else in the world. I love you."

I brought his hand to my chest, over my heart, and said, "Good, because I love you and I'm never letting you go, Rafe. You're stuck with me. Although..."

He raised his brows. "Although, what?"

"I still never claimed my favor for staying married to you..."

He snorted. "I honor my bargains. So what do you want, love?"

Leaning forward, I traced his jaw before placing my hand on his chest. "For you to love me, Rafael. Just love me."

He kissed me, and I melted as much against him as I could, considering we were in a car. When he finally let me up for air, I stated, "We need to get home. Stat. I'm not about to accidentally give my brothers a free show in the parking lot."

Rafe chuckled as he started the engine. "And as much as I want you right now, I'd rather be able to touch and taste and devour all of you. So let's see how quickly I can get us home without getting pulled over."

As he sped down the road, I placed a hand on his leg and squeezed before moving it up, up, up.

Rafe hissed. "Don't even think about it, Abigail. I don't want to crash into a tree."

Laughing, I removed my hand and fondled my breasts. "What about this?"

Rafe cursed again. "You're incorrigible, aren't you?"

"And you love me for it."

"For whatever reason, I do."

"Good. Then hurry up. I'm impatient to be fully incorrigible in our bed."

And so I managed to behave as Rafe drove us home in record time.

Chapter Forty-One

Rafe

Watching Abby stand up to the woman falsely claiming to be my wife had been something else. She hadn't wavered, and together we convinced that woman to help with our case against CGN.

By the time she asked me to just love her, I was impatient to get her alone, strip her, and claim her all over again.

But she'd been right—sex in a car would be quick and clumsy and ran the risk of our siblings seeing us. And so I'd driven as fast as I dared. Once we reached our house, I took her chin, pulled her close, kissed her, and then growled. "I'll give you a ten second lead. Now, run."

Laughing, Abby opened the door and dashed toward the house. She had made it inside by the time I'd counted to ten, and I went after her.

While my injuries from the accident were healed, my knee would never be at 100 percent. Still, physical therapy had helped, and I could slowly jog after her. I saw her reach the top of the stairs and then disappear into my room.

I took them two at a time, and when I reached our bedroom—yes, Abby now shared it with me permanently—I found Abby sitting naked on the bed. With a growl, I stripped as I stalked toward her. By the time I reached her, I was also bare.

Her eyes shot to my hard cock, and she licked her lips. However, right here, right now, I didn't want her mouth. So I tugged her up, pulled her close, and crushed my lips to hers. I took my time exploring every inch of her mouth, licking and lapping and twining my tongue with hers.

When her fingers wrapped around my dick, I sucked in a breath and broke the kiss. Abby murmured, "I want you inside me. Now. Save the foreplay for later."

Threading my fingers through her hair, I tilted her head back and nipped at her bottom lip. "Hmm, now I want to do exactly the opposite to tease you."

She tightened her grip on me, and I groaned as she replied, "Later. Right now, I want my husband to make me come. Hard."

I kissed her briefly before guiding her back onto the bed, until I lay between her thighs. She wrapped her legs around my waist and arched her back, her wet pussy rubbing against me.

Leaning down, I took one of her nipples into my mouth and suckled.

"Rafe. Please. I want you inside me."

After releasing her, I met her gaze again as I ran a hand through her center and then lightly stroked her clit. "As my wife wishes."

I positioned and thrust inside her to the hilt. "Fuck, you're so hot and tight and wet. So perfect, love."

She drew my head down and kissed me. Between the grip of her pussy and the sweet taste of her mouth, I couldn't hold back and moved my hips. I continued to stroke her clit as she matched my rhythm, and soon the sound of flesh meeting flesh filled the room.

Abby broke the kiss to take my face in her hands. At the heat and love in her gaze, I moved even faster. "Tell me you're close, love."

"Yes. Rafe, please, just a little harder."

I complied, and she soon cried out as she gripped and released my cock. Her little pulses sent me over the edge, and I spilled inside her before collapsing.

I didn't know how long I lay there, with Abby stroking my back, before she said, "I love you, but you're a little heavy."

"Sorry." I quickly rolled to the side, taking her with me, and kissed the top of her head. Holding her close, I took a second to revel in her heat and scent and the absolute rightness of the moment.

Abigail was my wife. She loved me, and we'd have

our fucking happily ever after one day, no matter what it took.

Eventually, Abby yawned and then said, "I love you and your cuddles. But right now, I'm so tired."

I pulled the blanket up and tucked it around us. "Get some sleep. I'd rather not have to face Grumpy Abby."

She playfully slapped my chest. "Be nice."

I laughed and hugged her tighter. "I love you, but if you think you have a guy who will never tease you, then you have the wrong husband."

She propped her chin on my chest and looked up, smiling. "I have exactly the right husband, even if he's a meanie sometimes."

I lightly smacked her butt and said, "We're an even match, love. It'll make life interesting."

"Yes, and I wouldn't want it any other way."

And as I held my wife, she soon fell asleep and began to faintly snore.

Yes, I had exactly the right wife. One who loved and accepted me, but never put up with my shit.

Life was almost perfect. And I was damned if CGN or her ex would ruin our future.

Chapter Forty-Two

Abby

Aunt Lori: Are you sure he's coming to the party?

Me: Yes, like I told you a million times before, Fernando is coming. The rest is up to you!

Aunt Lori: I'll try. Although who knows how many others I'll have to fight off just to dance with him.

Me: You say that, but he always smiles wider when he sees you, Aunt Lori. Be yourself, don't hold back, and you'll win him in no time.

Aunt Lori: Easier said than done. I haven't gone on a date in decades.

Me (typed but deleted): I wish I would've helped you earlier. I'm sorry.

Me (actual reply instead): You are amazing and

Fernando will be lucky to dance with you. Just be yourself. <heart emoji>

Aunt Lori: Thanks, child. But focus on your day. This is the wedding reception you should've had all those months ago.

Me: Thanks! Let's hope nothing goes wrong... <fingers crossed emoji>

T wo and a half months later, my husband finally led me out for our first official dance onto the temporary dance floor at the edge of my family's apple orchard.

Oh, I wasn't wearing a white wedding dress, and we'd been married for almost four months now. However, we'd decided to make it a party to remember instead of trying to pretend we'd just gotten hitched. And it'd been Rafe's idea to have it near the orchard since he'd missed the chance to propose to me there, as was the tradition in my family.

It also made me feel closer to my parents since they couldn't be there.

Once Rafe pulled me close, we moved to the music. My family cheered, and I couldn't help but smile.

Rafe said, "Are they cheering because they like seeing you happy, or because you won't be moving back home?"

I narrowed my eyes. "Do you want me to stomp on your toes? My boots can do some damage."

He chuckled and kissed me, mollifying me a little,

before whispering, "Hey, it's their loss and my gain if it's the latter." He pulled me a little closer. "You're my wife, Abigail. Mine. I'm not letting you go, no matter what happens."

While most of the harassment had stopped now that Travis was in custody for statutory rape—he'd seduced at least two students in the past twenty years, and I still shuddered to think I'd fallen for his false charm too—but things wouldn't fully calm down until our battle with CGN was over. It was going well, even if it was still a long shot.

To be honest, if they merely forgot about us, I'd be happy.

But today was about celebrating and not worrying about the past. I'd have plenty of time for that later.

So I tightened my grip on my husband and said, "Good, because I'm not letting you go, either. No matter how much you tease me."

"You tease me right back. Remember the singing flower delivery you ordered for the opening day of the training facility?"

A few weeks ago, I'd had a quartet come dressed in inflatable dragon costumes to sing before the official opening celebration for Rafe and Mark's business. "That was good, you have to admit."

He grunted. "Mark and your brothers are never going to let me live it down."

"Hey, it was an homage to your years with the Manchester Dragons FC. I thought it was cute."

"Cute isn't exactly what I'm going for. Reformed? Yes. Responsible? Of course. But not cute."

I grinned and moved a hand to squeeze his butt. "But you are cute."

"With you, maybe. But the last thing I need is for adolescent and teenage clients to hear you calling me cute. If you think I tease too much, you have no idea how much boys can josh each other."

"Josh each other? Are you like fifty years old?"

He poked my side. "Shall we call a truce? The dance is nearly over, and I don't want to have your brothers glaring at me later if I have to get revenge during the cake tasting."

"I thought you could handle my brothers?"

Even Zach had come back for the party. He'd been on the road for over a month already, and had been doing well. However, it was nice to have him around again to help lighten the mood. Zane had struggled a little when his twin had left.

Glancing to the side, I saw Zach and Zane whispering together about something. Oh no. That didn't bode well.

Rafe followed my gaze and said, "I don't even want to guess."

The music started to fade, and I stilled and kissed Rafe. "Will you go see what they're up to? Please? I don't want any Wolfe sibling shenanigans to turn this party into chaos."

I gave him my best puppy dog eyes, and he sighed. "Fine. But it means I don't have to do the chicken dance later."

"You're no fun." I gave him a playful shove. "But I'll

just do it with my friends. Now, go. They're sneaking off, and I don't like it."

As Rafe went after my brothers, Emmy, Katie, and Amber all surrounded me.

Emmy nodded toward the left and whispered. "Look at Aunt Lori."

I did my best to be discreet. She was talking to Fernando, and like he always did, he smiled and looked at my aunt like she was an oasis in the desert. "I wish she'd stop being so nervous when it's obvious he's interested."

Katie nodded. "Yes, but it's been a really long time since your uncle died. We'll just have to keep playing matchmaker until she sees how much that man wants her."

Amber shook her head. "I can't believe she's waited this long to even try dating again. I mean, my dad barely waited a year after my mother died before he remarried."

Emmy asked, "Did you ever find out why?"

Amber replied, "I was too little to remember, and I'm afraid to snoop into my own past."

I wrapped an arm around Amber's shoulders and squeezed. "Well, if you ever need our help, just say so. After all you've done to help us—not to mention the amount of baked goods you've made over the years—we're more than ready to help you."

She smiled. "Thanks."

Before I could ask if she was worried about something now, Rafe returned. Alone.

Amber shooed me, and I rushed over to him. "Well? What happened? Where are Zach and Zane?"

He smiled and kissed me. "It's nothing bad, I promise."

Before I could press further, fireworks shot into the air. One after another, an array of colors and patterns filling the sky.

Rafe turned me so he could pull my back against his front and wrap his arms around me. Placing my hands over his arm, I leaned back and watched the display in the arms of my husband. Surrounded by my family and friends, it was hard to believe even a year ago that I'd thought I would never have this.

But I'd mended relations with my family, stopped holding back with my friends, and finally fell in love with a man who'd never hurt me intentionally.

The future might not be certain, but that was okay. With so much love in my life, I could face whatever came my way.

Epilogue

Rafe

Aunt Lori: I need more pictures! And promise me you'll bring back as many chocolates and macarons as you can.

Abby: What about an ugly mug?

Aunt Lori: That too, of course. If such a thing exists in France. <monocle emoji>

Me: The tourist souvenir shops have some cheap, ugly stuff. Don't worry. We'll find one for you.

Abby: I already found a T-shirt for your boyfriend!

Aunt Lori: Fernando doesn't need any more souvenir T-shirts. He has about fifty of them. <sighing emoji>

Me: Nope, he's getting one. He needs to feel welcome.

Abby: Don't try to pretend that's the real reason, Rafe.

Me: I don't know what you're talking about.

Abby: This is for the rival team's jersey Aunt Lori got you for Christmas. Now you're out to get your own kind of friendly revenge. Friendvenge?

Me: Are you making up words now?

Abby: Of course. And it sounds better, too.

Aunt Lori: Hmm. I can't stop you, but if you buy him more than one shirt, it's game on, Rafe. And you'll have to wait to see what I do next.

Me: Bring it, Aunt Lori.

Abby: <sighing emoji> This isn't going to end well, is it?

Me: You'll just have to wait and find out. For now, I'm taking my wife to Versailles and am going to ignore my text messages.

Aunt Lori: <crying emoji> Noooo!!!

Abby: <laughing emoji> I'll reach out later, when I have a chance. <heart emoji>

Exactly a Year After Waking Up Accidentally Married in Vegas
Paris, France

Light kisses against my chest woke me up, but I did my best to keep still. I wanted to see how far Abby would go.

Her hot breath danced across my skin as she moved to my nipple and toyed with it. My already hard cock grew harder, and Abby finally said, "I know you're awake, Rafe. You're breathing too hard."

I opened my eyes to find my wife sitting above me, her hair dancing around her shoulders. I reached up and lightly tweaked her nipple. "You just want me to hurry up so you can go sightseeing."

"Well, we *are* in Paris."

I pulled her down and kissed her before replying, "On our anniversary-slash-honeymoon. Which means some of it is mandatory to spend in bed."

"Well, since we've been married a year already, I like to find a balance. Sex is good, yes. But I've always wanted to see the gardens at Versailles. And maybe dance in the outdoor ballroom."

Smiling, I said, "I already promised I would. But it's still early."

She straddled my chest, teasing me with her wet pussy against my skin. "The gardens open at 7 a.m. So we could leave now."

I placed my hands on her hips and stroked her soft, warm skin with my thumbs. "It's February. Do you really want to go out in the dark? The sun won't even be up until after eight."

She ran her hands across my chest. "Ah, but you see, we need to start getting ready now."

"Give me five minutes. That's all I need."

She shimmied down until she could move her center against my cock, and I sucked in a breath. "Ah, but getting ready includes riding my husband before sharing a shower."

Reaching up, I cupped her breasts. "Well, in that case, we should definitely start getting ready now."

And so my wife took her time riding me, teasing me, until we both orgasmed and lay catching our breath on the big bed of our suite.

Eventually, Abby spoke again. "You never did tell me the full reason as to why you agreed to take me to Vegas last year. Was it because you felt sorry for me?"

I rubbed circles on her back as I replied, "A little bit. But mainly, I wanted to spend time with you alone, away from all our families, to see if there was even a chance of us being together."

She lifted her head. "I was a mess, and you still wanted to spend time alone with me?"

"Ever since I returned to Starry Hills and saw you as an adult, I tried to resist you. And when the chance came up to be your knight in shining armor? I took it. And maybe my subconscious agreed to marry you in Vegas because I didn't want to ever let you go. Even then."

She moved up until she could kiss me. "I love you, Rafael Mendoza. More now than ever before, if that's possible."

"And I love you, Abigail Mendoza."

As we stared at one another, I still couldn't believe how lucky I'd been in life. Yes, I'd had tragedy and years of self-imposed loneliness. However, it'd all led to this woman. The one who understood me, loved me, and shared her troubles and joys one day and listened to mine the next.

With her ex being indicted on a number of crimes,

plus CGN going quiet after trying to create a scandal over a mega-billionaire a few months ago and my training facility running at capacity, the future truly looked bright.

And once we finally made it to the Versailles gardens, I danced with my wife in the outdoor ballroom and made yet another happy memory, one of many to come.

Bonus Epilogue

Abby

Me: I really wish you could've come and helped us with all the kids! <crying emoji>

Avery: I told you and Emmy to pick a day after winter break started at college.

Wyatt: And I won't be back from my horse auction for a few days. Dad and Uncle Beck knew that.

Me: Still, it's crazy. Ten children under the age of eight at Disneyland is hard. Even with all the adults.

Aunt Lori: I would've gone, except I broke my leg. <sad face emoji>

Me: I know, Aunt Lori. Take care of yourself. <heart emoji> And Avery, I'm sorry I messed up your winter break dates. I thought you'd be off by now.

Avery: We definitely need a family online calendar! Maybe now everyone will listen to me.

Wyatt: I don't need more reminders on my phone. <eye roll emoji>

Avery: I could snail mail reminders, like I did over the summer.

Wyatt: No. Just no. Fifty letters in a week was too many.

Avery: It just shows you how much I love you, brother. <emoji blowing a kiss and winking>

Rafe: Abby. Abby! Come to Snow White's Grotto at the side of the castle. NOW.

Me: Oh, no. On my way.

G o to Disneyland at Christmas time, they said. It'll be fun and beautiful and make a good memory, they said.

Ha! Maybe if it'd been just Rafe, me, and our two kids, it wouldn't have been so bad.

No, that wasn't right. Our daughter seemed to find more trouble than most of the rest put together. Beck and West said Sophia reminded them a lot of me as a child. But I didn't think I would've ever been able to sneak into a haunted house, hide, and scare the living crap out of my parents like she'd done with us when we'd finally found her this past Halloween.

The spires of the castle came into view, and as I rushed toward the side where the wishing well stood, I finally spotted Rafe. He held our younger daughter

Victoria on his hip as he gestured wildly toward the waterfall.

The waterfall had three levels, with Snow White and the dwarves spread across three tiers wearing a few holiday decorations. The bottom tier had a fake log running between the two sides of rock, and there was my older daughter, walking across it, singing as she went.

I reached Rafe's side. "What the hell happened?"

"I don't know! I was making a wish with Tori and the next thing I knew, Sophia was over the fence."

A security guard was drawing near, and I knew we were this close to being kicked out.

We might still be, even if I got Sophia back over the fence. But I didn't want to cut my kids' vacation short. So as my daughter reached the safety of the other side of the grotto—and was no longer balancing over the water—I did my best to keep my voice some-what even as I said, "What did we say would happen if you climbed up any of the landscape props in the park?"

She shrugged. "I get one less souvenir at the end. But it's worth it! I want to see Snow White, Mom! I can see the castle better from up there, too."

I gripped the rails of the fence, trying my best to stay calm. My daughter liked to challenge Rafe and I, and shouting would only make her dig in. "Do you want to go home? Because if you don't come back over the fence, Sophia, they'll kick us out."

In addition to the security guard talking into a radio, the rest of my family showed up, their kids in tow. We now filled most of the area around the well.

Zach and Amber's daughter, Luna, shouted, "Sophia, you shouldn't be up there!"

West and Emmy's son, Ben, scowled. "They'll take you to jail if you don't come back."

Beck and Sabrina's daughter, Charlotte, only stayed in place because Beck kept his hands on her shoulders as she said, "I want to climb up the waterfall too!"

Nolan and Katie's son, Bowen, was the eldest of the kids there and said, "I bet you can't make it to the top!"

As Sophia moved to climb up the second level, Rafe swore, handed me Tori, jumped over the railing and went after our daughter. He managed to catch up to her, scooped her up, and brought her back. Once she was back on the ground, Sophia tried to squirm away, but Rafe kept his hands on her shoulders.

I was torn between hugging her close and scolding her. Before I could utter a word, the three security guards moved closer and one of them asked us to go with them.

An hour later, Rafe and I had managed not to get banned permanently, only for the day, meaning we could thankfully return tomorrow. However, if any of our children climbed the scenery again, the punishment would be harsher.

Since West and Emmy were watching Sophia and Tori temporarily, I stopped Rafe just before we left the security building. He raised his brows and then pulled me into a hug. I sighed. "I'm going to be completely gray within the next year, aren't I?"

He chuckled and said, "Well, she is a lot like you,

love. And when two people are a lot alike, they tend to butt heads more."

I hugged him tighter. "Well, Tori is more like you. And once she's older, then she can give you more gray hairs."

"Let's hope she doesn't resort to a constant stream of casual hookups once she's older. Because I will dust off my baseball bat and chase them away."

We stood hugging each other for another minute before I raised my head and kissed Rafe. "We should probably head out."

"After we talk with Sophia, Emmy offered to watch them tonight to give us a break."

"She must miss the twins being younger because I can barely manage two kids, and she has two step kids and three with West. Five! I couldn't do it."

"Two is more than enough. Especially with the mini-Abby running around."

He sighed dramatically, and I playfully hit his arm. "Be nice."

"Well, I seem to remember falling in love with you and staying married to you and having two kids with you. I think that means I'm fond of you and anyone like you." He kissed me and continued, "Let's go back outside before security tells us to leave."

And so we exited the building and spotted Emmy and West and all the rest of my family gathered near a tree. When we walked up, Sophia held up an ice cream cone. "I'm sorry, Mommy. This is for you."

"Bribing me with ice cream, are you?"

I took it, and Sophia replied, "I didn't mean to break

the rules. But I just wanted to see the statues up close. And Bowen told me earlier I couldn't do it because I was too little."

Nolan raised an eyebrow at his son. "Did he, now?"

Bowen crossed his arms over his chest. "I didn't tell her to climb the waterfall!"

Nolan and Katie gathered their kids, said they'd meet us later, and herded them out of the park.

As Rafe and I did the same with our daughters, Sophia looked at me again. "I *am* sorry, Mom. I won't do it again."

"Well, we have to leave for today. And you've lost your remaining souvenir privileges, too." Sophia opened her mouth, but I beat her to it. "But maybe, if you behave the rest of the vacation, you can have one at the very end. But only if you're on your best behavior."

"I will be, I promise!"

Rafe spoke up. "And don't take every dare you get from you cousins, Sophia. Remember what we talked about?"

"To stop and think. And if I might get hurt, to say no."

Rafe nodded. "That's right." He pulled her against his side and gave her a one-armed hug. "We're just happy you're safe."

With his other arm, Rafe hugged me and Tori, too.

And as we walked out of the park, Tori said something to make us laugh, then Sophia moved between Rafe and I to hold each of our hands. And even though we'd been kicked out of Disneyland, it somehow was one of those perfect moments that I'd remember for the rest of my life.

Author's Note

I hope you enjoyed Abby and Rafe's story! Waking up accidentally married is alway fun, even if things became a bit more serious later on.

I had hoped to get this book out earlier, but this year I've not only lost two cats, but my father was in the hospital several times. A crazy personal life does not make for easy writing! Things have calmed down some now (my dad is doing better!) and I hope to get back to normal writing speeds.

This book is also when I finally stopped trying to be like popular authors on TikTok and went back to what I like to write—tighter stories with a little drama and suspense, plus plenty of humor and family (found or through blood). Around 80,000 words is my sweet spot, and I hate filler. I think I might've done that with the third book, to get to nearly 100,000 words. No longer! Even though I've written 60+ books as Jessie Donovan, contemporary romance is SO different. I think going forward, I can be better and more true to myself. Thanks for going along this ride into a new subgenre of romance with me!

The next story will be about Zach and Amber and will be called *Cherish Me Forever*. I'm unsure at this point WHEN it'll be out, but sometime in 2025. Because of my difficult year, I have a lot of catch-up to do with my other pen name (it pays my bills, so it gets extra attention).

I want to thank Ashley, Iliana, and Amy — three great beta readers who help me find typos and minor inconsistencies. Thank you!

And to all of you who've read this far, thank you from the bottom of my heart. Being an author is both the best and hardest job in the world, and it's only possible because of you all. I hope you'll come back to Starry Hills for Zach and Amber's story.

Until next time, happy reading! (And if you haven't read the story about West, Emmy, and the twins, turn the page for the blurb.)

~Kayla~

Stay With Me Forever
Starry Hills #2

He's a single dad who never wants to marry again. She's his little sister's best friend who can't stand him. But when a hotel reservation goes wrong and there's only one bed, things heat up...

After sixteen years away, I finally moved back to Starry Hills with my two kids, determined to heal the rift with my family and help with the family's winery business.

Slowly, my children and I are finding our place in Starry Hills. But then summer vacation arrives and my kids keep finding their way to *her* property.

Emilia "Millie" Mendoza, the wedding planner who is extremely close to my family.

Except she wants nothing to do with me. From the first time she saw me after I got back, she's glared and told me to leave her alone.

Which would be a lot easier if she didn't keep showing my children the kindness and attention they never got from their mother.

Every swim lesson, bedtime story, or word of encouragement chips away at my walled-up heart.

And then we're forced to work together at a wedding expo, they lose her reservation, and we have to share a room.

That one bed soon changes everything.

But making her fall apart with my hands and mouth is the easy part. Because Emilia has burdens of her own.

Ones that might keep us apart.

Except Emilia is the one I want to stay with us forever. And I'll do whatever it takes to win her.

Stay With Me Forever is available in paperback.

About the Author

Kayla Chase writes sexy, feel-good romance full of laughter, friendships, and family. Her stories usually include crazy get togethers, fun festivals or events, and communities you want to be a part of. She also writes happy endings because real life and adulting can be way too hard.

She lives near Seattle but also grew up in California, which gives her lots of beautiful places to include in her stories (such as Sonoma wine country). While she's also lived in Japan and England, she has yet to figure a way to get her characters to those places. (But she does travel on a shoestring when she gets the chance!)

When not writing, she loves to read, jog on her treadmill, fit in some yoga, or try new recipes in the kitchen. More often than not, her cats derail her plans and make things, er, interesting.

facebook.com/kaylachaseauthor

instagram.com/kaylachaseauthor